Jeff Sherratt

The Brimstone Murders

A Jimmy O'Brien Mystery Novel

Echelon Press

Publishing

THE BRIMSTONE MURDERS
A Jimmy O'Brien Mystery Novel
An Echelon Press Book

First Echelon Press paperback printing / February 2008

ISBN 1-59080-552-6
978-1-59080-552-7

Library of Congress Number: 2007942954

Echelon Press, LLC
9735 Country Meadows Lane 1-D
Laurel, MD 20723
www.echelonpress.com

PRINTED IN THE UNITED STATES OF AMERICA

10 9 8 7 6 5 4 3 2 1

ॐ   ॐ

This one's for my family. I have been blessed.

ॐ   ॐ

Acknowledgements

I'd like to thank Mike Sirota, writing coach extraordinaire, whose help polishing the book has made my writing shine. Also, I'm grateful to my friends and family for their encouragement, support and criticism. I want to express my gratitude to Tom Budds, retired Los Angeles County Sheriff homicide detective, for the many insightful hours he spent with me, explaining the ins and outs of police procedure and how real life murder investigations are conducted.

Chapter One

PENAL CODE SECTION 187: *Murder is the unlawful killing of a human being with malice aforethought.*

Robbie Farris was in jail. He'd be there a long time and there wasn't a whole-hell-of-a-lot I could do about it. His professor was dead and there wasn't a whole-hell-of-a-lot I could do about that either.

I threaded my way up the Santa Ana Freeway heading for the L.A. County Jail, going at a good clip until a couple of lunkheads, discussing their fender bender on the side of the road, had traffic snarled all the way back to the 710. They were hammering away at each other, but a few quick jabs from the bigger guy seemed to quell the debate. I crept by in my five year old '68 Corvette, steaming. My pants were pressed, shirt only worn once, shoes halfway shined, and I was even on time, but now the traffic would make me late–again.

My client, Robbie Farris–charged with section 187, one count–was waiting at the jail. He wasn't going anywhere. But I hated being late. I'd have to do better with these minor imperfections. Racking my brain, I could only think of a few, but the peccadilloes were part of my personality, and we wouldn't want to change that. My main fault–if it was fault–had to do with women. The first thought that crossed my mind when I met a woman, any woman, young or old, was what it would be like to sleep with her. I don't mean to imply that I'm obsessed with sex, and sex certainly isn't obsessed with me. But when you are thirty-five and divorced, a healthy male with an active libido, isn't thinking about sex normal, or what?

Contrary to my married friends' fantasies, bachelor life isn't all that thrilling. It's just lonely.

It was a hot Monday morning in October, about nine A.M., and the prisoner I was assigned to represent, in all likelihood, would be behind bars until the new millennium. It wasn't that I was such a lousy lawyer; in fact, I was damn good. It was just that Robbie Farris committed the crime, murdered his college professor, and now–after his conscience kicked in–demanded that I let him plead guilty.

After I'd agreed to take the case, three days ago, I had a short phone conversation with Robbie. And after listening to his incoherent babble, I hung up and phoned the judge, *Hissoner* Abraham J. Tobias, the guy who assigned the case to me. I asked for a continuance of the arraignment, or to be more accurate, I begged. The judge gave me an additional two days, until next Wednesday.

From my discussion with Robbie, I gleaned that he had found Jesus. I guessed he figured he could score a few brownie points with the Lord by admitting his deed in open court. I tried to persuade him it wasn't such a good idea. I told him it would be better to try to score a few brownie points with a jury, then if God wanted him to do life in prison, He'd let the jury know. What could that hurt? But Robbie was adamant and now my role would be to see that he got the best possible deal.

I figured, after meeting with Robbie this morning, going over the details of the arraignment and listening to his *mea culpa* for as long as I could handle the self-flagellation, I'd head over to the D.A.'s office and try to arrange some kind of plea bargain. But getting any kind of deal might pose a problem. When arrested Robbie had been screaming, "God, take my wicked soul and cast it into everlasting damnation, for I have sinned. I have killed Professor Carmichael." It was all on tape, and with a statement like that ringing in everyone's ears, I wouldn't have much to dicker with. The D.A. would know they'd have a slam dunk. Especially since, in addition to the taped confession, Robbie's bloody fingerprints were all over the knife found at the scene. But protecting my clients' rights and providing them–the guilty as well as the innocent–the best defense possible was my job and I always did what I could.

According to the police report, the professor had been stabbed twenty-seven times. The first one, slicing his heart, killed him instantly. Robbie's other stabbings were just an afterthought, a little something to remember him by.

After signing in at the Central Jail's attorney entrance and being patted down, I was escorted along a dingy tile-lined hall and shown into an austere, cinder-block room reserved for lawyer/client conferences. The room had a single metal table and two chairs in the center. The table was bolted down, but the chairs were free to move about. Fluorescents flickered overhead, casting the room in a ghostly bluish hue. A strong smell hung in the air, the mingled odor of industrial strength disinfectants, cleaning soaps, and human anguish.

The guard, an L.A. County Sheriff's deputy, a black guy with a cookie-duster mustache, gave the table a good shake, demonstrating its immobility. "Hey, O'Brien," he said. "Don't want shysters like you walking off with the table." His face was filled with a tooth-flashing grin.

"The name's Jimmy, but you can call me *Mr*. O'Brien," I answered, pulling out a rusty steel chair and sitting down. "Hey, sport, chair's not bolted down, might be just the thing for my apartment. Goes with the rest of my stuff, Early Incarceration."

"I don't know what's worse, you criminal defense lawyers,

or your clients. One in the same, you ask me."

"Nobody's asking. Now, Flip, go get my guy, okay?" I said. Flip Wilson, a comedian, was the prime-time rage of the moment, and the deputy, without the mustache, had a strong resemblance to the TV star.

Within ten minutes, Flip returned with my client. Another guard accompanied him, a heavy white guy bulging out of his uniform. One more donut and bam, buttons would fly.

There was no mirth between Flip and me this time. It was routine, just the perfunctory securing of chains strung around Robbie's torso to eyebolts embedded in the concrete floor. Robbie appeared washed out; his pallor had the patina of dry cement, and unlike most young guys his age he was lifeless and numb. A tall, lanky kid of nineteen, he had mousy hair, trimmed around the temples but long on top, the tip of which fell forward and curled into his gray vacant eyes. He wore the customary white jumpsuit with L.A. County Jail stenciled in India ink on the back. There were no pockets or belts for obvious reasons, and the jumpsuit was designed as a one-size-fits-all model. In Robbie's case, the designer had failed. Robbie's forearms dangled out of the sleeves. These jail guys have no sense of style, I pondered, as I sat there looking sharp in my mod, bell-bottom slacks and tattersall-patterned, polyester sports coat.

After a few moments of Robbie murmuring eerie prayers of contrition, bowing and raising as much as the chains would allow, I got down to business.

"Why, Robbie…. Tell me why you did it?"

Robbie turned and stared at me, blinked once, and without an ounce of emotion said, "He was a heathen…." A chill hovered in the air.

"You killed him because you thought he was a heathen?" I asked.

"He had no right to life...life is a gift from God, and he had to die." Robbie's demeanor was as cold as the steel chair I sat on. "He wasn't a Christian..."

"He was a Catholic," I said, taking a wild shot. I wasn't sure if the professor was a Catholic or not, but with his Irish name, it had to figure.

"That's what I mean."

"I'm a Catholic," I said. "You want to stab me, too?"

"If I was told to stab you, I would."

"Someone told you to stab the professor?"

"Yeah."

"Who?"

Robbie dropped his head and intently scrutinized his hands, folded on the table. "My friend, the only one I can talk to," he finally answered.

So that was it. There was an accomplice. It could be a woman, maybe not. But whoever it was, it might be someone I could hang this on. Someone who was manipulating this poor unfortunate soul.

"Your friend told you to stab the professor?" I asked.

"Yes, he did, Mr. O'Brien. He told me in a loud and clear voice. He said Carmichael had to die. "

I leaned closer. "Who is your friend?"

"The Lord."

Chapter Two

"Amazing grace! How sweet the sound that saved a wretch like me...."

My jailhouse conference lasted less than five minutes. After admitting the stabbing at the behest of the Lord, Robbie, his eyes rolling, climbed back into his bowing and scraping mode and started to sing. There was no point in sticking around. *Forgive me* wasn't part of any criminal lawyer's lexicon, and I had to get out before it started to rub off.

Regardless of how Robbie felt, it was obvious his mental capacity was diminished, and he wasn't the one who should be making decisions about how he was going to spend the rest of his life. From the report, I learned that Robbie was an only child whose father had been killed in a car wreck years ago. His mother lived out in the San Fernando Valley, somewhere way out in the Valley, almost to Ventura. After stopping at the D.A.'s office, I'd go see her, make the drive on the hot, crowded Golden State Freeway all the way to a dusty region barely in L.A. County, a neighborhood on the outskirts of Chatsworth.

Why did Robbie have to stab the guy at a time when the temperature outside was a hundred degrees? And why did his mother have to live out in the valley where the smog was thick and the air was as sticky as blackstrap molasses? Why couldn't the guy's mother live at the beach? Better yet, anywhere in Colorado.

The D.A.'s office was located in the new Criminal Courts

Building downtown, a typical government structure. And, like the people housed inside, it was gray, utilitarian, and long on function but short on imagination. Steve Webster, the deputy D.A. assigned to the case was no exception in the imagination department. But, after an hour of saying no to every creative proposal I came up with, I felt I was finally wearing him down.

"C'mon, Steve, let's get this thing over with. The guy's loony-tunes, for chrissake. We'll plead not guilty by reason of insanity. You can warehouse him in some state hospital–"

"No way, O'Brien. He could miraculously be cured; he'd be back on the street."

Steve sat behind his metal desk, which was painted gray— but of course, everything in the building was painted gray, as gray as the law I was trying to invoke. If Robbie had been insane at the time of the crime, then he wouldn't go to jail. Then again, if he happened to be in his right mind, he wouldn't have stabbed the guy. Yeah, the law had its Catch-22, and at times I felt like Yossarian, a little paranoid and thinking everyone is crazy.

Steve sat there shaking his head. Maybe this wasn't going to be as easy as I thought. Then suddenly, he dropped the bomb. "Your client has priors."

"What? There is nothing in the report about any prior convictions."

"Sealed. Juvie stuff, drug related–"

"I don't believe it. My guy's a holy roller."

"You'd better believe it. I saw the sheet," he said.

"Hey, Steve, that proves my point. He got whacked on acid as a kid, and now he's totally out of it. Not responsible–"

"Won't fly, O'Brien. Robbie Farris wasn't diminished when he signed up for his GED at Golden Valley College. Where the good professor taught, I might add, before your client turned him into sushi."

We came to that moment in every negotiation when both sides, refusing to give up points, sat and stared at each other. How long the staring would continue depended on several factors, not the least of which was the stubbornness of the combatants. Women were much better at this phase of negotiating than men. It wouldn't surprise me a bit if Barbara, my ex-wife, still sat there staring at the spot where I had been sitting when she unceremoniously asked me to leave the house and never return.

But, of course, one way to break the logjam was to change the subject. I glanced around the room, taking in the functional furniture, the filing cabinets, and Steve sitting there with a dismal look on his face.

"Hey, Steve, your tie isn't gray."

He dropped his chin, glanced down and fingered his coffee stained knit tie. "It's blue. So what?"

Now, back to the negotiation. "Got a deal for you. We'll get this case behind us."

"What about my tie? You don't like it? Shit, look at you–"

"I'll plead my guy not guilty, insanity. You hold off requesting a trial date until a shrink checks him out. If he's nuts, you accept the plea. Sounds good?"

Webster stopped fiddling with his tie and looked up. "And, if he's sane, sane in the legal sense of the word?"

"Then we work out a new deal."

"You're the one who's nuts, O'Brien. If the shrink says Robbie Farris is sane, then he pleads guilty..." Webster paused for a moment, making a steeple with his fingers, flexing them in and out.

"Okay, it's a deal," I said. "At the arraignment, we'll ask the judge to postpone–"

"Not so fast, O'Brien."

Oh-oh.

"We use the county shrink," he said.

This was going better than I figured. It is obvious Robbie wasn't in his right mind when he killed Professor Carmichael. Any competent doctor would see that. But I had to nail this down before Webster changed his mind.

"No deal, Steve. We use an impartial guy. No county doctors." I didn't give a damn about the doctor. I just didn't want to appear that I was too eager, or a pushover.

"Cost money," he said.

"Cheaper than a trial."

"Okay, O'Brien. I'll go for it. I'll make the motion at the arraignment, but no tricks. No last minute complications. Capish?"

"Aw, Steve, trust me...have I ever.... But there is one small thing—"

"There you go. Goddammit, O'Brien, same old bull pucky."

"Calm down," I said. "I just have to flag the deal by his mother. Need her approval. Don't worry, I'll nail it down."

The deputy D.A. peered at me in silence. His eyebrows formed a distrusting V, and there was skepticism in his eyes.

"It's a formality," I said.

"See that she goes along."

The drive out to Chatsworth, bordering Ventura County on the far side of the San Fernando Valley, killed what remained of the morning. Steve Webster supplied the unlisted phone number and I had called Hazel Farris from a pay phone in the lobby of the court building before I left. After about forty rings, a boozy voice answered and confirmed that she was

Robbie's mother. She agreed, reluctantly, to a meeting. I told her I'd be there in a couple of hours.

The directions she gave over the phone made no sense, but after digging out my moldy, five-year-old Thomas Brothers, and wasting ten minutes jumping from one page to another with no apparent logic to the map book, I finally found her street. At least I found it in the book. She lived off a side street called Larkin outside the city limits of Chatsworth in an isolated area of Los Angeles County. After cruising up and down Topanga Canyon Boulevard looking for Larkin and spending another fifteen minutes trying to find her place, I finally pulled into a trailer camp straight out of the thirties.

These were no holiday get-away jobs. Cobwebs stringing the wheel wells, the flat tires, and the expired license plates told me they hadn't been moved in years.

I knocked on a few doors, but only one guy answered. He told me how to get to Hazel Farris's unit. She lived in a beat-up Airstream parked at the end of a dirt road that weaved haphazardly through the camp, the last one by the exit. Her trailer was hunkered down in the center of a weed-infested patch of dirt. It rested on a haphazard scattering of cement blocks acting as a feeble foundation. The trailer's oxidized aluminum siding was torn in spots and peeled back like a cast-off, rusty tin can. In fact, the trailer looked like a big old tin can, a can of Spam, the large economy size.

I slid out of my Corvette. To the distant sound of a barking dog, I trudged through the weeds to what I perceived to be the front door cut in the side of the Airstream. I rapped on the flimsy tin, not too hard, not wanting to knock the trailer off its blocks. I waited and was just about to knock again, when the door opened a crack. A bloodshot eyeball peered at me through the opening.

"Whadda ya want?"

"It's me, Mrs. Farris. Jimmy O'Brien, remember I called?"

"You're the lawyer man, the guy supposed to be helping Robbie?"

"Yes–"

She opened the door a little bit more, her eyes flicking from side to side. "Get in here fast, before they get you!"

"Who?" I said, glancing around.

"The spooks, you numbskull."

She scraped the security chain across the slot, unlatched it, and banged open the door. With a quick movement of a withered, liver-spotted hand, she grabbed my shirt and pulled me inside.

"You'll be safe in here," she said, staring at me with wild eyes, her body pressed flat against the door.

The interior wasn't much of an improvement over the outside, worn and used up, and the place smelled like a wet dog, a mongrel. Her decorator wasn't schooled at the Boutique d'Interieur; more like Boutique d'garbagé. But what caught my eye were the empty whiskey bottles littering every flat surface. Mrs. Farris took a little nip now and again.

She was maybe fifty or so, but it was hard to tell with alcoholics. The red and purple spider-web capillaries covering her face masked her age just as effectively as cosmetic surgery masked women on the other end of life's spectrum. Her green eyes had lost their luster and she was a little heavy now, but before the bottle took over her life, she could've been a knockout. She had a certain air about her; maybe it was the way she looked at me when she fingered her thin, flower-pattern housecoat clinging loosely about her voluptuous figure. She had the essence of a woman who in a past life knew what sex was about and how to use it. She turned and moved away from the door, leading me deeper into her lair.

"Sit down, lawyer man."

"Please call me Jimmy. Is it okay to call you Hazel?"

"We don't stand on formalities 'round here."

I shrugged out of my jacket, loosened my tie, and found a spot on the ratty sofa. A cat jumped up from nowhere and hissed at me for an instant, before screeching away out of sight.

"Tom don't cotton to strangers. Maybe he knows you're a lawyer." She nodded knowingly and plopped down on an old wood rocking chair across from me. Then she reached for a half-empty bottle of Jim Beam resting on an end table next to her.

"Want a little drinky-poo?" She held the bottle out about an inch from her body. Without waiting for a response, she raised it to her lips and took a healthy swig.

"No, thanks," I said.

Hazel wiped her mouth with the back of her right hand, holding the now almost empty bottle in her left. "No thanks, what?"

"I don't drink. Used to, but I quit."

"I quit too, yesterday. Didn't take a drink all morning. Well, 'til almost ten a.m., but goddammit, I didn't see no point to it. I'm not a drunk or nothin' like that."

"Of course not, Hazel. Just a little nip now and then for the chill." It was 102° outside, but what the hell.

"Yeah, that's it, for the chill…" her voice trailed off. She glanced around with barren eyes and gazed off into the distance, her face a blank slate. Then she gulped down another belt, for the chill.

We sat quietly for a moment. Then she struggled out of her chair and walked unsteadily with one hand out in front of her body as if she were blind, feeling her way. She went to the kitchen area and stopped at a small dining table. The table was set for one. Resting on the Formica with the plate and a few tarnished eating utensils was a small glass vase with a single flower in it. The flower, a long-stemmed white lily, had died days before and the petals, now dark and shriveled, were lying where they fell. Next to the vase, in a wooden frame, was a black and white photograph. She picked up the frame, holding it carefully by the edges, and looked at the photo for a long moment. Then she meticulously set it down in the same spot. When she turned back to me, her eyes were red-rimmed and misty.

I felt sorrow. Sorrow for her, sure, but more sorrow for a society that casts off women like Hazel who, without marketable skills, are left to rot like worm-eaten fruit in an isolated orchard. I didn't ask, and she didn't tell me about the man in the photograph. It wasn't Robbie. The man in the photo was older, maybe her dead husband.

Finally she said, "Robbie's a good boy." She turned away and sat down in her chair again without waiting for my response. She retreated to her secret place, a place in her soul where the pain wasn't so deep. "Did you see them?" she asked in an emotionless voice.

"Who?"

"They are going to get you, too, you know."

"No, Hazel, I didn't see anyone."

"They watch me. They want to silence me." She began to rock slowly in her chair, humming a tune I didn't recognize.

I could sit there chatting with Mrs. Farris all afternoon, but if I wanted to beat the rush-hour traffic back to my office in Downey, I'd have to get down to business, get her to sign the power of attorney granting me temporary custody of Robbie. I kept a blank form in my jacket pocket for occasions such as this.

"Tell me, Hazel..." I paused, wondering how I could phrase this delicate subject in a manner that wouldn't offend, especially in view of her condition. "Don't you think Robbie's a little crazy? I mean, killing that guy and all."

"Oh, damn you," she said, still staring off in the distance. "Robbie's a good boy."

"Yes, I'm sure he is, and that's why I'm here. See, if we can prove he's a little nutty, then we can keep him out of prison. You'd like that, wouldn't you?"

She gulped down the remaining Jim Beam and let the bottle slip from her fingers. It rolled off her lap and hit the floor, where it made a thumping sound. The thump startled Hazel. She came out of her trance and turned to me. "What did you say?"

"Robbie. I'm talking about Robbie."

"What about him." An angry scowl mushroomed on her face.

"Well, as I said, Mrs. Farris." I kept my tone soft and pleasant. I had to tread lightly. "He needs a little help, mental help, and–"

"Hey, Mister, are you saying what I think you're saying?"

"Calm down, Hazel."

"God damn it, Robbie's not crazy. Don't be telling me that. You goddamn lawyers come in here and demand money. Get out!"

It was beginning to look like I would be there all afternoon. "Listen, Hazel. I don't want any money. I just want to help Robbie."

"I said, get out. If you don't leave right now, I'll sic Tom on you."

I glanced around; there didn't seem to be anyone else in

the trailer. Unless he was hiding in her bedroom. But the door was open, and all I saw was a small, rumpled bed. "Tom?"

"My cat, you asshole!"

It took a bit of doing, but I finally convinced her to think about what I was trying to do for Robbie. Her mood improved after I made a run to the Liquor Bin on Topanga Canyon Boulevard and returned with a couple fresh bottles of Jim Beam. Before long, she began to see my point. She opened up and started talking when I poured a dinking glass full of the amber liquid and held it out for her. An hour later I had what I came for, the signed document, and I had a better understanding of Robbie and his troubled life. When she passed out in her chair, I put a couple of my business cards on her table and quietly left.

It was almost dark after the three-hour drive when I pulled into my office back in Downey. I patted my jacket pocket where the power-of-attorney rested, folded and signed by Hazel Farris, mother of the defendant. I smiled.

The lights were on when I cracked open the door and peered in the office. Mabel, our firm's business manager was gone for the day but Rita, my young associate, was there. She was leaning against the desk, talking.

"No, I told you, I don't know where he's been."

When she noticed me coming through the door, she turned away from the two men in suits standing ramrod straight off to the side.

Her face was white. "Jimmy, these guys are homicide detectives. They want to talk to you," she said in a hushed tone.

"Why?"

"A patrolman from the Valley called them, said they found your business card in a dead woman's trailer. Do you know someone named Hazel Farris?"

Chapter Three

An hour later, I was in East L.A. being grilled at the sheriff's headquarters by a couple of beefy homicide cops. No glaring lights, no rubber hoses, but I was in the hot seat and Rita was at my side. They knew I was at Hazel's trailer just before the murder. The first cops on the scene had found my business card in her trailer and these guys said someone reported spotting a beat-up red Corvette leaving the area around the time of her death. Probably the guy who pointed out her trailer to me. I didn't deny being there, but, of course, I denied any knowledge of her murder. Rita had insisted on accompanying me to the interview.

"Isn't that what we always tell our clients, Jimmy?" Rita had said back at the office. "Don't say anything unless your lawyer is present? Well, I'm going to be your lawyer, tonight."

I knew she was right and it felt good having her with me.

Although Rita was single and beautiful, with dark flowing hair, sparkling eyes and a figure that would melt rocks, there was no office hanky-panky going on. She was much too young for me, twenty-six. And, even though she never put it into words, I was sure she looked up to me as her mentor. I was delighted having her at my side. Maybe she'd gain some experience by being here, learn how to handle a homicide interview.

We followed the cops—at their strong suggestion—in Rita's yellow Datsun to the Sheriff's headquarters in East L.A. After being escorted to one of the homicide division's interrogation rooms, Rita and I were informed that Hazel Farris had been shot through the forehead while sprawled in the same rocking chair in which she'd sat when I visited her. We were seated at a scratched, wooden interrogation table in a stark air-conditioned cubbyhole down the hall from the homicide squad room. Sergeant Joe Hammer, and his partner Butch something–I didn't catch his last name–started questioning me about my meeting. But first, I demanded to know who'd called them. I wanted to know the name of the person who saw my car at Hazel's trailer. Maybe I could ask him if he saw someone else.

When they refused to divulge that information, Rita stood and told them we were through cooperating and we were now leaving. At that point, they let on that the call was anonymous.

"There you go," I said, starting to stand again. "Whoever made that call was obviously the killer."

"Sit down, O'Brien. We need to ask you a few things. We don't need the guy who called it in. You admitted you were there at the time of her death."

"Hold it Hammer–" I started to say.

Rita piped up. "Don't say anything, Jimmy. And just sit down." Turning to the big cop, she said, "What my client is alluding to…what he started to say was Ms. Farris, the decedent, was alive when he left."

"Yeah, that's what I was going to say. Hazel was passed out in her chair–"

"Put a sock in it, Jimmy. Don't say anything until I say it's okay." There was a slight edge in her voice.

Hammer paced the linoleum floor. He started tossing out questions, beginning with the obvious one, what was I doing there in the first place. Officer Butch stood silently in the corner taking notes, jotting in his police-issue interview pad.

Rita explained my reason for visiting Hazel at her trailer. She told Hammer how I needed her signature on the power of attorney.

Hammer's face began to curl into an ugly grimace. "Let me get this straight, O'Brien," he said to me, ignoring Rita. "You're saying you just went there to get her to sign some kind of legal document regarding her son, a murderer, now in custody. Is that correct?" Hammer looked like a Rhodesian ridgeback with a gas problem, but his tone was perfunctory.

I hunched up close to Rita and we had a small conference. Because I was going to use the insanity defense with Robbie, I felt, and Rita concurred, that I would not be violating attorney/client confidentiality by telling the police the details of my meeting with his mother. Rita advised me not to embellish, but go ahead and tell the cops exactly what happened in a straightforward manner.

I told them how Hazel Farris mentioned that Robbie was once a good boy. How she'd told me that when they moved to the Chatsworth area after her husband was killed, Robbie fell in with a bad crowd, teenage hoodlums who did drugs. "He turned bad and raised all kinds of hell," Hazel said.

After loosening up, she'd told me more. She had discussed Robbie's problem with Elroy Snavley, the pastor of her church, The Divine Christ Ministry over on Winnetka Avenue. It was decided that Robbie should be sent away. At the pastor's urging, she agreed to send him to a Christian intervention center somewhere in the desert, outside of Barstow.

According to the rules the center had imposed, she wasn't allowed to visit her son, or have any contact with him whatsoever.

But, when Robbie returned home after a six month stint, he was a different person. "He was cured of drugs, all right," she'd said. "But his head was filled with that religious mumbo-jumbo those goons taught out there."

She didn't know what was worse, his lifeless state while on drugs, or the hyperactive ranting about his newfound salvation. "The Lord this and the Lord that, all day and all night. How much of that fire and brimstone crap can I take?" she'd said.

It wasn't long after Robbie returned that he left, again. That was about a year ago; she hadn't heard a thing from him since, and until I broke the news, she knew nothing about Robbie stabbing the professor, or about his mental condition. She didn't have any idea of what may have caused him to snap.

"What's all of this garbage have to do with the old woman's murder, O'Brien?" Hammer asked.

"I don't know. Maybe nothing," I said. "I'm just telling you what happened while I was there. Hey, maybe the spooks got her?"

"Spooks? What in the hell are you talking about?"

"Yeah, spooks, you know, ghosts, little goblins running around." I did a little finger wave. "Wooo...she saw them all the time."

Hammer gave me a hard-cop look, eyebrows arched with his chin jutting out. "What kind of horseshit are you feeding me, O'Brien?"

"You're embellishing, Jimmy," Rita said.

"Hey, I'm just telling him what she said."

Hammer leaned down and got into my face. "Yeah, some boozed up old broad tells you she sees ghosts, and you believe it?"

"Hey, Hammer, she was alive when I left. If you call being passed out in a chair living."

"You're saying she was out, dead drunk when you left? Is that it?"

"She was breathing," I said.

"You don't get a big fat hole in the center of your forehead from booze, at least from the stuff I drink." The cop turned and snapped a finger at his partner. "Butch, listen up. What time did O'Brien say he left?"

"About four in the afternoon," I said in a firm tone.

"Hold on a sec," Butch said, coming to attention and thumbing his interrogation pad.

"Four o'clock," I said again, louder.

"Here it is!" Butch beamed and proudly announced, "Four p.m., said he was there until four, Joe. But, hey, are we gonna take his word for it?"

Hammer turned back to me. "The call came in at 5:17. Some guy walking his dog went by her trailer. The door was open and he could see the old lady dead in her chair. Called the local law enforcement. The officers at the scene found your card on the floor by the body. They called us and here we are. Now, you're admitting you were there. That means you, O'Brien." He made a symbolic gun out of his fist and forefinger, cocked his thumb, and shot me with it. "You were the last person to see her alive."

"Objection!"

All eyes in the room turned to Rita, who sat calmly with her right arm partially raised.

"The killer or killers unknown, perhaps the supposed dog walker, was the last person or persons to see the decedent alive." She stood. "Now, gentlemen, you have my client's statement and nothing more can be gained by further discussion of this tragic affair. So, we will be leaving now." Rita tapped me on the shoulder. "C'mon, Jimmy, let's go."

"Hold up a minute," Sergeant Hammer shouted. "Little lady, he's not going anywhere until I say he can go."

Rita darted around the table, charged into Hammer's

space, and all five-foot four and one-hundred twelve pounds of her reached up and jabbed her finger into the stomach of the two-fifty pound pile of ugly muscle.

"You hold on, big guy," she said. "You either charge my client and book him right now, or we're outta here, understand?"

"Hey, back off, sweetheart." Hammer looked down at Rita's tiny finger poking his belly.

"*You* back off, sugar buns. And, listen up. You can address me as counselor, Ms., or hey you, but not *sweetheart*," Rita said. "Chrissakes, show some class."

She cast a quick glance in my direction, winked, then turned back to Hammer. "We're leaving now. Have a nice evening."

As we strolled down the hall outside the interrogation room toward the exit, I heard Hammer's voice booming somewhere behind us: "Hey, O'Brien, don't leave town."

Rita glanced over her shoulder and tossed out an insolent, "Ha."

We continued walking.

It was quiet on the Santa Ana Freeway as we drove back to Downey. I glanced at Rita, in the driver's seat of the cramped, little Datsun. Her skirt had slipped up to mid-thigh, and I wondered why I hadn't noticed before what lovely legs she had.

She turned my way and gave me a nice smile.

"Sugar buns, Rita? You called that hairy ape sugar buns," I said, and she laughed.

Then we both fell silent again, wondering why anyone would want to kill a washed-out alcoholic like Hazel Farris.

Chapter Four

At precisely 9:30 a.m., Judge Abraham J. Tobias marched in, ascended three steps, adjusted his robes, and plopped his ample backside into the seat of the black, high-back chair. He wiggled a little, getting comfortable on his throne, and with the unmistakable gleam of self-importance, he gazed out at the people gathered there. Harrumphing, he glared at us as if we were his subjects ready to do his bidding.

We were assembled in Judge Abe Tobias's courtroom, Arraignments, Division 6 C, on the third floor of the Criminal Courts building in downtown Los Angeles. The deputy D.A., Steve Webster, and I were all set to act out our prearranged roles.

I sat at the defense table with Robbie. He wasn't cuffed, but he still wore the jailhouse jumpsuit. There was no need for street clothes at this point. This proceeding would be held in front of Tobias without a jury present and the prisoner garb wouldn't prejudice the judge regarding my client's guilt or innocence. We all knew that.

Webster sat alone at the prosecutor's table on the right side of the courtroom. His hand scribbled notes on a yellow tablet. He had to be working on one of his other cases; our deal was cut, chiseled in stone. The court reporter, a young and attractive woman in a loose white blouse, sat at her small table in front of the bench. Her fingers, forming claws were fixed above the keyboard of the gizmo in front of her, poised to transcribe our pearls of wisdom, fresh and pure, as they rolled glibly off our tongues.

The bailiff and a deputy sheriff stood close behind Robbie, guarding their prisoner.

Today would be routine. I would ask for a continuance of the arraignment until a psychiatrist had a chance to examine Robbie. Steve Webster would make a verbal motion not to set a trial date until the psychiatrist provided the court with his evaluation. Earlier, before the beginning of today's proceedings, I met Webster in the snack bar downstairs in the lobby, where he handed me a list of psychiatrists who would be acceptable to the people. I was to choose one and get back to him within a day or two.

At this morning's arraignment, the judge would agree to our plan, and the whole affair would be over in a matter of minutes. Even with the hour drive back to Downey, I'd be out of here and back my office in plenty of time to interview a new client Mabel had scheduled for eleven.

And after listening to the new guy's woes–something about his troubles with a bank he tried to stiff–I'd still have time to catch up on a little paperwork before I headed out for a leisurely lunch with my best friend, Sol Silverman. Yeah, today's arraignment was going to be a snap. Hey, were barbecued ribs the special today at Rocco's?

When I broke the news to Robbie about his mother's murder, he had little response, just mumbled something about eternal damnation and continued with his praying. The only time he seemed to come out of his prayer-induced spell was when he asked if he could speak with the pastor of his mother's church. I knew that neither Robbie nor his mother had any assets, cash or otherwise, and I assumed he wanted to ask the pastor to say a few words on his mother's behalf at the funeral, which the county would provide. I told him I would arrange the meeting, or at the least a telephone conversation. Robbie told me the guy's name, Reverend Elroy Snavley, and we moved on to the next order of business. I explained the arraignment procedure by rote while he slipped back into his prayer mode, not listening to a word I said.

"Docket number 73-4654, the People of the State of California versus Robbie Farris, Section 187, Penal Code, murder in the first degree lying in wait." The clerk called our case. The *lying in wait* kicker was an afterthought, which bounced my client's crime from second to first degree. They say he was lurking in the dark, waiting. It was nighttime; where else could he lurk, for chrissakes? But it didn't matter. It was moot. My plan was in high gear, and I'd be out of here in a matter of minutes.

Webster and I stood. Robbie remained seated, his hands folded on the table in front of him, his gaze directed at the ceiling, his lips going a mile a minute in silent prayer.

"O'Brien for the defense, Your Honor," I said, adjusting my tie.

"What's wrong with your client? He's crippled or something? Can't stand up?"

"No, Your Honor, he's insane and I'd like–"

"Objection, Judge." Webster jumped in. "That has not been determined yet. We don't know if he's sane or not. But, the people will agree to postpone the arraignment until the defendant has been examined by a duly certified psychiatrist–"

Judge Tobias held his hands out in front of him. "Say no more, counselor. I get the point." Tobias looked down at his desk, filched a gold pen from its holder, and started jotting on a form of some kind. Without looking up he said, "Does your client agree to the postponement of the plea, O'Brien?"

I glanced down at Robbie sitting there, consumed in

prayer. But before I could respond, he jerked his head up, gawked at me for an instant, and with fury in his eyes rose from his chair.

"I'm guilty. I demand to be put to death at once!" he shouted at the top of his lungs.

The judge banged his gavel several times while Robbie continued to invoke the Lord's help in his pursuit of the great beyond.

"Oh, Lord, show them the way. Tell them to strike me down like a rabid dog!"

The guard and the bailiff were at a loss, not sure of their next move. "Oh, Lord, take me now. Take my wretched soul." Robbie was on a roll, screaming hysterically, his arms flailing about. "Cast me into Hell. I have sinned."

What in hell is he doing? He's going to screw everything up.

Webster sat down. He stretched his arm across the back of the chair next to him, an amused spectator at a full-blown revival.

Bang! The gavel hit wood. "O'Brien, control you client, or I'll have him removed!"

I turned to Robbie, who was now hopping up and down on one foot. I firmly placed both of my hands on his shoulders.

"Calm down, son," I said.

Although I had attended Catholic schools as a youth, I've never been much of a believer in anything religious, but I felt this might be the perfect time for a prayer of some sort, a prayer Robbie could comprehend. I squeezed hard on the soft tissue and ligaments adjacent to his shoulders and spun him around until we were face to face.

"Look at me, Robbie, look into my eyes."

He brought his head up. His eyes were fiery, blazing with

intense loathing, like those of a wild beast captured in a horrible trap.

I shifted my gaze to the heavens. "Oh, Lord, calm thy servant, Robbie." I chanted in a deep full voice, giving Robbie my best impression of Billy Graham.

"I killed the heathen. I have to die—" Robbie whimpered. My prayer seemed to be working. He was running out of steam.

I continued: "Tell thy servant, Robbie, that he'll be joining you soon enough, but also tell him that Jimmy O'Brien is going to take care of things for a while. And tell him to shut up, so I can get this hearing over with."

Robbie had a perplexed look on his face. He studied me, searching for some meaning to my words, or perhaps waiting for further instructions from above.

Judge Tobias banged the gavel once more. "This isn't a church, goddammit. This is a court of law. No praying allowed."

I didn't mention to His Honor that more prayers, fervent prayers of a heartfelt nature, were probably uttered in the criminal courts of our land than in any church ever erected; didn't think it would shed any light on the proceedings.

"Bailiff, remove the prisoner." He banged the gavel again.

The judge could not rule on Webster's motion until Robbie agreed to the deal, but if Tobias had him removed from the court before he ruled, then I'd have to come down here sometime in the future and go through the process all over again from the top.

At the very least, I'd have to fight the traffic and pony up another five bucks to park. But, worse, who knew what could happen in the meantime. Webster could change his mind about accepting my insanity defense, and Robbie would most likely spend the rest of his life buried in a cell at San Quentin.

I faced the bench. "Judge, please give me a moment. Let me confer with my client." I loosened my grip on Robbie's shoulders, and he started hopping up and down again, but not as high as before. "I'm sure I'll be able to calm him down so we can get on with this."

"I have a dozen arraignments lined up, and that's just the morning session. I can't waste any more time on this nonsense."

"Judge, give me a few minutes. Let me talk to my client." I dug my fingers into Robbie's shoulders, hard. He stopped hopping. "You can move on to the next case while I explain to him what this is all about." I was practically begging. "He'll listen to me, Your Honor, I promise."

The judge sighed. "All right, O'Brien, you got ten minutes. Not one second more. If you can't get him under control, we're postponing until he's fit." He turned to the deputy sheriff. "Guard, stay with O'Brien and the defendant. I'm leaving the bench. Court's in recess for ten minutes."

"Thank you, Your Honor." I said to the judge's fleeing back as he hurried to his chambers door. He probably had to take a leak. If it weren't for the judge's weak bladder, Robbie would do life.

Webster, the court reporter, and the bailiff all scurried out of the courtroom, bolting for the snack bar, I assumed.

I leaned into Robbie and whispered in his ear. "Now, shut your goddamn mouth, and quit jumping around, or I bust your chops. Understand?"

He nodded his head, slightly.

I motioned for Robbie to sit down, grabbed my briefcase, and plopped it on the table.

He fell quiet and sat hunched over, rocking back and forth, mumbling a little. I wondered if, when the proceedings began again, he'd start acting like a baboon.

"Stand up, buddy," The guard said, hovering over Robbie, reaching behind his back for handcuffs kept in a pouch hooked to his Sam Browne belt.

"Give me a minute, deputy. He's okay now."

I considered the possibility that all the uniforms, chains, and guns might be spooking Robbie. I believed I might be able to get through his mental barricade if it were just him and me, one on one. Prior to becoming a lawyer, I was a cop, LA PD. At times, I had to use my finely honed skill at negotiation to worm my way out of a jam or two.

"No way. When court's not in session, he's got to be hooked up. Rules."

"Look at him, he's harmless."

"Yeah, sure, they all are. Squeaky Fromme, one of Charlie Manson's girls, is up there." He gestured in the direction of the courthouse cellblock, one story above us "She's in our lockup waiting for her appearance down the hall, playing gin with one of the female deputies, calm and cool as can be."

Robbie slowly got to his feet. The deputy turned to grab his arm. Robbie leapt at him. In a blur, he grabbed the deputy's service revolver and yanked it out of the holster. He whipped the gun furiously across the deputy's face. Blood erupted. The guy went down.

Before I could react, Robbie jammed the gun barrel tightly up against his right temple and started backing slowly through the bar gate. He moved steadily toward the courtroom door.

"Don't come near me. I'm leaving. I'm going to meet the Lord!" he screamed.

"Robbie, don't!"

I glanced down at the deputy. He stirred. I made a move toward Robbie.

He leveled the gun at me, waving it erratically. "Stop, heathen!"

I stopped in my tracks. The word 'heathen' sent a jolt up my spine. I knew what happened to the last guy he thought was a heathen.

Robbie inched backward, one cautious step after another, the gun dangling from his unsteady hand. "Oh, Lord, forgive me for what I'm about to do." Fear blanketed his face.

He kept moving, his eyes wide and fixed on me in a cold stare. The scraping sound his feet made as he slowly shuffled away grated my nerves like fingernails raking a blackboard. If I stood stark still, maybe Robbie wouldn't shoot me. But if he got away, the judge would kill me for sure.

While I stood there helplessly, Robbie disappeared through the doorway.

Chapter Five

I stared at the deputy lying on the floor. He managed to hunch up to his hands and knees. Turning his head, he tossed me a scornful look. "You'd better get that son-of-a-bitch back here, O'Brien. It's your ass. I'm not going down for this." He swiped his hand across his cheek and looked at the blood. "Go! Damn it."

I raced to the courtroom door, grabbed the handle, then stopped. Robbie had a gun. He might be laying in wait for me. He could be lurking just outside in the hall, waiting for me to blindly follow him. I tossed a quick look back at the deputy.

"Get going," he shouted, as he struggled to his feet. "Follow him, but don't get shot."

Yanking the door open, I stuck my head around the edge of the wall, ready to jerk it back at the first sight of a gun barrel pointed in my direction. Down the hall, I saw the stairwell door at the far end slam shut.

"I'm going for help," I heard the deputy shout behind me. "We'll have to block the building's entrances. It your fault, goddammit."

"Yeah, sure," I said more to myself than to the deputy, as I shot though the doorway and made a beeline for the stairwell.

Pausing cautiously for a second, I pulled on the stairwell door. Again, Robbie could be waiting, ready to send a doubting Thomas like me to meet his maker. But I could wait no longer. I slipped tentatively through the opening, pressing my body tight against the cold, hard wall.

"Robbie, it's me. I want to help you." I waited and

listened, but heard only the sound of my heart thumping in my chest. "Anybody in here?"

There was no response, just my voice echoing off the concrete walls, bouncing up and down the stairwell.

I had to find him and I had to find him fast.

Closer to the steps, I quietly listened again. I heard no sound, no running footsteps on the stairs, nothing. He could have dashed to the next floor and charged out into the hallway there. He could be running around flashing the gun, scaring the hell out of everyone, or...he could have shot someone by now. There were a lot of heathens to choose from in the Criminal Courts Building, and I didn't mean just the lawyers.

If he went up, he couldn't get out of the building. The cops would catch him sooner or later. I bolted down the steps, three at a time.

I exited on the second floor, ran into the hall and took a quick look in both directions. Everything seemed normal. People going on about their business, no crazed gunman terrorizing the citizens.

After charging down the next flights of stairs and running out into the hall, I stopped for an instant to catch my breath. I was on the ground floor, and again I glanced in all directions— no luck, he wasn't there.

Then I ducked into the snack bar and asked several people if they had seen a guy wearing jailhouse whites. Nobody had. Damn, I mumbled and continued roaming the marble lined lobby. I asked an elderly lady, who had just emerged from the one of the restrooms, if she saw Robbie. The woman had a feather boa wrapped around her neck, partially obscuring the undulating folds of flesh drooping there. With her elbows flapping, she gave me a haughty look and kept on walking, feathers flying.

I heard a man's raspy voice coming from somewhere down the main corridor. "Hey, buddy, you lookin' for the dude in the white outfit?"

I turned around. Nobody was there.

"Psst, over here."

I turned again and saw a guy wearing dark glasses. He held a white cane while leaning against the wall. A tin pail rested at his feet. "Yeah, that's right, me. Over here, Jake," he said out of the corner of his mouth.

"Do you know something?" I didn't ask if he saw Robbie.

"Cost you a buck."

"For what?"

"I saw him. The escaped con."

"You saw him?"

"Sometimes I can see," he said.

"Nobody else saw him," I said.

"The good citizens thought he was a janitor. Ya'know, wearing the white coveralls. People don't notice guys like that. Just 'cause he had L.A. County Jail plastered in big letters on his back, don't mean he mops up the jail."

"For chrissakes. Where'd he go?"

"Cost you a buck," the blind pretender said again, louder.

I ripped a dollar bill from my wallet. "Okay already, here's a buck," I said, flinging the bill into his pail. "Now what about my guy?"

"He charged out of the stairway door," he said with his boney finger pointing at the stairwell. "Then, he looked around for a couple of seconds, you know, like he didn't know what to do..." his voice trailed off. He stared straight ahead, his eyes hidden behind his dark glasses.

"Go on. Then what?"

"Costya a buck," he said, running the words together in a

well-practiced manner.

"Christ, am I going to get this on the installment plan?" I gave him another dollar. "Now tell me where he went."

"He went to the glass doors in front, waited a moment or two, then ran outside and waited on the steps. I followed him…"

I turned and started for the front doors.

"He ain't there now. He's gone," the beggar said to my back.

I tuned around. "Yeah, then where is he?"

"Costya a buck."

I grabbed the guy by his T-shirt. "Dammit, tell me where he went." I glanced around. Maybe I shouldn't have been so rough. People were giving me dirty looks. That's right, folks, I'm Jimmy O'Brien, a lawyer, and I'm beating up a blind guy.

I let go, reached into my wallet, pulled out a five and gave it to him. "Now, I want the whole story, okay."

"Hey, Clyde, not so rough. Guy's gotta make a living, ya'know," he said, his face all scrunched up.

"Yeah, maybe so." I felt a touch of remorse for being a bit hostile. "Now, c'mon, where is he?"

The guy lowered his glasses about a half inch with the tip of his right index finger. He gave me a squinty-eyed look up from under his stringy, bent eyebrows. "You're not a cop. I can tell. Your shoes aren't shined."

I glanced down. He was right. "C'mon, guy–"

"Hey, I know," he said. "You and the con are working together. Is that it? You let him take off. What happen, he run out without coughing up the *dinero*?"

"No goddammit, it is nothing like that," I said. "Now tell me where he went."

"Okay, Mac, okay. He waited outside for about five

seconds. All at once, a black Ford passenger van zooms up to the curb. Then the wrecking crew jumps out–"

"Wrecking crew?" I asked.

"Yeah, broken-noses in suits." He pushed his nose to one side. "Ya'know, leg breakers."

"Hired thugs?"

"Yeah, two big guys. Well, anyhow, your boy sees them," he said, pulling off his dark glasses and polishing the lenses with the end of his T-shirt. "I think he knew who they were. Then the suits rushed up and hustled him to the panel truck. They shoved him in the backseat and split." He put the glasses back on and glanced around, nodding.

"My God, you mean the guys in the suits kidnapped him?"

"Nah, I wouldn't say that. He didn't put up no fight or nothin', he just went with them."

I had to think. Could the guys in the black van be helping Robbie escape? Could this be a setup? If it was, then it had to be planned out in advance and that could mean Robbie wasn't crazy after all. His holy-roller routine could have been an act.

"You didn't see the thugs pull out weapons, or anything?" I asked.

"Didn't see no guns, no strongarm stuff."

"Did you get the license plate?"

"Nah, it was too far away."

I rushed out the main door and down the steps and stopped at the curb.

Wait a minute. Have I just been taken?

In the harsh sunlight, the story told by a swindler, a guy as genuine as a Tijuana Rolex, about Robbie being snatched and hauled away in a black van seemed utterly bizarre, like a bad movie. And I fell for it. Cost me seven bucks. But still, as illogical as it seemed, I looked up and down Grand Avenue several times. There were no black vans in sight.

I turned back to the court building. The cops had the front doors closed and the building was sealed off.

Chapter Six

Late again! The arraignment should have been history at around ten and now over an hour after that I was just getting on the freeway, rushing back to my office where my eleven o'clock client waited. The guy might think I'm not reliable. But hey, how was I to know Robbie would pull a trick and vanish like Harry Blackstone's donkey.

I grappled with my mind as I drove, confused about the events swirling around me, and wondered how much deeper I was going to be sucked in. All the bits and pieces, rattling debris, churning in my brain had my mind in turmoil. Robbie, my crazy client–who might not be crazy–ranting and raving about the Lord; his dead mother in a trailer and the cops questioning me about her murder as if I were some kind of suspect, and now a judge who was going to be on my ass.

When Judge Tobias assigned the Robbie Farris case to me and I saw that Robbie was mentally deficient, I knew the only defense possible would be an insanity plea–but I also realized an insanity plea wouldn't be easy. Only one percent of all criminal cases made use of the insanity defense and it was practically impossible to win one without the D.A. concurring. I had Webster convinced, tentatively, to go along with me but now I felt sure the deal was out the window.

I had to get to the office fast and find out just how upset the judge was. Why is it, when I'm in a hurry the traffic is always jammed up and I'm locked behind a cement truck moving at about two mph?

But, after mulling it over during the two hours it took to

drive from the Spring Street underpass to the exit at Paramount Boulevard in Downey, a distance of fifteen miles, I concluded that Judge Tobias might not be upset with me after all. He's an okay guy and he's known me for a while. He'll understand.

Surely, he would realize it wasn't my fault that Robbie got happy feet and took off. Nah, I wasn't in trouble, but just to be on the safe side, I'd phone the judge when I got back to my office. I'd phone him as soon as I was finished with my eleven o'clock client and patiently explain the details of Robbie's escape. Yeah, that's it; I'd simply explain how, after chasing around the court building looking for Robbie, unfortunately without success, I ended up on Grand Avenue. I'd tell him how I tried to get back inside, but by then the cops had the building sealed off. I was sure he'd understand. I'll calmly tell the judge to call me when the police found Robbie, and I would gladly pick up the case where we left off.

I wheeled into the office lot, parked the Vette, and glanced at the clock in the dash as I slid out. One-thirty six. Christ, I had kept my client waiting over two and half hours.

Mabel gave me her usual uplifting, cheery greeting when I entered.

"Where in the hell have you been? Your client took off, and damn, we need to get some cash in here. The bills are stacking up."

Mabel was in her middle years, her middle earlies, as she always said. She wore too much makeup, her carrot-top hair needed a touchup every now and then, and she had about as much class as hot dogs at the opera. But I liked her, I liked her a lot, and she worked miracles every day just keeping our law firm up and running.

"What do you mean he took off?" I asked. "Didn't you tell him I'd be here?"

"How long did you think he'd wait, for chrissakes?"

"Didn't you give him any coffee? I figured you'd give him some coffee."

"That's when he left, when he finished the coffee."

"Jesus, Mabel, you should've given him some more."

"We ran out. He drank three pots," she said.

"The guy drank three pots of coffee?"

"Yeah, he was kind of wired when he left."

"Call him again," I said. "Tell him I can't represent him unless he sticks around long enough for me to get the facts." I shook my head. "What do these clients think? Can't even wait a few minutes. Well, I guess that's why they're always in trouble, irresponsible," I said as I walked in my office and closed the door.

I told Mabel to hold my calls. I wanted to relax for a little while. It was too late for lunch. Sol wouldn't have waited; besides, this whole mess destroyed my appetite.

I slipped off my shoes, put my feet on the desk and started massaging my temples. I felt a headache coming on, and I wanted to put it to rest before the minor throbbing became a full-blown migraine.

Why is it, when Mabel makes the coffee, it is so good? But when I make the coffee, it tastes like Royal Triton motor oil? I guess that's just one of those mysteries of life not worth wasting my time trying to figure out when I had so many pressing matters to concern myself with. I continued kneading my head.

After a couple of minutes of grinding my temples, the headache started to wane.

The intercom buzzed. I grabbed the receiver while doing a couple of neck rolls. "Mabel, I said to hold my calls."

"You have an emergency on line one. I told him you were

in a meeting. He said he didn't give a damn. Said to put you on the line. Said it was a court order."

"Who said?"

"Hissoner himself, Judge Abraham Tobias."

I jumped and put my stocking feet on the floor. Oh, Christ, I forgot to call him. "What's he want, Mabel?"

"Ask him." Mabel hung up, and I pushed the flashing button with one hand while working a foot into one shoe with the other.

"This is O'Brien."

"I want you to surrender your client, right now. Don't mess with me, O'Brien." Judge Tobias sounded peeved, even a mite angry, and my headache roared to life, pounding like a jackhammer.

While wiggling my other foot into the loafer, I described the events in his courtroom after he left. I explained calmly how Robbie had grabbed the cop's gun, how he took off, and how I made a valiant effort, at risk of personal injury, to find him before he fled the building.

I didn't mention the blind guy or his story about the two thugs who drove up in the van and hauled Robbie away. I didn't know if I believed the story myself, and at this point, I didn't want to confuse the issue.

"That's not what I heard," Tobias said when I paused for a moment. "Officer Lisowski, the guard, said you helped the defendant escape."

"That's absurd," I said, trying without success to remain unruffled.

"I shouldn't be telling you this–"

"Telling me what?"

"Webster is pissed. He hasn't yet, but he's thinking about bringing you up on charges. He has Lisowski's sworn statement. Lisowski said you distracted him so Farris could grab his weapon."

"That's not true–" That son-of-a-bitch cop warned me. But, somehow, I couldn't hold it against him. A cop losing his weapon, especially to the bad guys, is about the worst that can happen.

"Webster also found out you're a suspect in a murder case, which occurred Monday, which just happened to be the defendant's mother. Who you, O'Brien, just happened to be visiting at the time she was killed. And," he said, his voice taking on a deep ominous tone, "when the homicide detectives wanted to talk to you, you lawyered up and refused to cooperate."

"Judge, you know me better than that."

"I thought I did, O'Brien, but now I'm not so sure..."

"Aw, Judge–"

"Webster's hot on this. He's talking about nailing you with a Penal Code Section 32."

My mind started to wind up, heading for the spin cycle. "Accessory? Aiding and abetting?"

"Congratulations, you know the law," the judge said with scorn in his voice. "You're lucky if he doesn't try to elevate it to conspiracy, a felony as you well know. But at a minimum, you'd lose your ticket to practice law and, frankly, it appears as if he has a damn good case."

It's my ass on the line now. The hell with the cop. "That's crazy. The deputy is lying. He's just trying to save his skin."

"Personally, I don't think you're guilty of murder, but I don't know what to think about the Section 32 charge. You've been known to be very aggressive defending your clients."

"Aw, Judge, you know me better than that," I said again, almost pleading. "I'd never do anything illegal. But, anyway, what's wrong with being aggressive? That's our system."

"You've been known to bend the rules," Judge Tobias said.

"C'mon, Judge, I've always stayed within the law–"

"So you say, but I have my doubts. You are facing serious charges, O'Brien. The way I see it, you've got only one way out of this mess, and that is if your client surrenders before Webster can get an indictment against you. You got three days, maybe four, that's about it. Dammit, listen to me. I'm not going to bat for you on this. Am I making myself clear?"

"One more thing, Judge, before you hang up," I said.

"Yeah, what?"

"I left my briefcase in your courtroom. Can you save it for me?"

He slammed down the phone.

After I hung up, I leaned back and thought, this just isn't my day. But, at least, the worst is over.

The intercom came to life. Mabel's voice filled the room. "Jimmy, there's a couple of homicide cops out here. They want to talk to you."

Chapter Seven

"Do you own a gun, a .38 caliber?"

I did, my police special, a .38-caliber revolver left over from my days on the L.A. police force. And these two cops knew it.

"Why? Was she killed with a .38?" Dumb question, but I felt I had to say something.

Both guys were standing, facing me across my desk. When they entered the office, I stood but did not come from behind the desk to greet them, and I didn't offer any of Mabel's wonderful coffee. One, we didn't have any, and two, I wouldn't have offered it even if we did. This was not a social call.

"Where is it?" Sergeant Hammer asked. He stood there, muscles rippling beneath his tight Italian-cut suit. His partner, Butch, leaned against the wall in the corner by the window with his interrogation pad out. He wore a cheap polyester sports coat: probably bought it at Sears. That's where I got mine.

"Whoever offed the old broad was a crack shot. They planted the slug dead center in her forehead." Hammer paused for a moment. "We checked your record. When you were on the job, you qualified as a sharpshooter on the range."

"C'mon, Sarge. You know anyone who could squeeze the trigger qualified."

"Give it up, O'Brien. If your gun's not the murder weapon, you're off the hook. See, we're on your side," he said, tossing out the remark to his partner. "Aren't we Butch?"

"Yeah, we're on his side. But if he doesn't cough up the

weapon, we're gonna be on his bad side," Butch Something said.

"You gonna turn the weapon over voluntarily, or do we have to get a warrant?" Hammer asked without rancor. "We got probable cause."

Again, I found myself in that phase of a tense negotiation where there was a lot of staring going on. I stared at him and he stared at me. But I really didn't have any major concerns about letting the cops have my gun. After all, my .38 wasn't the murder weapon. However, being a criminal lawyer, I knew that sort of thing just wasn't done. What kind of an example would I set, caving in to the cops like that after telling my clients to clam up when dealing with them? I'd be the laughingstock of the Criminal Lawyer's Don't-Answer-That Society.

I kept the revolver in my top desk drawer here in the office, but I kept the gun's cleaning kit and a box of bullets in the bedroom closet, top shelf, at my apartment. I brought the weapon to my office after receiving a telephone threat on my life concerning an old case. The man who'd made the threat won't be making any more nasty calls. Let's just say that his phone has been permanently disconnected.

And now I wasn't about to give up the revolver. If the cops wanted my gun, they'd have to get their warrant.

All three of us turned when we heard the door bang open. Rita marched in.

"Hey, what's going on?" she asked. "You guys questioning my client without me being present? That's against the rules. Now, get out."

Hammer cast a sidelong glance at Rita as she swept toward us wearing a bell-bottom pantsuit with a delightful sweater vest, her breasts stretching the fabric in a tantalizing way.

"Missy, I knew you were going to be trouble from the jump," he said.

"Move it, big boy," she responded.

The cops, knowing they were going to get nothing more, and now that the odds were even–two against two, lawyers versus cops–they turned to leave. But before they did, I had to find out what Hammer meant when he said they had probable cause. "Hold it," I called out.

Hammer shrugged. "Yeah, what?"

"Shut up, Jimmy," Rita said.

Rita reacted as any good criminal lawyer would have, but she had only been a member of the bar for about a month with one small case under her belt. I had been a lawyer for a couple of years now with several cases. I had concerns. I didn't know if she had what it took to handle a thing this heavy.

"Rita," I said. "Hold on a minute. I want to talk to these guys."

"Let me handle this. I'm your lawyer." She turned to the cops. "You guys still here? Take a hike."

"Goddammit, make up your mind," Hammer said. "You wanna cooperate, or not?"

Rita and I silently stared at each other. Abraham Lincoln's moldy adage flashed through my mind: "*A lawyer who represents himself has a fool for a client and a fool for a lawyer.*" There was no doubt I was in trouble and I needed a lawyer oh, did I need a lawyer. I studied Rita's face; she seemed awful young to be a top-notch attorney. But, gosh, she's so pretty...

Rita peered at me out of the corner of her eye, waiting.

I turned to the cops. "You heard my lawyer. I'm through talking."

"It's your funeral, O'Brien. C'mon, Butch, let's go get that warrant."

I knew I would feel more secure with some weathered old guy acting as my attorney, an experienced trial lawyer with a golden tongue and a bear-trap mind. A guy like Charles Laughton in *Witness for the Prosecution*. Rita did not look like Charles Laughton.

"Rita," I said, "I'm thrilled that you're my lawyer. What's next?"

"Before this thing gets totally out of control," she said, "we need a plan."

Chapter Eight

"Let me have a crack at it," Rita said, walking to my office window and glancing down at the traffic rushing by on Lakewood. When she turned back, her face was solemn, her eyes focused and sharp. "Jimmy, I want to be your lawyer. I'll do anything. I'll do everything with every fiber of my being to get you out of this mess."

"I know you will," I said and I meant it. *But will that be enough?*

She and I discussed my situation for about an hour more before we realized that the day had slipped away. We were both getting hungry. Each of us had skipped lunch, Rita working a DUI with her perennial drunk, a client named Geoff, while I was stuck behind the cement truck on the Santa Ana Freeway. We decided to grab a bite somewhere and continue the discussion.

I discovered Rita loved pizza with anchovies as much as I did. "So, Luigi's here we come," I said as we hopped in my car.

Luigi's Italian Deli was located a few minutes from the office on Paramount Boulevard in Downey, but when we walked in, we could have been entering a pizzeria in a country village somewhere in Italy. Luigi's was a refreshing change from the corporate, sterile, stainless steel pizza joints springing up around the city. Cured salami and strong, aromatic Parmigiano Reggiano hung in mesh bags from the ceiling. Chianti bottles with melting, shimmering candles sat on the tables, casting the restaurant in a soft warm glow. Colorful maps and pictures of the old country lined the walls.

Over the edge of the menu, I stole a look at Rita sitting across from me. In the candlelight, her cream-colored skin was flawless and her face was radiant with a youthful glimmer. I'd noticed before how lovely she was, of course. I'd noticed her petite, perfect figure and her beautiful features, but I'd never seen her quite the way I saw her tonight. She looked like an angel and now she wanted to be an angel, my guardian angel.

We ordered the pizza, and while waiting for Luigi to bring our food I tried to explain the reality of a being a criminal lawyer. "It's not all that glamorous like on TV..." I started to say, but when she gave me a wary look, I changed my angle. "It's not that rewarding–"

"Come off of it, Jimmy. I've made my mind up. Criminal law is where I belong."

"Actually, Rita, maybe you'd like corporate law better. Think it over. The best of both worlds. The clients will still be crooks, but, hey, they pay their bills."

"No way, Jimmy. I'm thrilled to be with you and with the firm. And now I'm really excited. My God, you are my first client with serious problems. Isn't that wonderful–oops." She put her hand over her mouth, but I could still see the glint in her eyes.

I smiled. "I know Rita, but–"

A shadow swept across her face. "What's the matter? You don't want me?"

"Oh no, of course I want you. How could you think that? I was just concerned about your career. That's all. Really. "

Luigi brought the pizza and Cokes. He came just in time, saving me from delving deeper into my concerns about Rita's experience. After we silently ate a few slices, I made up my mind. "Okay, Ms. Criminal Lawyer, where do we start?" I said.

She took one more nibble on the crust of her pizza slice,

put it down, wiped her hands on the paper napkin next to her plate, and quickly took a sip of her Coke. Then she leaned into me, and with a determined look etched on her face, she said. "All right. Here's the way I see it."

"Okay," I said, watching her eyes dance.

"The cops are looking at you for the murder. They've got evidence."

"Yeah."

"But their evidence sucks. Alone, it can be explained away."

"Think so?"

Rita leaned back and twirled the straw in her glass. "Yes, what do they have? You had a legitimate reason to be at Hazel Farris's place, and just because you own a .38 means nothing. After all, your gun wasn't the murder weapon."

"I haven't fired the gun since I was a cop," I said.

"Okay, but it's the other thing that bothers me, the Section 32 thing."

"Robbie's escape."

"Yes," she said and took another sip of her Coke. "If they tie the two together, and they will, then–"

"Then I'll be in deep trouble," I said, finishing her sentence.

She raised her head. "Jimmy, it would go to motive for the murder."

"Maybe they've already tied the cases together. Hammer said he had probable cause. That could be it. They'd figure I killed his mother and somehow Robbie knew about it. They'll say I let him escape so he wouldn't rat me out. But why would I kill her in the first place?"

"Doesn't matter, Jimmy. They'll only need enough to get an indictment. And how do we prove you didn't kill her." It was a rhetorical question. When I didn't respond, she continued: "You've got no alibi and we can't prove a negative."

"Looks bad."

"True, but I have a plan," she announced, her eyes sparkling.

"Go."

"We find Robbie, bring him back, and prove he's insane. Just as you said all along. That will show that you didn't help him escape in the first place. Once we do that, there'll be no reason to tie his disappearance to the murder, no motive. Ergo," she said, with a lilting smile, "no reason to figure you contributed to Mrs. Farris's untimely demise."

I sat thinking. There were a couple of loopholes in her plan.

"What do you think, Jimmy? Good plan?"

"Better than average."

I didn't want to mention it, but the problem with her plan was, just how were we supposed to find Robbie in the first place? God only knows where he could have gone.

Rita's soft voice interrupted my thoughts. "I know what you're thinking. How are we going to find Robbie?"

"Well, not really."

"We'll get Sol Silverman, the world's greatest detective, to help us. You know he'll do it. He won't even charge you."

"Think so?" I asked.

"Yes, he's your dear friend. I know he'll help. Try not to worry."

"I'm not worried. With Sol helping out, and with you as my lawyer, how can I miss?"

I wasn't worried; I was scared. After all, I was being questioned in connection with a murder. Who wouldn't let that gnaw at his guts? And I had real concerns about Webster filing the Section 32 charge. Even if the homicide detectives found out I had nothing to do with the old woman's death, assuming they found the real killer, I could still be convicted of the Section 32 violation, aiding and abetting. I'd lose my license to practice law.

Even though I wasn't guilty of a crime–stupidity maybe, but a crime, no–getting off the hook wasn't going to be that easy. Webster had the cop's statement, and as Rita pointed out, how do you prove a negative? In other words, how do I prove I didn't do it?

Oh, all the inspired rhetoric flowing from lofty sources said a person is not guilty until proven so in a court of law. And they always say the accused does not have to prove his innocence. Bullshit.

Yes, Rita's plan was a simple one. Find Robbie, bring him back and prove to the judge that he's insane. That would work, and as she said, Sol would help. Rita thinks he's the world's greatest detective. Why did Rita think that? I mused. Because Sol told her so, that's why.

We left the pizzeria. The moon, a silver crescent drifting in the night sky among a scattering of gleaming stars, was high in the east. We walked silently to my Vette.

"Look at the moon, Jimmy," Rita said. "It's right next to that star. Isn't it beautiful?"

I was dying inside and my lawyer was gazing at the moon. But I glanced up. The tip of the lunar crescent was pointed at the planet Venus, shimmering bright in all its splendor. Was that an omen, the moon pointing at Venus that way? Was the moon telling me to get out of town and move far away, preferably to another planet?

"Yes, Rita. It's beautiful."

When we pulled into the parking lot, back at the office, we

lingered a moment.

"I know you will do everything possible on my behalf, Rita, and I'm grateful."

She gave my arm an affectionate pat and hopped out of the car. She did not have to say how concerned she was; the worry was in her eyes.

Chapter Nine

Sol took a sip of Krug Champagne and set the flute glass down on the tablecloth. "So tell me, Jimmy, what's this all about."

When I'd called and asked for help finding Robbie, Sol suggested we discuss the situation over lunch, and now we were at Rocco's. After we ordered, I told him the whole story, filled him in on the murder of Robbie's mother, and mentioned how the homicide detectives were looking at me like some kind of suspect. Then I explained how Robbie had vanished at the arraignment. I told him that Webster had the guard's statement, and now he was going to file charges, which could cause me to lose my license and could possibly land me jail.

"Frankly, Sol, I'm getting a little antsy about the whole affair," I said.

"That's how it is being a lawyer, Jimmy," Sol said in a convivial manner. "Got to take to the good with the bad. Here, taste this veal." He reached across the table with his fork. A morsel of veal was impaled on it. "It's terrific, veal Oscar, named after King Oscar of Sweden or someplace like that," he said. "You see, this king guy was..."

My guts were churning and Sol kept rambling on about some goddamn king and his goddamn veal.

"Sol, forget the king, I've got a problem here, and I need your help."

"Not until you taste this stuff." He jabbed the fork at me.

"Don't want any damn veal Omar, or what ever the hell you call it–"

"Eat it!"

"All right, then we work on my problem." I took the fork and stuck it in my mouth. "Okay, now here's the plan–hey, this stuff's pretty good."

Sol, his finger whirling in the air, signaled for Janine, our waitress.

After I finished a plate of veal Oscar and Sol his second helping, we got back to why we were there in the first place.

"So, anyway, Sol, I need your help. We gotta find the guy," I said. "Rita and I had dinner last night and–"

"Thought you were going out with that flight instructor. What's her name again?"

"Susie. But she got a job with an airline, a puddle jumper somewhere in the Midwest. She left a month ago. Anyway, what's this got to do with finding Robbie?"

"You hitting on Rita now?"

"No, damn it. I work with her, for chrissakes. Anyway she's my lawyer now."

"*What!* Rita's your lawyer?" He started to laugh.

"Yeah, but Sol, she just wants to help."

"Yeah, but nothing, Jimmy. You need a real lawyer." Sol said. "Cute little Rita, with her nice little tushy, Jimmy's lawyer." He continued laughing. "Hey, don't worry; I'll bring the veal Oscar on visiting days."

"Sol, knock it off. This is serious. It's a murder charge."

Suddenly he became somber. "What's for dessert?"

"Oh, for chrissakes."

I should've known that it would do no good to discuss my case with Sol while food was on the table, but finally dessert was finished.

I sipped the last of my coffee, and Sol peered at me with one eyebrow cocked. He sat back and put his wine glass on the table. We were now ready to discuss my *tsores*, his word for troubles. Now was the time to put Rita's plan into action.

"Okay, Jimmy, just what is it you want me to do?"

"I need to use your contacts. I've only got a few days."

Sol had contacts, a vast network of people on his payroll, *off the books*–paid in cash–informants in key places. He called them his spies. I wanted to make good use of his sources.

"My spies are your spies."

"See if you can find out what Webster's up to." As I asked for Sol's help, I wondered if there was anything in the canons of legal ethics about using paid informants to spy on the D.A. I supposed there probably was, but I was getting nervous with the deadline, and all. "Can you get a copy of the guard's statement; find out if Webster has enough to file a complaint?"

"Of course, my boy, but you knew that. In the meantime, I suggest you turn your daily work, your caseload over to sweet little Rita." He chuckled and shook his head. "You don't want her as your lawyer, but she can help. She can free you up so you can concentrate on getting out from under this mess. And, Jimmy," he reached across the table and patted my arm, "when you need a lawyer, don't worry, I'll get you Morty."

Sol had powerful friends. I wondered if he was referring to Morton Zuckerman, the highest priced criminal defense attorney on the coast. "Morty who?"

"Morty, my wife's nephew." Sol slowly shook his head. Then he looked up. "Hey, Morty's not a nitwit. He just needs a client to show what he can do."

So much for Zuckerman. I didn't want him anyway. Rita was my lawyer. "Yeah, thanks, Sol."

"Good. But can Rita handle your caseload?"

There was no use explaining to Sol that Rita handling my clients wouldn't be a problem. I only had one. And who knew if he'd be back...unless he liked Mabel's coffee, that is. But Sol was right: I needed to keep my mind free until this thing was behind me, and I knew Rita could act as my lawyer and still handle my day-to-day duties without breaking a sweat.

"Yeah, good idea, Sol. I think she might be able to handle my caseload. Of course, if she gets bogged down or needs my advice, I can always help. But you're right. I've got to get myself out of this mess."

I left Rocco's feeling optimistic. I knew with Sol's help

we'd find Robbie, and in spite of all of his oddball characteristics, Sol was the best.

When I arrived back at the office, Mabel reminded me that Rita had a trial appearance in West L.A regarding her client, Geoff. She wasn't expected back for the remainder of the day.

I walked into my office, sipped coffee, and gazed out the window watching the line of the cars turn into Stonewood Shopping Center. Must be a big sale at the Broadway. Life goes on, I guess.

I needed to see Rita to explain the transfer of my workload, my one client…big deal, a nothing case. The guy was charged with credit card fraud. She'll cut a deal, have the guy promise to pay his debt, they'll drop the charges. No sweat.

It was well after seven when I got up from my desk ready to leave the office. Rita hadn't returned, but I hadn't expected her to. That's okay. I'd catch her tomorrow.

I lived close by, and at that time of night there wouldn't be much traffic. The drive took less than five minutes. I had a nice two-bedroom apartment on Cecilia Street. I needed a spot where I could relax and unwind at the end of the day, so I had converted the second bedroom into a study. A hardback chair stood in the center, a guitar leaning next to it. That's all, just the guitar and the chair. I didn't like things cluttering up my life.

Tonight, I'd soak in the tub, forget my problems, and maybe practice the guitar, a Beatles number I was working on, "Let it be." I wasn't sure; I thought John Lennon had preformed the song on the sixties hit record, but a beautiful girl I had met at Rocco's one night told me the singer was not Lennon but Paul McCartney. Though very convincing, she was probably wrong. I wanted to ask her out. But she was from out of state, just visiting a friend. And besides, she was engaged; at least that's what she'd said. She may have been wrong about that too.

I made the turn onto Cecilia. "Oh, *Christ*, what now?" I exclaimed. My apartment door was open. I saw the flashing lights of several squad cars parked haphazardly at the curb.

Chapter Ten

I parked, vaulted the stairway three steps at a time, and rushed to my apartment on the second floor. Cops were all over the place. Hammer and Butch Something were in the living room. Hammer directed a couple of Downey cops who were getting ready to search the living room. Butch was braced in the corner by the TV, smoking a cigarette.

"You got the warrant, I guess," I said to Hammer.

"Yeah, want to see it?" He removed the document from his inside jacket pocket and handed it over.

I took a quick glance: a no-knock search warrant signed by Judge Frisco. This meant they didn't need a whole lot of compelling evidence to get the warrant. Frisco, an ox D.A., was known for being a law-and-order judge. He'd sign anything the cops set before him.

The police had the right to search my home looking for my gun and—if found—the warrant allowed them to seize it. A *no-knock warrant* meant they could walk right in, bust down the door if necessary, and tear the place apart. To get a no-knock warrant, the police would normally have to provide an affidavit certifying that they were afraid the evidence was in imminent danger of disappearing. I doubted they even told Frisco what they were looking for. They filled in the blanks, and he signed it. Why didn't he just give them a rubber stamp with his signature? Maybe he did.

"You can save yourself a lot of grief, O'Brien, if you tell us where it is."

The law stated I couldn't interfere with the search, but it

also said I had the right to keep my mouth shut and not say anything that would aid them. But if I didn't tell them where the gun was, they'd continue ripping my place apart.

"We found your gun kit and some bullets in the closet next to a cowboy hat," he said," But no gun."

"I was going to ask about the hat," Butch Something piped up from the corner. "You some kind of cowboy, O'Brien?" He flashed a lewd smirk. "Like to ride 'em bareback?"

I ignored Something's remark and started for the bedroom.

Ducking my head in, I almost gagged. Everything in the room was in shambles, mattress torn apart, all my clothes scattered on the floor, drawers pulled out and flung around the room.

I stood stark still, shocked, at the point of paralysis. Then the rage started to build like pressure in an old boiler. All of a sudden, I lost it. I lurched at Hammer; the two uniforms jumped in and grabbed me before I could get to him. "You son-of-a-bitch, you're going too far!"

"Cough up the weapon, and we won't search the rest of the premises."

I read the threat and struggled to get free of the two big cops that were latched onto my arms. "Goddammit, let go of me."

Butch ground his cigarette butt on my carpet. "Interfering with a lawful search pursuant to a warrant is a crime."

"Shut-up, Butch," Hammer snapped. "He's a lawyer. He knows the law." Then he said to me, "If you don't behave, O'Brien, I'll hook you up."

I kept quiet, the angry burning inside.

"Let him go," Hammer told the uniforms. "Now, damn it, O'Brien, where's the gun? Where did you hide it?"

"I didn't hide it. It's at the office."

"I think it's here. Or maybe you hid it somewhere. If you don't cough it up, we're going to search this place from top to bottom." Hammer scowled. "We won't be so neat and tidy this time."

They were using the gun excuse to go through my living quarters with a scorched earth vengeance. The warrant only gave them the right to look for my gun but if they found something else they could use it against me as well. They'd find nothing but my place would be a shambles. "Hammer, if I was going to hide my gun, do you think I'd be stupid enough to hide it here? Look," I said, "just cool your heels, I'll go to the office and get the gun. I'll bring it right back."

"Better hurry."

I heard a ripping sound, and turned. One of the cops was tearing the back off of my sofa. "Hey, knock it off, that's a brand new sofa. Cost me fifty bucks." I spun around. "Goddammit, Hammer, tell your storm troopers to back off."

"You're interfering. Step outside or you're taking a ride."

My nerves were stretched tight and Hammer was plucking the strings. One more twang and they would snap. I needed to cool off.

I knew if I stuck around, I'd do something reckless. Being frogmarched to the Downey lockup with my arms cuffed behind my back wasn't going to help matters. I needed to get out of that apartment fast, go to the office and get the gun and bring it back. If I did, then the cops would have no excuse to tear my place apart.

I jumped in the Vette and peeled away from the curb. By the time I hit Paramount Boulevard the speedometer needle was swinging through its arch, bouncing off 80.

I clipped the light at Florence Avenue and shot up onto the Santa Ana Freeway. Swerving to miss a pickup truck, I almost went into a sidespin, just missing a couple of nuns who drove a Dodge station wagon going about five miles an hour. I realized that racing around like a madman wasn't going to help, but I had to get the gun back to Hammer before they did any more damage to my home.

I swerved off Cecilia Street, bounced the Vette into my parking spot, and rushed to my office door. It wasn't locked. Damn, I was careless. Mabel was always on me about locking up, but I didn't have time to think about that now.

I charged to my desk and pulled the drawer open–no gun! I ruffled through all the drawers, still no gun.

Where in the hell is it? I know, it's in Mabel's desk, she took the gun, would feel safe with it. Couldn't blame her. We had a client list filled with bad guys. That's how it is being a criminal lawyer, I thought, as I rushed to her desk. I went though her drawers. Not there either. *Damn, someone stole it*!

The gun was gone. I spent the next twenty minutes rummaging through all the desk and cabinet drawers with no success. I knew someone came in here and snatched it. I was desperate to get to the bottom of this. If someone took my gun, what are the odds that it was used to murder Hazel Farris? If it was my gun that killed her, then that meant someone was trying to set me up for sure. Who...and why me?

I had to go back to my apartment and face the heat like a man, like an officer of the court, like a person who believed in our system of justice, which sooner or later would make things right. Without the law, who was I? Just another two-bit hustler out to make a buck off of some poor sap's misery. But what's the use? Hammer would be gone by now and my apartment would be destroyed.

I got in my Corvette and drove home.

When I pulled up to the curb this time, sure enough, the

cops were gone. The patrol cars had left, but Rita's yellow Datsun was parked there. I climbed out of the Vette but didn't bolt up the stairs like before. I felt downhearted and it would show. I wanted time to improve my attitude before seeing Rita. I was her mentor, after all, and I had to be strong.

As I climbed the steps, I wondered why she'd stopped by. But I felt glad she did. Maybe I just needed to see a friendly face, someone on my side for a change.

Reaching the top step, I stood still and thought for a moment. Other than Rita and Sol, I really didn't have many friends. Oh, there was Bobby Pollard, my buddy all through high school, but when he graduated from college he got a job with an insurance company and moved to Chicago. The last time I talked to him, he tried to sell me a whole-life policy. Double benefits if I got run over by a train.

The front door was open. Rita stood in the middle of the living room, hands on her hips surveying the damage. My TV was smashed, stuff overturned, furniture torn apart. The kitchenette, the bit I could see out of the corner of my eye, had been ransacked and looked as if a tornado had hit it–a tornado named Hammer.

Rita turned when I walked in. There was a moment's silence, a warm acknowledgment of our friendship.

"Oh, Jimmy, your apartment is a mess."

"Cops," I said.

"I know. They were still here when I arrived. Hammer gave me a copy of the warrant. I'm sorry, Jimmy."

"Hey, Rita, I planned on doing a remodel job anyway, and now it's done–Early Cop." I laughed an empty laugh.

"They're looking for your gun."

"They knew it wasn't here. They were looking for something else too, a fishing expedition. But, I'm really worried now…. I looked in the office, my gun is gone…someone stole it."

"Jimmy, this could be trouble."

"Yeah, I know. The gun all of a sudden goes missing, and a woman is murdered with the same kind of weapon. I don't like coincidences."

"My God," she said. "Do you think someone took your gun and shot Robbie's mother with it?"

"I don't know, Rita. I don't know what to think."

"You didn't just misplace it?"

"Nah, I put it in my desk drawer a few months ago. Haven't touched it since. But I know one thing."

"What?"

"If my gun is the murder weapon, as sure as I'm standing here, it will turn up."

Rita covered her mouth with her hand and whispered, "Oh, my God."

Chapter Eleven

I woke up, tangled in the sheets, the blanket in a heap on the floor. Stumbling into my kitchenette with the sheet draped around my middle, I rooted through the junk scattered all over the floor and found the coffeepot. I glanced up at the open cupboard; the cops had dumped out my Yuban. A small heap of coffee was on the floor next to a broken jar of strawberry jam. I wasn't upset about the jam, it was moldy anyway, but I was pissed about the coffee. I scooped up enough for a cup and while waiting for it to brew I called my office. No one was there, but Rita had left a message on the answering machine.

She had an early appointment scheduled with a deputy D.A. in Pacoima and would touch bases with me later in the day. I was to leave my client's file with Mabel, and she would review it before she phoned the guy. She wished me a good day and said, "Keep smiling, boss. It will work out." Yeah, I'll keep smiling, I mumbled, and poured myself a cup of freshly brewed dirt.

I drifted into the bathroom, showered, shaved, and after dressing–chino pants and a sport shirt–I left the apartment.

I called the office again from a pay phone outside of Dolan's Donuts. This time Mabel answered. I told her where to find the client file for Rita and said I would be tied up for a while. She said, so what, I didn't have any client appointments anyhow. Before hanging up, I asked her if she saw my gun somewhere, and of course, she said no.

After the call, I headed north on the Santa Ana Freeway toward Chatsworth, then made the transition to the Ventura Freeway. The traffic was a breeze, and forty-five minutes after I'd left my office I turned off at Winnetka Boulevard.

Gene Krupa, the great jazz drummer, told us a long time ago that *the big wind blows and brings the big noise from Winnetka*. There were no big noise coming from this Winnetka, just a lot of small noise, traffic noise, busy people being busy noise, and the noise of strip malls going up on every corner. I was in the San Fernando Valley, not Winnetka Illinois.

On my right, halfway between the freeway and Devonshire Avenue, just past Nordhoff, I saw a closed up White Front store that had been converted into the Divine Christ Ministry church. The plain, vanilla-white building, with its huge arch soaring over the entrance, was set back beyond a million acres of cracked blacktop, the old store's vast parking lot. There were only a few cars there scattered around, but I imagined on Sunday the lot would be jammed and overflowing. Salvation was a hot ticket these days. Parked at the front, in the shade of the building, was a black Mercedes 600 stretch limousine.

I pulled up to the main entrance, parked next to the limo, and glanced up at a new sign mounted over the doublewide doors. Painted in red letters on a white background was the church's name, Divine Christ Ministry. Directly below that in script were the words: *A day without Jesus is like a day without sunshine*. I wondered who came up with that slogan. It seemed a bit trite. I shook my head. Hey, we are talking about the Almighty here. It seemed to me they could have picked something a touch more magnanimous, something like, "Give money, or go to Hell." Tell it like it is, I always said.

Walking to the building's entrance, I noticed the limo driver, a giant of a man, leaning on the fender reading a newspaper. I nodded when he looked up. He pinned me with his hard eyes.

I pulled open one of the doublewide glass doors and entered the building. A long hallway led to the main auditorium. A few pictures hung on the walls, photographs of dour looking men, and farther down at the end of the hallway was a large portrait of Jesus–his beard was trimmed and neat, his long hair styled and combed to perfection. He had the look of a movie star. I wondered if he bought his cloak and tunic at Sy Devor's on Vine Street.

Several doors were cut into the hallway. I tried the one marked *Office*, but it was locked, so I continued on to the end of the hall, which opened into a large auditorium.

The place didn't look like any church I'd ever been in. It looked more like a basketball arena, high exposed-beam ceiling and wood floors, but there were no hoops in sight. And unlike a basketball court, the floor was covered with row upon row of gray metal folding chairs. At the north end, a large stage extended the width of the auditorium.

Up on the stage a small group of men and about a dozen young and attractive women stood in a circle. A guy standing in the middle of the group, wearing a pinstriped double-breasted suit, seemed to be getting all the attention. I walked purposefully toward the stage, as if I belonged there. One of the men, a tall, long-limbed guy dressed casually in denim pants and a short-sleeve white shirt, saw me coming.

"May I help you?" he called out.

I kept walking toward the stage, about thirty feet away. "Looking for Reverend Snavley," I hollered back at the guy.

"I'm Reverend Elroy, Elroy Snavley, but we're a little busy right now. Do you have an appointment?"

"Just need a second of your time." I skirted the front row of chairs and moved to the center of the room. Nearing the edge of the stage, I looked up at the group. "Hey, I like your slogan, outside on the sign." A little friendly banter to break the ice.

The other man, the one in the suit, stopped talking and made an irritated, shooing gesture directed at Reverend Elroy. He obviously wanted the reverend to get rid of me.

Elroy came to the edge of the stage and, squatting, looked down at me. He was about forty; a pleasant looking guy, lightly freckled face, disheveled sandy hair, but his nose was too large to fit comfortably between his close-set eyes, which kept blinking.

"Oh, do you like my slogan?" he said. "I paraphrased Cicero. You know, 'A room without books is like a body without a soul.' "

"Kinda sounded a little like the Gallo wine commercial, too," I said. "You know, 'A day without wine…'"

"Yeah, that too," he said with a hint of irritation.

I didn't want to tell him what Sol's friend, a comedian, had said: 'A day without sunshine is like night,' didn't want to get on Elroy's bad side right out of the gate.

"Hey, Elroy, can we get on with this?" the man with the suit demanded.

The reverend glanced at the suit, then quickly back at me. "I'm sorry, sir, but as you can see—"

The man in the suit stood stiffly with his chest puffed, glaring at me. He was in his mid-fifties, a little paunchy, and he had a large head with an abundance of silver hair, leonine in its grandeur. The man had an expensive barber, and his suit cost more than my car. The limo outside must be his, I presumed.

"It's about Robbie Farris," I said.

Elroy bolted upright and swiveled to Mr. Suit, the man obviously in charge.

The suit glared at me. His gaze felt like a blast from a hot furnace. "Come on, let's talk," he said.

Chapter Twelve

The rich guy's name, I found out, was J. Billy Bickerton. I'd heard of him. Who hadn't? He owned a string of evangelical TV stations across the nation. These religious, *non-profit* stations made a lot of money and Bickerton was very rich indeed.

"Okay," he said, "let's get to the point here. Just what do you want from us?"

I ignored Bickerton, addressed Reverend Elroy, "Reverend, I'm a lawyer, a member of the bar, and I'm defending Robbie Farris–"

The good reverend blanched. "I don't know anything about him."

Reverend Elroy's plain, threadbare-carpeted office wasn't much, maybe twenty-five feet long and about twelve feet wide with a small wood desk jammed at one end. We sat at a card table at the opposite end, away from the desk. Bickerton, the big shot, took a seat across from me. The Reverend was perched in his chair, on my right, nervous like a twittering finch.

"Hey, Mr. O'Brien, he doesn't know the guy. So I don't see how we can be of any help to you."

"He knows Robbie…" I turned to Reverend Elroy. "…and I need a little information."

"Yes, I knew him." The reverend's eyes darted around the room. "But I had nothing to do with him. And now, I hear he's in trouble, disappeared." He paused when I didn't say any thing, then added, "Hey, it was in the papers."

"He came here for help, and you sent him away–"

"Now look here, O'Brien," Bickerton said. "You come

waltzing in here all bent out of shape about some kid. Telling us you're a lawyer, member of the bar, and all that crap. I hate lawyers, leeches.... May I call you Jimmy?"

"Sure."

"Okay, Jimmy. Now what's your fee? What do you charge for your services?"

"Fifty dollars an hour."

"Same price as a Vegas whore."

"Plus another fifty for Rockin' Robbin."

"Who's that?"

"My pimp."

He let out a guffaw. "I like your attitude young man, but, you see, we're real busy around here. Tell him Elroy. Tell Jimmy just how busy you are."

"I'm putting together a TV special," Reverend Elroy said. "Very exciting, it will teach troubled kids that Christianity can be fun, more fun than drugs and rock 'n roll. But the show will have the type of entertainment they can relate to. Mr. Bickerton has agreed to air the show on his network."

"Tell him about the dance number you wrote for the show, Elroy. Don't be modest."

The Reverend's eyes blinked. "It's called 'Get Down and Funky With Jesus.'"

"It's a hoot, I'll tell you that," Bickerton added. "All those cute little Christian gals shaking their booties for the Lord. Can't miss."

"That's nice, Reverend, but didn't you advise Mrs. Farris that her son would be better off going to a drug treatment center–"

Bickerton jumped in. "Are you here to cause problems for Elroy? He's already told you he had nothing to do with the kid."

"I don't want any trouble. I just want information about Robbie, his connection with the church, stuff like that. Might help in my search for him."

"It's a sad case, yes indeed, very sad." Reverend Elroy shook his head. "But when he came here, he was too far gone, beyond even my ability to save him. As a last resort I recommended the intervention center to his mother, Mrs. Farris."

"Jimmy, Reverend Elroy would rather not discuss any of this, isn't that right, Elroy?"

"Why not?" I asked.

Bickerton went on to explain that going public about Robbie, talking about his membership in the drug rehab program, would not only be embarrassing, but it might jeopardize the church's ability to acquire corporate sponsors, whose cash was desperately needed to help save wayward teens. He said the reverend's failure with Robbie was unique. Reverend Elroy Snavley worked with hundreds of teens and one was bound to slip though the cracks. Why jeopardize the entire program because of one incorrigible misfit?

"Yes, Robbie doing those crazy things…well, it just might make Elroy look like a failure," he added.

While he rattled on, I wondered what a big shot like Bickerton was doing here at this nothing Van Nuys church in the first place. I'd read in the *L.A. Times* that his outfit, The Holy Sprit Network, was huge with forty or more stations, and they were looking to acquire an additional broadcasting outlet or two in the lucrative Southern California market. But why was he here now with Elroy Snavley? Anyway, I was getting a little tired of him jumping in every time I had a question for the reverend.

"Reverend Elroy," I said, "just what does Mr. Bickerton have to do with all of this stuff about Robbie? Why is he in this meeting?" I glanced at Bickerton. "No offense, sir."

Bickerton dove in again. "Oh, I understand your concerns,

Jimmy. But we're all friends here. Nothing to hide. Isn't that right, Elroy?" He pulled a cigar, a huge one, from his suit coat pocket. "Here, Jimmy, have a cigar." He leaned forward and handed it to me across the table.

The cigar was the size and shape of Fat Boy, the atom bomb used in World War II, and from the looks of it had probably cost as much. "Thanks, Billy. I'll smoke it later." I slipped the thing into my shirt pocket. I'll score a few points with Sol when I hand him this baby, I thought.

"Nonsense!" Bickerton pulled out two more cigars. "We'll smoke them now. You don't mind do you, Elroy? Of course not. We want to loosen up and have a nice chat with Jimmy, here." He tore the wrappers off, slid one to me, jammed the other in his mouth and talked around it while he patted his breast pockets. "Elroy, dang it, get me a match."

Elroy jumped up, dashed to his desk, grabbed a lighter from a drawer, rushed back and torched Bickerton's cigar. He came around to me. What the hell, I stuck the thing in my mouth. Elroy held the flame under it while I puffed. It felt good.

Bickerton and I leaned back in our chairs, gazing at the ceiling, puffing away. The room, filling with blue smoke, had the polite smell of money burning. Elroy let out a cough, which he tried without success to stifle.

After a few seconds I leaned forward, took the cigar in my hand and held it in front of my face, examining it. "Hmm," I said, as I'd seen Edward G. Robinson do many times in the gangster movies on the Late Show. "Hazel Farris is dead. Murdered, see."

Elroy cried, "What!" He gawked at me, slack-jawed. "Dead?"

"Yep, murdered." I kept my eye on Bickerton, who toked

on the stogie. The news didn't seem to faze him.

"Happens," Bickerton finally said. "What does that have to do with Elroy here? Maybe you're a little off base, Jimmy. He knows nothing about any murder." Bickerton faced Elroy. "You don't, do you, Elroy?"

"No. Why would I?"

Hazel's death probably had nothing to do with Reverend Elroy, but he was the one who'd recommended the drug intervention center to Mrs. Farris. I needed the name and the address of the place, and I needed a knockdown to the person in charge of it. Maybe Robbie went there when he escaped, or maybe he had a friend there he'd confided in. Or maybe there was a connection between the center and the black Ford van— the van that allegedly picked him up outside the court. Or maybe it was nothing, just a lot of maybes, all smoke and maybes, like the smoke that filled the office with every puff we took.

But if people at the center were involved in Robbie's escape, I doubted I'd get any cooperation from them. Of course, the van thing was a longshot; a story told by a phony blind guy. A phony that I didn't even believe. Anyway, why would people managing a drug intervention center want to help an escaped murderer? It didn't add up. But here's what *did* add up: my ass was on the line and I had to find Robbie, and the center seemed like a good place to start looking.

"Hey, Elroy," I said, "why don't you tell me about the drug center?"

Elroy paced the room, wringing his hands, mumbling words I couldn't hear.

Bickerton shook his head. "No way. Can't give any info out. Confidential."

"What do you mean, confidential?"

"You ought to know what that means, being a lawyer." Bickerton, it seemed to me, was becoming a little churlish.

"No offense, J. Billy, but I asked Elroy here a question. This doesn't concern you," I said. "Hey now, Elroy, I need the address of the center."

Elroy instantly stopped pacing. He stood still, stiff, eyes bulging like a frozen fish.

Bickerton roared, "Damn it, O'Brien. I said the information is privileged!"

I guessed his majesty wasn't used to having his commandments being questioned.

"Why are you butting in?" I asked. "And, anyway, what's so confidential about a drug center, for chrissakes?"

"Watch you language, wise guy. We are in the house of the Lord." Bickerton waved the cigar around like it was a burning, out-of-control flying turd. "And, mister, I'll tell you why I'm butting in. I own this goddamn church."

"Thought it was the Lord's house."

"Don't get cute."

My welcome at the Divine Christ Ministry Church had started to wear thin. Billy Bickerton and the Reverend Elroy Snavley grew exceedingly tired of dodging my questions about the center, but I kept pounding away. And of course, it was only a matter of minutes before I was asked to leave. When I wouldn't stop the interrogation, the chauffeur was summoned. He politely showed me the door.

The chauffeur's nose would heal, but my shirt was beyond repair and that fine cigar in the pocket was now in shreds.

Chapter Thirteen

First, I stopped at a J.C. Penny's on Nordhoff and picked up a new shirt, an OP Surfer, featuring scenes of palm trees, ocean waves, and a Woody parked by a sunny beach. Not too lawyerly, but what the heck, I liked it. Then I headed out. Turning off Winnetka, I swung into in a Shell gas station and used the payphone next to the restrooms. My call went to Joyce, Sol's private secretary. Her smoky, almost ethereal voice greeted me with a pleasant, "Good morning Jimmy. It is still morning, isn't it?"

"I think so, Joyce. Is Sol around?"

"No, but he left a message. Said that it's important that he speak with you."

I didn't like the sound of that. Sol seldom said anything was important unless it had to do with food. But I felt certain this message was about Webster's investigation, not lunch. "He didn't say what it was about, did he?"

"No, he just said you'd know, but he'll be returning this afternoon. Will he be able to reach you?"

"I'll have to call him. Robbie's mother had mentioned that the drug center is out by Barstow. There's something funny about the place. So I'm heading there now to snoop around. Tell Sol it has to do with Robbie's disappearance. The center and his disappearance could be related. Will you tell him that, Joyce?"

"You bet, Jimmy."

Barstow was about a hundred-forty miles northeast of Chatsworth, halfway to Vegas. Traffic in L.A. was a tangled mess, but the trip went fast once I departed the basin. I rolled on the down side of the San Bernardino Mountains, covering the last fifty miles of Highway 66 from Victorville in thirty-four minutes, not a record, but not too bad.

It was after three in the afternoon when I pulled into the desert town, crawling along Main Street. I had no idea where I was going or what I was going to do. I just knew I had to do something, and the drug center seemed to be the logical place to start. I randomly turned left on First Street, continued until I came to Riverside Drive and then turned left again.

On my left, I spotted a tumbledown café sitting in the middle of a dirt patch in front of the Santa Fe Railroad switching yard. I pulled into the lot. I needed a cup of coffee and maybe a bite to eat but, more importantly, I'd ask someone if they knew anything about the intervention center.

It occurred to me that I stood a better chance of getting information by stopping at a café off the beaten track, away from the tourists. I figured the locals knew more about what was going on in their town than the people that just stopped for a tank of gas and a piss before heading back on the highway and zooming to Vegas. If the folks here were anything like the ones in Downey, I doubted they would appreciate a drug intervention center being built in their community. It might even be the talk of the town. But, after a moment's reflection, I knew I was being optimistic. The way Bickerton refused not only to give me the address, but to even discuss the center, told me that the outfit had to be keeping a low profile.

The screen door banged shut after me when I walked into the Bright Spot Café. A ceiling fan spun listlessly above, harassing a tiny squadron of houseflies engaged in a tight formation flight on the periphery of the revolving blade's arc. The café, with the fan and sweltering heat, could've been the setting for the movie *Key Largo*. I glanced around; Bacall was nowhere in sight but a grizzled old guy, cigarette dangling, sat at the counter. He bore a striking resemblance to Bogart. I didn't ask for his autograph; didn't want to gush.

All eyes turned and looked at me as I walked across the scuffed linoleum floor and sat at the far end of the counter. Other than Bogey, a half-dozen men slouched at the few tables placed haphazardly around the café. The men all wore bib overalls, and two had baseball caps pushed back on their foreheads, the Santa Fe Railroad logo prominently displayed above the bill on both caps.

A pretty girl with dark hair, wearing a white apron over her checkered shirt and tight fitting jeans, wiped a table across the room. Her back was to me, and she was bending slightly. Her hand moved across the table with a slow, mechanical rhythm.

The girl had to be about eighteen with the firm, tight, nascent body of feminine youth, which never failed to tantalize old guys like me.

The girl peeked surreptitiously at me. When she saw that I noticed her, she quickly looked away and continued with her chore.

I plucked the menu, a single sheet covered in plastic, from its metal bracket clamped to the edge of the counter. The front side of the menu listed the café's offerings: bacon and eggs, hamburgers, that sort of stuff, but typed on the back was a blurb, a short history of the Bright Spot Café.

The white clapboard building–the menu read–was built in 1930. "*John Steinbeck stopped right here at the Bright Spot Café when traveling Route 66, doing research for his great novel,* Of Mice and Men. *It's about a bunch of Okies coming to Calif.*"

The waitress, a woman of undeterminable age but a hell of a lot older than me, brought me a chipped coffee cup, the handle of which ringed the pinky of her left hand. She held a coffeepot in her right hand.

"*Grapes of Wrath*," I said.

She dropped the cup on the counter and, with an exaggerated sigh, turned to the food delivery slot in the wall behind her. "Hey Gus, we got another one of them intellectuals here."

"Hey, buddy, don't want no trouble," a heavy voice growled from the slot.

"Nope, no trouble." I already had to buy one shirt today. "Must have been mistaken, sorry," I shouted back at the slot.

"S'okay."

I decided to drop the issue and not delve any further into Steinbeck. It was obviously a sore point at the Bright Spot. Who was I anyway, a literary critic? I needed information about the drug intervention center and I wouldn't get any cooperation by upsetting the natives. Besides, maybe George and Lenny did travel through Barstow on their way to the Salinas Valley...

The waitress turned back to me. Her chin was tucked in and she looked at me cautiously. She filled my cup, stepped back a couple of feet as though I might explode, and slowly withdrew an order pad from the pocket of her white but filthy uniform. "Want something to eat?"

I was starved. "Nah, not hungry," I said. "Just coffee, thanks."

She started to move along the counter. "Wait," I called out.

She stopped dead in her tracks, really uptight. Christ, that intellectual who came in here must have been hell on wheels.

"Got a phone book?" I said.

It was like she deflated, kind of slumped. Then she dashed to the cash register, reached behind it and pulled out the thin book. She slid it along the counter toward me.

A male voice from behind me, one of the men at a table, spoke up. "Looking for someone in town, mister? I've been here nigh on forty years. Know everybody in town."

I swiveled on the stool. An older guy without a baseball cap nodded.

"Ben Moran," he said. "Yep, came here from Kansas in thirty-three. Depression, you know, heading to L.A. Had to find work. Got this far, ran outta money. Been here every since. Still outta money." When he said that everyone in the place, even the waitress, let out a loud guffaw.

Ben sat hunched over his coffee cup alone at the table. Even seated I could see that he was a large man, a giant with more fat than muscle. His shapeless form filled the chair and parts of his backside spilled over it, curling around the edges. The man's stringy gray hair was thin in front but long and wavy in the back and on the sides. He wore a handlebar mustache under a banged up nose, which was too large for his face. His mouth was a jagged slit cut into his molting, liver-spotted skin.

I nodded. "Jimmy O'Brien, glad to know you."

His pale, watery eyes, hooded by a thicket of salt and pepper brows, peered at me. "You ain't really one of them professors or smarty-pants fellows, are ya?" he asked.

"Not me," I said. "Just a guy trying to make a buck here and there." I didn't want to tell him I was a lawyer, God forbid.

"Didn't think so. Don't look the type. Well then, come on over here. Bring your coffee."

I picked up my cup and moved to his table. When I got close, Moran kicked out a chair. I sat down, and we shook hands.

We—or I should say Ben—talked about his town and the people in it. He seemed to know everyone and was determined to tell me all of their life stories. He had everyone in the café enthralled with strange tales of his forty years in this strange town. Everyone but me, that is. He chortled and slapped his hands on his denim clad legs when he told me about Vera Olson, an eighty-year old-spinster, who was rumored to have been a communist in the thirties and now subscribed to *Ms* magazine. Vera was the town's leading proponent of women's lib. He figured she was defiantly bent and he figured she was bent in the wrong direction. "And like Tinkerbelle," he did a finger wave, "Vera had scattered a little pixie dust in her day." The crowd broke up at that last crack.

But as enlightening as his narrative was, it had to end. It was getting late and I wanted to find the drug center before dark. Ben's jocular mood shifted when I changed the subject. "Tell me, Ben, What do you know about a Christian teen drug center out here somewhere?"

The café instantly became quiet, and the people in the room pretended not hear my question. They all looked away.

"You some kind of government agent?" Ben asked menacingly.

"No, not at all."

"Why you asking about the center?"

"Heard about it. That's all."

He leaned closer and peered intently at me. "You're the lawyer."

"Why…do you say that?"

Without saying anything he pushed on his chair, and slowly his enormous bulk rose. Then he turned and galumphed out of the café without looking back.

I glanced around; everyone was ignoring me.

"Hey, buddy, we need your spot at the table," the voice from the food slot called out. "Got a big group coming in. Be here any moment now. So, why don't you be a good guy and hightail it outta here."

I climbed out of my chair, surveyed the room, and in a loud voice, said, "Hey, c'mon. Don't you people know anything about a teen drug center right here in your midst?"

Everyone in the café sat there gawking at me. Their eyes were dead, their faces masked with blank expressions. There wasn't a murmur, hardly a sound, just the whining noise of the ceiling fan. It needed a new bearing in the motor.

"Where is it? Damn it, someone tell me!"

Not a peep, just the staring.

I continued to stand with my back stiff, rooted in the center of the room. My eyes tracked the vacant, lifeless forms. These people were frightened. But frightened of what? That old fat guy, Ben Moran?

After long seconds of dead silence, the food slot pleaded in a hushed tone, "Come on Mack, leave us alone. Get going."

"Why don't you come out from behind that wall and make me leave?"

The food slot was beginning to grate my nerves. In fact, the whole joint was making my skin itch.

"*Grapes of Wrath*. Do you hear me, damn it? It's *The Grapes of Wrath!*" I stomped out of the café.

In the parking lot around the corner of the building, I noticed a payphone. Stepping in and closing the door, I dropped a coin in the shot, dialed O, and when the operator came on, I asked to make a collect call to Sol Silverman at Silverman Investigations, Inc. in Downey.

Joyce came on the line. She accepted the call and said, "Oh, Jimmy, I'm glad you called. Sol has been pacing the floor. Hang on a minute, please."

The line clicked and there was a moment of static.

It was stifling hot in the booth. I turned to open the door a crack and that's when I saw her. The teenaged girl from the café stood just outside the booth staring at me with the same blank expression as the people inside had. I swung the door open all the way. "Can I help you miss?"

She stood there motionless and silent.

"Miss?" I said.

"You want to know about the center?"

My heart thumped. "Yes."

She took a couple of quick glances in both directions. "Meet me behind the old Harvey House in five minutes. But I can't wait. I'll leave if you're not there." She started to back away.

"The what? What house? Where?"

"You'll find it," she whispered over her shoulder as she turned. She moved like a shadow, slipped around the corner of the building and disappeared.

"Jimmy," Sol said on the phone. "I'm glad you called. I have news–"

I hung up the phone and ran for my car.

Chapter Fourteen

I jumped in the Vette, raced out of the parking lot, and shot into the first gas station I saw, a Standard Oil just off First Street by Riverside Drive.

A craggy-faced, weathered guy hobbled out of the office. He had on the Standard Oil uniform, white pants and shirt, black bowtie, and a garrison cap like those worn by soldiers in World War II. The old guy looked like he had fought one too many battles. The battle of Gas Pump Island popped into my head.

I asked directions to the Harvey House. He didn't say anything, just kept moving toward me with a lumbering gait. Jumping out of the car, I rushed to him and asked again about the old house.

He stood there deep in thought. Finally, he drew an oil-stained orange rag from his hip pocket and slowly wiped his brow with it. He looked off into the distance, started to point, and then said, "Nah." He stared at the rag in his hand; forever, it seemed.

I mentioned that I was in a hurry and glanced at my Timex: two minutes had passed since my encounter with the girl.

Suddenly, like in a cartoon, the light bulb lit up. Not only did he know what and where the Harvey House was, but he was bent on giving me the entire history of the place. I tried to interrupt, but the guy wouldn't shut up about the old house. He kept rambling on, said the house was once used as a location for a 1940s movie, *The Harvey Girls*, but now it was in terrible shape.

He kept on talking, grousing that someone should turn the

place into a museum. "Maybe they will someday. You know, it reminds me of a story…"

I was getting frantic. If the girl took off, I'd never find the teen drug center. It could be anywhere in the billion square miles of desert out here. How foolish to think I could drive to Barstow, cruise around, and find it.

What did I expect? Did I think there would be signs pointing the way? Signs like the Burma Shave ads posted every mile or so I saw driving up here: "*The monkey took…. One look at Jim…. And threw the peanuts…. Back at him…. Burma Shave.*" Even the Burma Shave pundits didn't think I had a chance.

This was hopeless. I'd better forget about the center and head back to Downey. But before I left Barstow, I'd call Sol and see if he had any news. Maybe he could find out, through the authorities, something about the center. It had to be licensed, I was sure. But where would he begin? I didn't even have the name of the place. Oh my God, it suddenly dawned on me that I had hung up on him.

I cast a quick glance in all directions and spotted a phone booth. I was about to make a dash it when I saw the gas station guy pointing to the west, at what appeared to be an abandoned train station just down the road about a hundred yards.

"What's that?" I asked.

"The Harvey House."

"Where? I don't see any house."

"The Harvey House is the old railroad depot and hotel right next door," he said. "Ain't that what you were asking me about?"

I had only thirty seconds before the teenaged girl would leave. Jumping in my car, I cranked the engine and stomped on the gas. I swerved to miss the fence separating the gas station lot from the dilapidated hotel, then stood on the brake. In a cloud of dust, I skidded to stop in front of the antiquated hotel-depot. Ten seconds to spare.

The sun was low in the western sky when I darted around the corner of the building and ventured into the dirt yard behind the derelict building. I stopped and glanced around. The girl wasn't there.

The atmosphere was eerie, unnaturally quiet. The trash-laden yard was blanketed with long murky shadows. I watched carefully as I walked to the other end of the building amid a minefield of debris. Rusted oil drums, a banged up refrigerator, a jumbled nest of broken pipes sitting next to a worn out sofa with its fibrous stuffing pulled out in spots like the straw from a long-standing scarecrow, littered what was once, I imagined, the manicured grounds of the old mission-style building behind me.

A spotted lizard, no bigger than a Tiparillo cigar, scurried from its position under a rock, stopped once with its head raised, as if listening for a distant train that would never pass this way again, then quickly vanished behind a rusty hubcap.

Still no sign of the girl. I stopped again and glanced up at the building's façade. Six large Spanish arches ran the width of the outer wall. The portals gave access to a ghostly promenade. Halfway down the building, opening into a dark, foreboding interior was the main entrance, a black gaping maw situated behind a row of fluted Roman columns.

I took a few more steps and heard soft clicks. Light footsteps repeated behind me. I spun around and listened: nothing. Starting back to the corner, where I'd come from, I heard the footsteps again. But when I stopped, they stopped.

A slight breeze kicked up. A scrap of yellowing paper fluttered at my feet like a butterfly before settling down again. I felt a chill in the shadows behind the building and I shivered a little. But, it wasn't the breeze that caused me to shudder. It was the ghostly, decaying place itself.

What the hell was I doing out here in a town in the middle of the Mojave Desert anyway? Looking for a drug center that probably had nothing to do with Robbie's escape. Standing behind an old dead hotel waiting for a teenaged girl who was obviously pulling a prank. She was probably laughing it up right now back at the Bright Spot with her buddies, the Barstow Steinbeck Society.

I had to get back to Downey, find Sol, and apologize. Sol lived like a potentate, only more so, and he always bragged, "No one hangs up on Sol Silverman." Well, he won't be able to say that anymore and he'll be pissed, that's for sure.

I took one last glance at the old derelict behind me. "Bye, Harvey," I said and started to walk back to the car. But just then, out of the corner of my eye, I caught a slight movement; a figure stood in the gloom behind one of the arches inside the building. It was her, the teenaged girl. She slipped out to where I could see her and stood silently, staring at me in the dim light just in front of the last arch.

It startled me for an instant, seeing her there unexpectedly. I must have jumped. "Whoa—"

"Did I scare you?" she asked in a slow, emotionless monotone.

"Startled me for a second, that's all. What's your name?"

The girl was kind of spooky but she had pretty features, sapphire blue eyes, and pure white skin that contrasted with her coal-black hair. She could have been Snow White in the movie except this girl was real, not something from the imagination of an artist with a fine point brush.

"My name is Jane. Do you like me?"

Oh-oh, with all the problems swirling around me, I didn't need some mixed-up adolescent coming on to me. "Look, Jane, I'm kinda in a hurry."

She turned and faced the dark inner recesses of the hotel. Maybe I shouldn't have been so abrupt. "Look, Jane, I like you. But I'm old enough to be your father." I wasn't that old, but it was a good line.

She spun around. Her soft demeanor was gone, replaced by wrath. "He dead!" she screamed.

"Who—"

"My father."

"Oh, I'm sorry. I didn't know," I said with as much tenderness as I could muster. "What about your mother? Do you live with her?"

"He killed her."

"Who killed her?"

"He did. Then he killed himself."

"Oh, my God! You poor girl. I had no idea." I stood there not knowing what to say. I just stared into the deep blue eyes of this disturbed young woman, a child, really.

"That's when they took me here..." Her voice trailed off and she stood still, almost as if in a daze. But her eyes were focused intently on me.

"To Barstow? You live here with a relative, an aunt, or someone?"

"No, they took me to the base. I work in the kitchen. They send me to work here at the café, too." She said no more than that, but I knew there was more she wanted to tell me. She took a step forward.

"They took you to the base?" I felt my throat tighten. If I handle this right, she'd take me there. "The base is the teen center?"

"Yes, that's what they call it. I was small when they took me away. There was nothing I could do."

"Did you do drugs? I mean, after your folks died, is that why they sent you out here to the center? Drugs?"

"No! No drugs. My body is a temple, belongs to the Lord." She quickly looked away and just as quickly turned back to me.

I had so many questions for the girl, but also a strong sense that at any moment she would leave. I knew I had to tread lightly.

"Why did you ask me to meet here? Is there something you wanted to tell me about the center?" I asked with trepidation.

"It has to be closed."

"Why?"

"Because it's evil," she said calmly, as if she were telling me the time of day, but her eyes held a burning intensity and remained fixed on my face. "I'm scared to be here," she added. "They will give me a beating."

In spite of the chill in the air, I started to sweat. "Jane, why? Why would anyone beat you? *Who* would give you a beating?"

"The old man you were talking to. He will tell them to beat me."

"Ben Moran? The guy at the café? He has something to do with the center?"

Before she could answer, a car, a black-and-white squad car–the police–rounded the corner of the Harvey House.

I shifted my gaze away from the girl for a moment and took a quick look at the cop car. A uniformed officer was starting to climb out.

I glanced back at the arch. The girl had vanished.

"Oh, Christ…"

The tall cop came closer, his polished boots crunching on the trash and twigs. His right hand rested on his holstered gun.

"Your name O'Brien?" he asked.

I wondered how he knew that. "Yeah, why?"

"Let's see some ID." The cop wiggled his fingers in a gimme manner. "That your Vette out there in front? Registered to one James O'Brien. Is that you?"

I handed over my license. "Yeah. What's the problem?"

He pulled a flashlight from his hip pocket, flicked the light on my face for a couple of seconds then shined the beam on my license. "Suppose you tell me what you're doing back here."

No way I would tell him that I was here meeting a teenaged girl. And with the reaction I was getting every time I mentioned the drug center, I felt it best to keep my mouth shut about that as well. "Just looking the old place over," I said.

"Yeah, why? This is private property."

"Thinking about buying it. Turning it into a museum. Did you know the old movie, *The Harvey Girls*, was shot here?"

The cop said nothing. Did he see through my story? I'm not that good of an actor, am I?

"No kidding, a movie. Hmm," he said at last. "I didn't know that." He handed over my license. "It's getting dark. Maybe you'd better come back tomorrow."

"Yeah, I was just leaving."

The cop lumbered off and I started walking back to my Vette. When I turned the corner of the building, the cop stood at his black and white with the door open. He started to climb in, but suddenly stopped. He shouted, "Hey, O'Brien, hold it."

I froze. "What?"

"One more question"

Oh, Christ, what now? "Yeah?"

"What was the name of that movie, again?"

My breathing resumed. "*Harvey Girls*, you know, like the building."

He nodded, climbed into the car and took off.

My hunch was stronger than ever that the drug center was tied into Robbie's escape, and now I felt that the blind guy's story about the black van whisking him away could be true, which meant Robbie's mental condition had to be an act. It was plainly a diversion designed to relax the security surrounding him, and I fell for it.

It was after eight p.m. when I finally got back on Interstate 15 driving to Downey. I'd spent two hours cruising around the town on the off chance that I might spot Jane. No luck there. I also had no luck driving the outskirts, back streets, and side roads of Barstow looking for anything that might appear to house a drug center. I stopped at the payphone in the Standard Oil station lot and phoned Sol's office. He had left for the day. I tried his home number: no answer.

I'd also looked in the Yellow Pages and found a listing for a teen center, but not a teen *drug* center. I had nothing to lose, so I called the number and was connected with the local Catholic Church's parish facility, where teenagers could hang out and have fun. I asked if they knew anything about a drug center in the area. They said no, but invited me over to their place to say the rosary. I politely declined.

After ten, I pulled into my apartment. I figured I'd sleep on the floor until I got around to fixing the damage caused by the police. When I opened the door, I was stunned. The place had been straightened, organized, the bed made, and on my pillow was a note from Rita: "*Mabel loaned me your spare key. So Hector, my cousin, and I stopped by and sorta fixed the place up. Thanks for giving me the chance to work on your case. Sol could have gotten you some big time guy, someone like Zuckerman, but you chose me. Wow!!! Sleep well, Jimmy.*"

I glanced at the answering machine sitting next to my phone. The red light was blinking furiously. Five messages, three from Sol's secretary, Joyce. She asked me to phone him as soon as I walked in the door, but then there was a message from Sol himself.

"*Call me in the morning. I tried to tell you when you phoned earlier, but somehow we got disconnected. Webster, the DA, turned all the files he had on you over to the sheriff's department, to Detective Hammer. He gave the homicide cop the file containing his investigation of the Section 32 charge, aiding and abetting, and everything else he had. Jimmy, my boy, maybe we should do something. As you know, you're being investigated for the murder of Hazel Farris. But you're the only suspect. If they find anything new they're gonna come and take you away.*"

The fifth message was from George Biddle, my insurance guy. My car insurance was overdue. I put down the receiver.

Chapter Fifteen

I couldn't sleep. I worried about Sol's message, worried about my missing gun, and worried about what would happen when the cops found it. But I knew what would happen. I've been part of the system long enough, first as a cop, and now as a lawyer. I'd be dragged to the slammer, locked in a cell, and everyone including a jury would assume I was guilty.

After several hours of those pleasant thoughts rattling around in my brain I got up, sat by the window, and stared out at the darkness until the sun peeked over the mountains. "*Hello darkness my old friend, I've come to talk with you again...*"

It was still too early to phone Sol. I'd wait until a decent hour, then call him from my office. I dressed and headed to Dolan's Donuts on Brookshire, down the street from Downey High, where I ordered two glazed and a large coffee and grabbed a copy of the *Southeast News*, Downey's local paper. I thought I'd take a half hour, maybe forty-five minutes and just enjoy my breakfast. I was very good at compartmentalizing my problems, and anyway why should I ruin my morning worrying about the cops? By now, they must have found new evidence, something that pointed away from me and steered them to the real killer. I squeezed into a plastic booth by the window and unfolded the paper.

"*Oh my God!*" I exclaimed. I don't have many clients as it is, and now this. The newspaper had my picture plastered on page one under the headline, "Downey Man Suspected in Brutal Murder." I knew I was a suspect, and because of Sol's message I knew I was the only suspect, but seeing it in print made my skin crawl.

I scanned the article. It told about the sheriff department's investigation of the Hazel Farris murder and that the police had me in their sights. The reporter quoted detective Hammer: *"There is a definite connection between the murder victim and O'Brien. He was the last known person to see her alive. We don't have sufficient evidence right now to arrest Mr. O'Brien, but we're digging. The case could break wide open at any moment."* What they reported was true, including Hammer's remarks, but none of it proved my guilt. Still, anyone seeing the story would assume I was a cold-blooded killer.

I slumped down in my seat. Where would this end?

"You having heart attack? Go outside!"

I looked up. The Asian guy behind the counter was screaming at me.

"What is your problem?" I said.

"No die in here! Bad *fu*." He scrunched up his face and made a shooing motion with his hands, like he was sweeping me out along with the used-up coffee cups. "Bad *Fu*, you go now."

I began to get peeved. "I'm not having a heart attack."

"Why your face all white? And you shout!"

"The coffee's too hot."

I had no idea what bad *fu* meant, but I figured whatever it was, I probably had a dose of it. I took my tray with the donuts, coffee, and newspaper, dumped it all into the trash and walked out. Only 6:30 and the new day was already starting off sick, like one of those take-three-aspirins-and-call-me-in-the-morning kind of days.

Five minutes later, I unlocked the office. I knew Mabel wouldn't be there that early, so it was a surprise to see a full pot of freshly brewed coffee sitting on the counter. I ambled over to pour myself a cup, wondering who had made it. Had to have been Rita. She must've had an early appointment.

I was irritated that I let the counterman at Dolan's get on my nerves, making me waste the donuts and almost a full cup. It wasn't his fault that my nerves were shot. But the photo pushed me over the limit, reminded me that I was still a target and that my problems wouldn't go away until I somehow brought Robbie back.

"*Psst*, Jimmy…over here."

I set the cup down and glanced around. It sounded like Rita, but no one was in sight.

"*Psst*, Jimmy, your office, quick."

I saw her peeking out from behind the slightly opened office door and walked to where she stood. She pushed the door open all the way, pulled me in, and quickly closed it behind us. She looked tense.

"Rita, my God, what's the matter?"

One hand covering her mouth, she stood with her back to the door and jabbed her finger toward the filing cabinet across the room.

"Did you see a mouse?"

She dropped both hands. "Oh Christ, Jimmy, gimme a break. Your gun is behind the filing cabinet."

"What?"

"Yeah, your gun."

I rushed to the cabinet and pulled it out a little. Sure enough, a .38 revolver sat there, as if someone had carelessly dropped it into the space between the cabinet and the wall. I ran to my desk, found a wire coat hanger, fished out the gun, and held the hanger with the .38 dangling by its trigger guard.

Rita grabbed her purse off my desk and held it open in front of her. "Don't touch the gun, Jimmy. Quick, drop it in here."

Suddenly a bag of emotions, sadness, and guilt rocked my consciousness. I knew what she was planning. Rita was going to hide the gun, not turn it over to the police.

We both figured the gun was the murder weapon. The cylinder held five live rounds and one spent cartridge. By concealing the weapon she would not only be violating her personal code of ethics, she'd be breaking the law. If caught, she'd not only lose her bar license, she'd go to jail. Rita was going to risk all of that for me.

"No, Rita–"

"We don't have much time. Gimme the gun!"

"Go call Hammer. Tell him you found the murder weapon."

She didn't move. She just stood there silently, holding her purse open. She looked small and vulnerable and hurt. My head throbbed with frustration. We stood there eye to eye for what seemed like a long time, but was only a few seconds.

"Rita," I finally said. "How did you know it was there?"

She lowered her purse. "Last night when I was getting ready for bed I started thinking about the gun, and what you said about it being the murder weapon. Remember, you said how the real killer would hide it where the cops would eventually find it and it would be somewhere that would make you look guilty?"

"Yes, I remember."

"Well, I climbed into bed, turned out the lights, but it kept nagging me. I couldn't sleep. Something was missing. Then it hit me. Where else could the real killer have planted the gun to implicate you?" She was quiet for a moment, giving me a chance to absorb what she was saying.

"My God, Rita you're right. It could've been behind that cabinet since the murder."

"I got up and rushed here. I wouldn't be able to sleep until–"

"Until you came to the office, searched, and found the gun."

"It only took about five minutes to find it. The killer would bring it back to your office. Finally, I peeked behind the cabinet. Bingo. But here's the scary part."

"What?"

"The police already searched all around the crime scene, your apartment, and heck, they even scoured the trash bins. Now they'll get a warrant and search the office."

"It was easy for them to get the no-knock to search my apartment," I said. "But to get a warrant to search a criminal defense lawyer's office would be a lot harder. They would have to get a special master to accompany them."

"He'd have to oversee the search," Rita said.

"Yeah, client privilege, our files are sacrosanct. To get one they'd need solid evidence. The D.A. would have to be involved. Even Frisco wouldn't sign a warrant assigning a special master without a compelling reason. Too many watchful eyes."

"Jimmy, the very fact that you were the last known person to see Hazel Farris is enough to convince a judge. But, getting a special master would delay the search. Maybe only for a day or so, though."

"The cops could show up sometime today."

"That what I figured. That's why I had to be sure your gun wasn't here. But it was…."

"And the murderer left it here. My God, he was here in my office twice, once when he stole the gun and again when he brought it back."

"He came in here, got the gun, drove to her trailer, shot her, and came back," Rita said. "He had to come back to hide the gun. He just waltzed in and out like he owned the place. You never lock the doors at night, Jimmy."

"Maybe it was one of our clients."

"Don't be silly, boss, we don't have any clients. But the killer had to have been here both times. He had to be here when you weren't sitting behind your desk. He had to know your routine. And he had to know you were defending Robbie. Maybe he was following you…or, maybe, there were two guys. One guy who stole the gun–"

"Aw, Rita, nobody followed me. Anyone could've come in here and taken the gun, and brought it back during the day, even."

"Like who?"

"We'll ask Mabel if any delivery guys happened to drop by when neither of us were here," I said.

"Oh, Jimmy, I hope it's not the pizza guy. He's cute."

"Rita, he's a pimply-faced kid. You can do better, for crying out loud," I said with a disingenuous smile. "Anyway, Hazel Farris was killed with a bullet, not a bad anchovy."

"That's not funny."

"I know...." We fell quiet again. Finally I broke the silence. "And now, young lady, you are going to march into the other room and call Hammer. You've got to call him before he gets the warrant and comes barging in the door."

"This is all they'll need, then they'll come looking for you. They'll arrest you. I'm not going to bury you."

"Then I'll call him myself."

"You do," Rita turned and pointed, "and I'll walk right out that door. You'll never see me again." Her voice was filled with strong determination and she waited for me to make my move. I knew Rita and I knew she meant what she said. She wasn't bluffing.

"Rita, listen to me. I'm your boss–"

"And, I'm your lawyer, and I'm–"

"Listen to me, please! It might not even be the murder weapon..."

Her face taut, she looked at me. "Wanna bet?"

"Rita, I couldn't live with myself if I let you violate your personal code of ethics, not to mention break the law. When you first became a lawyer you told me that when the time comes, the time when you have to make the hard choice, you'd do the right thing."

She stood there and stared silently at her shoes.

"Do you remember saying that?"

"Yes."

"Are you going to make the call?"

Her head snapped up. "No! And I'm not kidding, I'll walk!"

Chapter Sixteen

After my discussion with Rita, I left the office and drove back to Dolan's to grab a dozen glazed. As the counterman quickly tossed the donuts in a bag, he looked at me with his eyes wide as if I were about to drop dead...or maybe he figured he saw a ghost. I thought about making a scary face, but that wouldn't be a dignified way for a lawyer to act, so I just said boo. Then I headed directly to the ten-story office building that housed Sol's corporate security and investigations firm, Silverman Investigations, Inc.

Joyce escorted me along a marble-lined hallway leading to Sol's private office at the end of it. I amused myself with his lava lamp until he appeared promptly at nine a.m.

I apologized about the disconnected phone call. He frowned and commented about how someone who didn't know me might feel as if I had hung up on him. I chuckled. "Imagine that," I said. We shared the donuts, washing them down with a gallon of Sol's special grind of *Kopi Luwak* coffee. He wouldn't tell me the secret method that the growers in Sumatra employed in the bean's preparation. But I didn't care how it was made, the coffee tasted great.

While we ate the donuts and drank the coffee we discussed the murder investigation. Without bringing up the discovery of the gun–the less said about that the better–I told him my reasons for the Barstow trip. I explained how I'd tried to find the teen drug center. I mentioned the old man in the Bright Spot Café, and told him about my meeting behind the Harvey House with Jane, the strange teenaged girl. And, of course, I added how the girl had been afraid of being punished, how the old man, Ben Moran, allegedly ordered beatings. We both agreed that the center was the key to solving the mystery of Robbie's escape, and that Robbie's escape was the key to Hazel Farris's murder.

"Now all we have to do is find the center." Sol started to rise out of his chair. "And we can't do that sitting here on our fat asses."

I gingerly placed the donut in my hand back in the box.

He summoned the Deacon, his number one operative, and Cubby, his principal driver, and soon the four of us were in Sol's big black limousine. We cruised northeast, rolling at a hundred miles per hour on Interstate 15 heading for Barstow and the Bright Spot Café.

The mobile radiophone buzzed. The Deacon, sitting on the jump seat in the back of the big limousine, reached out with his massive arm and lifted the receiver from its cradle. After he listened for a moment, he handed it to Sol. A few moments later Sol replaced the radiophone receiver in its cradle and turned to me. "That was Joyce. Mabel phoned her. She had a message to give you."

"Yeah, what was it?"

"Said the cops came to your office with a search warrant looking for a gun."

My stomach did a little samba. I cleared my throat. "What did they find?" I asked with all the calmness I could muster.

Sol's eyes bored into me. "Nothing. But why would they expect to find a gun there?"

My heart sank. "You mean they didn't find it?"

Of course, I was relieved that I wasn't going to be arrested the minute I showed up back in Downey, but at the same time I was disappointed. After a serious discussion, Rita and I had come to an understanding. We agreed that we'd put the gun back where it was found. I'd explained that it wasn't her responsibility to do the cops' job, searching for evidence, and as long as the evidence wasn't tampered with it, she had no obligation to tell them what she knew. When the cops finally got their search warrant, and found the gun...well then, so be it. We'd fight the section 187 charge, and we'd win. She reluctantly agreed and gave me her word she wouldn't dig the gun out again and hide it. Now it troubled me to realize that Rita hadn't kept her promise.

"Hey, buddy boy, you said nothing about a gun. What gives?" Sol asked.

I blurted out the whole story, the cops looking for my gun, Rita finding it, and our agreement.

"*Gott in himmel,*" Sol shouted. "You mean to tell me you had the gun in your hand? The murder weapon, the piece of evidence that could put you in jail for life, and you wanted to leave it there for the cops to waltz in and pick up. You schmuck! Thank God for Rita, at least someone in that *feckockteh* firm has a brain."

With a wave of his hand, he indicated his immediate need for a drink. I was glad Sol wasn't holding the gun at that moment; he probably would've shot me with it. He was that angry. And I couldn't blame him. After all, he had my best interest at heart and he was doing his utmost to help me find Robbie so I'd stay out of jail. But I was still disappointed in Rita, breaking her word.

The Deacon opened the sliding door of the small bar built into the seatback and started to fix Sol a drink.

"Sol, listen," I said. "I couldn't let her do it.... But she did it anyway."

The Deacon handed Sol the drink, his signature martini,

one-hundred-proof vodka in a glass.

Sol took a sip, then put his arm around my shoulder and tousled my hair. "Ah, Jimmy, my boy, you big oaf," he said. "That's why you couldn't make it as a cop, too damned softhearted."

"Yeah, should have run you in when I had the chance," I mumbled with a weak grin, but the expression on my face must've mirrored my feelings. While Rita had violated my trust, she'd done it for me, and the thought of that tugged at my heart.

"Hey, O'Brien, quit with the long face. We'll get to the bottom of this. We'll find the drug center. The Deacon will explain to those jokers at the Bright Spot that we'd really like to know where that dad-blamed center is," Sol said, oblivious to the real reason for my sudden shift of mood. "Isn't that right, Deacon?"

"Right on, boss," the Deacon answered.

The Deacon, a nickname he acquired when he was an All-American defensive end for USC–named after the great Deacon Jones of the L.A. Rams, whom he emulated–was a powerful black guy about six-two and two-hundred-twenty pounds. He had arms of steel and his shoulders were like the crossbeams that held up the Vincent Thomas Bridge. After a tour in Viet Nam, Special Forces, decorated for valor twice, and a stint in the Secret Service he joined Sol's team of talented and formidable agents. It wasn't long before the Deacon became Sol's prime operative, often accompanying him on special missions where muscle and diplomacy were needed in equal proportions.

The Deacon wore an expensive Italian-cut business suit with all the accessories, monogrammed dress shirt, Magnum .45, and a Hermes tie, the Magnum being tucked into a designer crocodile holster.

While Sol took another call, I stared out the window at the vast desert wasteland rushing by. I wasn't focused on the sun-bleached rocks or scorched mountains. I tried to comprehend where and how I'd gone wrong. I thought about the terrible mess I was in: Robbie's escape, Judge Tobias and his disappointment in me, and now Rita sacrificing her ethics. It was too much. Thoughts of quitting the law crossed my mind. Yeah, maybe it would be better if I gave up the law business, got a real job. But quitting the law, canceling my bar card, would probably be a moot point before long anyway.

"By the way, Jimmy," Sol said, after he hung up the phone. "Mabel had something else to tell you."

"Yeah, what'd she say this time?"

"Seems she found a goddamn mouse in your office."

"A mouse in my office?"

"Yeah, imagine that. When she came to work this morning, Rita and you were in your office talking. Mabel left and came back when you two were gone. Later, when she went into your office to get a file, she noticed that someone had moved the filing cabinet. She went to straighten it. And guess what? She found a goddamn mouse. That's what she said, a goddamn mouse behind the cabinet. She said it's now in her purse."

I hadn't been paying much attention to Sol, but suddenly it dawned on me what he was talking about. "Mabel did *what?* Rita wasn't there?"

A mischievous grin appeared on Sol's face. "Why would Mabel put a goddamn mouse in her purse?" He glanced at the Deacon. "Why would she do that, Deacon?"

"Don't know, boss."

"Maybe she didn't want the cops to notice how untidy a

law office can get. Things like that laying around. Disgusting."

Sol dusted his hands in an exaggerated fashion, mocking my gloom, which now departed at a fast gallop. Rita hadn't removed the gun after all. She had kept her word.

"Yeah," the Deacon said. "A goddamn mouse, imagine that."

"With a goddamn .38 caliber asshole," Sol said, "that shits bullets."

Sol and the Deacon broke out laughing. I laughed too, hard. And it felt good.

We roared up to the Bright Spot Café, jumped out of the limo, and dashed into the white clapboard building.

"All right, everyone up against the wall!" Sol strutted around the room, walking tall, flashing his P.I. badge. He waved it around at arm's length. The Deacon stood next to the wall, in front of the window, holding his gun at his side, pointed at the floor. Cubby stayed with the car. I stood by the door.

Sol wanted to make a dramatic entrance, get the people's attention, he'd explained earlier.

The same group of men slouched in the café, but the teenaged girl, Jane, was nowhere in sight. Everyone looked up and started moving slowly to the edge of the room. Everyone, that is, except Ben Moran and his buddy, a new guy I hadn't seen before.

The new guy was a bear of man, a redneck brute of about forty. He wore no shirt and his hairy, ursine back and chest were exposed beneath his bib overalls. Even while he sat, I could see that Moran's buddy had to be about six-foot-five and in a weight contest he'd top a black grizzly. He was no Winnie the Pooh.

The redneck and Moran sat calmly at the table drinking coffee, oblivious to the action surrounding them. Finally, the bear looked up. "Hey, gumshoe. Tell your boy to put his peashooter away before I have to get out of my chair and shove it up his ass." He spoke with a thick cracker accent.

Ben Moran's eyes flashed and he said, "Shut up, Buddy." He said it fast, before Sol could react to the redneck's comment. "We're going to have a friendly little chat with these gentlemen. Then we'll ask them to leave, nice and polite like." He turned to Sol. "C'mon over and sit down. Have some coffee." He looked at me; there was a hardness in his eyes I hadn't seen before. "You too, O'Brien. You can tell me about your plan to buy the Harvey House."

"The Deacon," Sol swaggered toward the men at the table, "doesn't like to be called *boy*. Makes him real upset, no telling what he'll do." Sol then charged the table, got up close to Moran's pal, and said, "I'm a Jew, wanna make something out of that?"

Buddy the bear sprang to his feet and roared back, ready to let fly an amazingly huge fist in the direction of Sol's face.

Moran grabbed Buddy by the straps of his bib overalls. "Calm down, friend," he said. Then he turned to Sol. "You too mister gumshoe. Christ said—"

"I don't give a damn what Christ said. I wanna know where the girl is."

"What girl?"

I walked to the table and answered for Sol. "Dark-haired teenager named Jane."

"Never heard of her." Moran turned to the customers lining the wall, the men guarded by the Deacon. "Any of you boys know some girl calls herself Jane?"

I watched their dead eyes as they lied, shaking their heads

in unison.

Then I marched to the counter, hopped over it, and peered through the food slot into the filthy, drab kitchen behind the wall. No one was back there. I turned to the waitress who stood motionless, taut, next to the cash register. "You know who we are taking about. She works here, was wiping tables."

The waitress shook her head vehemently, but her eyes shifted downward. I followed her glance. Her hand was held out open below the counter; hidden from the group in the café. In it she held a small scrap of paper. Quickly, I snatched the paper and jammed it into my pocket.

"Where's the owner of this place? I want to see the employment records," Sol said.

"I own it," Moran said. "Ain't got no records. Don't believe in them."

"Government says you gotta keep records."

"Government's got no right poking their nose in my businesses."

"Didn't Christ say something about rendering unto Caesar?" Sol said.

"Caesar's dead–and soon all the Hebrews will be dead too, along with the Roman heathens and descendents of Cain. Dead and gone once the day of reckoning is upon us." Moran raised his head. "Amen, I say amen!" I thought I noticed a smirk hiding in his dark eyes under those bushy brows.

The men at the wall joined in, chanting *amen* and waving their arms as they moved closer to the Deacon.

I came out from around the counter. "In the meantime, you can tell us where the drug center is located."

Moran lowered his arms; the chanting stopped. His eyes shifted from the men lined up at the wall to the Deacon, then to Sol.

Buddy the bear slowly hoisted his three hundred pounds of flab and attitude out of the chair. He pinned me with a defiant scowl and then focused on the Deacon. His face had the hue of a hot brick. Any minute he'd explode. Tension filled the room; you could squeeze it with your fingers and it would bleed.

"Hey, *boy*!" Buddy the bear yelled at the Deacon.

The Deacon spun around, exposing his back to the men lined up behind him.

Then it happened.

"Get 'em men!" Moran shouted.

At once all five of the men attacked the Deacon.

Buddy the bear sprang on the balls of his feet–lightning fast–and pounced on Sol.

One of the guys at the wall pulled a toad sticker from his coveralls pocket, flicked open the six inch blade, and eyed me cautiously for a split second before he charged, the blade glittering in the light.

The Deacon's gun clattered to the floor. Ben Moran grunted, pushed his massive bulk out of the chair, and scrambled after the revolver as it slid across the room. He looked up. Cubby, who had silently slipped into the café, had his foot on the gun. He wagged his finger. "Sit this one out, old man, before you get hurt." Moran moseyed back to his table and settled in, an innocent bystander at the Bright Spot rumble.

I stepped back. The guy with the blade flew past me and sprawled on the floor, after he tripped on my outstretched foot. He banged his head on the wall, stuck himself in the leg with his knife, and didn't get up. He sat there and stared at the blood that started to pool under his thigh. I toyed with the idea of tossing him the washrag that sat on the counter.

The ruckus continued. The Deacon had made short work

of the first three guys and now was pounding the last hooligan into hamburger.

And Sol, his jaws clenched, was busy with the redneck. He had the big bear in a hammerlock, thumping the guy's head on the table.

"Hold it," Moran shouted. "I think these city folks have had enough."

Sol looked up. Surprise was written on his face. "Yeah, guess we're not as tough as we thought." He dropped the redneck and the guy rolled slowly to the floor. Then with his hand, he made a slashing motion across his neck indicating to the Deacon and me–like a director making a movie–*cut, the fight scene is over*.

I strolled to the counter and tossed the rag to Mack the Knife, still on the floor by the wall. The bloody mess was becoming unsightly.

The room became quiet and Moran said in a loud voice, "That girl, the one you called Jane, she just wandered in here, hungry, wanted food." He nodded. "Gave her some, and she cleaned tables for an hour or two. That's all I know about her."

Sol dabbed at a cut on his lip with a napkin he grabbed from a table. "Why didn't you tell us that before?" he asked.

"You folks come in here throwin' your weight around, itchin' for a brusin'. I figure why spoil the fun?"

Sol looked at me. We both heard the whooping sounds of sirens off in the distance. It sounded like they were converging on the Bright Spot. "Where can we find the teen drug center?" I said to Moran.

He turned to me. "What is it with you? There ain't no damn teen center out here. Where'd you come up with that notion?"

Before I could answer, Sol jumped in. "I think he's right

Jimmy. I think the party you spoke to about the center could have said it's in *Bakersfield*, not Barstow. Don't you think?"

The sirens were getting louder. "*Bakersfield*?"

"Yeah, Jimmy, Bakers...*field*. I guess if it's not there, then that's the end of the line."

Moran climbed out of his chair bit by bit. "If you folks just leave town, nice and quiet like, then there'd be no sense in pressing charges. Provided you don't come back and bother us about this nonsense no more."

Whoop, whoop, whoop. The sirens were blaring just outside the café. The police had the place surrounded.

"*Come out with you hands in the air*." A bullhorn-filtered voice growled, the words bouncing off the café walls.

Sol's eyes locked on Moran who stood with pursed lips, stoically, as if challenging Sol. Sol nodded once, then turned and marched outside. "Whaddya want?" he shouted into the circle of squad cars that surrounded the café.

The Deacon picked up his gun, tucked it away, and helped people to their feet. Their fun was over and they wouldn't be causing any trouble. Cubby settled in at one of the tables and tried to get the waitress's attention. He wanted a cup of coffee and a hamburger. I stood in the doorway and watched the scene in the parking lot unfold.

The bullhorn again. "Put your hands in the air."

A half dozen of Barstow's finest were crouched behind their black-and-whites with guns in their hands, the hands rested on the hoods of the cars, and the guns aimed directly at Sol's chest, not a small target by any means.

Sol pranced closer to the cop cars. "Who's in charge, dammit?" he shouted. It sounded like he was becoming upset again.

An angry voice flew out from behind the barricade. "Hey

fella, hold it right there–"

"It's all right Burt," Ben Moran shouted through the window. "We had a difference of opinion, that's all. And now these gentlemen are leaving."

A swagbellied cop, with more decorations dangling from his khaki uniform than Napoleon wore at his coronation, popped up and motioned vigorously for his troops to holster their weapons. He sauntered toward the café, tugging at his John Brown belt, which had slipped to his ass during the standoff. "What was the trouble in there?" he asked, the question directed at Sol.

"Food sucks," Sol answered.

"Well, hell, what do you expect in a dump like this?"

"Burt, knock it off. It's all over," Moran hollered to the police chief. "These gentlemen are leaving."

"Ben, we got a call. Said the old place was being held up," the chief shouted back.

"You fool, there's no money in here, what the hell you talking about? These guys are leaving town, won't be back." Moran said. "Now, do as I say and let them go."

"Okay, Ben, you're the boss. I ain't gonna hold 'em. Just want to have a few words with this guy. That's all."

"Hey, Chief, I'm Sol Silverman. Everything is under control. We were just heading out for Bakersfield...." I heard Sol say before he lowered his voice and stepped closer to the big cop.

Chapter Seventeen

Sol and I huddled outside by the limo for a few moments while Burt, the chief of police and his men pulled out. Sol told me he'd assured the chief that we were heading directly out of town and would leave posthaste without beating up on anyone else. He said it seemed easier to agree to that stipulation than to post bail and go through the rigmarole.

But we were intrigued with Ben Moran. He was obviously the kingfish in town. We speculated why he wanted us out of Barstow so badly. And how he seemed to lighten up when Sol mentioned Bakersfield.

"Bakersfield, Sol?" I asked.

"Yep, a lovely town. Don't you think, Jimmy?"

Bakersfield was an oil boom town in the 1920s, but its glory had faded when the price of oil started a steady decline in the late '50s, and now was a struggling working class community about a hundred miles north of Los Angeles. I had nothing against Bakersfield and in light of the Yom Kippur War oil prices might rise yet again, but I doubted that Sol was serious when he said that the drug center could be located there. "Bakersfield's fine, I guess; that is, if you like the sight of rickety oil derricks on every empty lot."

"Yeah, it's lovely–"

"Moran's not that dumb, Sol. He knows we aren't going to Bakersfield. Why didn't he have his cop buddy, the chief, hook us up? I mean, we did mess up his joint."

"He doesn't want to create waves, just wants us out of town. I just said that stuff about Bakersfield to help him save face. But you're right Jimmy, I can feel it. Something's going on out here and Moran is smack-dab in the middle of it."

"I think he's afraid that we'll discover something about the girl that would prove to be unsavory for him in light of his religious fervor, or at least his image of it," I said.

"Could be, but I think he figures we'll take off and not come back. Because if we do, he'll have the police pick us up and hold us. What kind of snooping can we do from a jail cell?"

"He has it both ways. We're gone, and won't be back, and there is no fuss, no need to get a judge involved." I paused for a second. "Who is he anyway, Sol? He's not just some old fogey who sits around the Bright Spot all day waiting for famous writers to pop in."

Sol glanced at the white clapboard building, then he turned back and mentioned that it would be worthwhile to run an R & I on the old guy. I told him he sounded like Joe Friday of *Dragnet*. He gave me a playful tap on the shoulder. I'd have a bruise for a week.

Before climbing into the limo, I fished the waitress's note out of my pocket. In a tiny female script was written the girl's name, Jane Simon and under that was what I assumed to be the name of the local newspaper, the *Barstow Sun*.

We kicked around a few ideas about why the waitress slipped me the note, and why the girl's name would be associated with the newspaper. But Sol and I agreed, we'd come this far, might as well check it out before leaving town. After prying directions from a different gas station guy than the one I'd talked with before–we wanted to get there sometime today–we drove east on Main Street looking for Sweetwater Road. When we came to it, we turned left and pulled up in front of a well maintained, painted cinderblock building. An old fashioned sign hung above the entrance, *The Barstow Sun*, the words being cut into the wood.

Cubby and the Deacon waited in the limo with the motor running in the event it became necessary to make a fast departure. Cubby would tap the horn if he spotted any cop cars approaching.

Inside the paper's business office, a striking woman who appeared to be about thirty-two, thirty-three, with a figure you'd bow down to, walked to the counter. Her voice was crisp and businesslike, but her eyes, dark and gleaming, revealed a passion burning inside. Or was it my imagination? Slender women with dark eyes always have passion, I told myself. And like the others, I doubted that this gorgeous woman would be an exception.

"Hi, I'm Jimmy O'Brien, and this is my friend Sol Silverman," I said. "And you have a passion–"

"What?"

"Ah…. I mean…we have a passion for the truth. And that's why we came to the *Sun*."

"Wise choice," the beauty said.

"For chrissakes, Jimmy, get to the point." Sol interrupted. "Sweetheart, we need some information. Is your boss in?"

"Hi, Sol. My name is Cathy Rogers. I own the paper." The lovely woman reached across the counter and offered her hand to Sol.

I beat Sol to the outstretched hand and shook it. "Hi, Cathy," I said, "maybe you can help us. We are looking for a girl by the name of Jane Simon–"

Sol jumped in. "Miss Rogers, what my young friend here wants to know is do you have an employee by the name of Jane? Simon could be her last name. She's a dark-haired teenager who might be working here. We have reason to believe she may be in some trouble."

"No, I'm sorry, we don't hire teens. My husband, Tom, and I run the paper and…" At the mention of a husband, I deflated a little, but she still had passion in her eyes. "Wait, what did you say her name was?" Cathy paused. "A dark-haired girl? Did you say Jane Simon? My God, fair skin and deep blue eyes?"

My pulse raced. "Yes, yes, that's her! Do you know the girl? How can we find her?"

"No, it can't be. No.... I'm sorry, gentlemen, I know of no one by that name. Now if you'll excuse me." Cathy started to turn away.

Sol leaned on the counter. "Wait a minute, my dear. Couldn't you help us, please? The young girl is in serious trouble and we're here to see what we can do for her, that's all," he said with tenderness in his voice, a gentleness he rarely displayed.

Cathy turned away from us. I wasn't sure, but I thought I heard a muffled whimper. Was she crying? "Cathy, we're sorry, we didn't mean to upset you."

A man with tousled sandy hair standing next to a clanking printing press in the back of the shop looked our way. He paused for a few seconds before he walked cautiously toward Cathy. His eyes pinned Sol and me as he approached. When he got close, he studied Cathy's face. "What's the matter honey? Are these guys brothering you?" He gave us a puzzled look.

Cathy raised her head. "No, no, Tom. It's not that. It's about Jane. Something they said reminded me of her, that's all."

Tom wrapped a loving arm around Cathy's shoulder and his eyes shifted first to Sol and then to me. "Did you gentlemen know Jane?"

Chapter Eighteen

The ten-year old headline in bold, black type screamed at me: *Air Force Man Kills Wife, Daughter, Self.* I started to shake. But, it wasn't the headline that shook me. It was the picture below it—a man, a woman, and a little girl posed in the shade of a plain stucco house.

I bolted out of my chair and pointed at the picture. "That's her. Same dark hair, eyes, and my God...the girl I met has a striking resemblance to the mother in the newspaper photo."

Sol and I sat with Cathy and Tom in their modest office at the rear of the print shop. Cathy's antique roll top dominated the room, but there was a small worktable in the center, and we all sat there staring at the ten-year-old edition of the *Barstow Sun* spread out on top of the table. After we'd told them why we came, explaining about my meeting with the teenaged girl who called herself Jane, and after I showed them the scrap of paper from the waitress, Tom had dug out the old edition from their archives, a closet next to the restroom.

He calmly explained that the photo printed below the headline had been taken a few months before the tragic murder-suicide. But I was almost positive that the small girl standing next to her mother and father was the same girl I'd met, the same Jane Simon. The girl in the photograph was a pint-sized version of the teenager.

"Impossible," Tom said. "She's been dead for ten years now."

Cathy's hands were on the table, folded tight in front of her. "I saw her body and went to her funeral," she said to no one in particular.

"Are you sure Jimmy, absolutely sure that's the girl you met behind the building?" Sol asked. "That's an old picture. The girl's just a kid."

"Sol, I think so. I couldn't swear in court." I studied the newspaper photo. "But Jane, the girl from the café, told me about her father killing her mother. She was very convincing. I don't think she was lying."

"Look, Jimmy, you met someone, a dark-haired girl, sure. But the story about the murder and suicide was in the papers, anyone could've–"

"Sol," I said. "It has to be her. It's the same girl. Too many things match up. The family resemblance, everything else. Besides, why would a dead girl try to convince someone she was alive?"

Sol shook his head. "Irish logic?"

"You know what I mean." I pointed at the picture again. "I'm convinced. That's the girl I met. I don't know how to explain it, but it's her."

Tom and Cathy listened to our exchange without saying a word.

Sol and I fell silent for a moment.

Cathy moved her hand and partially covered her mouth. "It can't be. It just can't be. I can't believe she's alive."

Tom added in a quiet voice, "I don't believe in ghosts."

Although I was now convinced the teenager I'd seen in the café and met later behind the Harvey House was the same girl who was supposedly killed ten years ago, I still had no idea what all of this had to do with Robbie Farris's escape and his mother's murder.

The four of us sat looking at one another not knowing exactly what to say. Cathy started talking, telling us about Jane

Simon. She explained her involvement with the little girl, and why she'd *lost it* out in the front office. We sat silently and listened to her story.

"When I was a teenager myself," Cathy said, "I babysat for the Simons and naturally Jane and I became close, almost like I was a big sister to her. As she grew older, she had a difficult time adjusting to her parents' constant bickering and arguing. Her father was an officer in the Air Force. They had a house here in town, but he was assigned to the old military base at Rattlesnake Lake. It's closed now. They closed the base shortly after...after the shooting."

Cathy paused to gain her composure–or maybe to gather her thoughts. She glanced at her husband, Tom. He nodded silently and she continued. "Most days Jane's father stayed out at the base, but when he came home, there was hell to pay. Jane couldn't handle it. When her parents started fighting, she'd call and ask if she could come and stay with me. Well, of course, I always said yes..."

She stood and walked slowly to her roll top desk. "On the night of the shooting, Jane had called; and when she did..." Cathy spun around. Her eyes were filled with dread. "I told her she couldn't come over...I had a date."

The implication was obvious. Cathy still held strong feelings of guilt. Jane would still be alive, if only...

I now believed that Jane hadn't been murdered that horrible night, but Cathy had agonized about the girl's death for ten years and she wasn't about to accept the word of a stranger who said the girl was alive and living at a teen drug center right here in Barstow.

"Do you happen to know a kid named Robbie Farris?" I tossed out the question not just to change the subject, but in the slim chance that they might know something that would tie him to Jane's appearance. As expected, neither Cathy nor Tom had heard of him.

"How about the drug center? Do you folks know where it could be located, or anything about it?" Sol asked.

They both shook their heads, and unlike the people in the café, Tom and Cathy seemed sincere when they disavowed knowledge of the center.

"Is there an old school or maybe a campground that could have been converted?" I asked.

I drew blank stares. Tom said, "Jimmy, again, nothing like that comes to mind. But the Mormons, and the Catholic Church over on Mountain View, both have teen recreation centers. No kids live in either place, at least that I'm aware of."

"No," I said. "I have the impression that the drug center would have to be a fairly large facility, large enough to house and feed many youngsters–"

Cathy interrupted. "What makes you think there's a place like that in Barstow? I'm sure we'd know if it existed."

"A certain old lady told me, and the girl–"

"The girl is obviously an imposter," Cathy snapped. "For crying out loud! I identified her body at the morgue. Not only that Burt Krause, the chief of police, told me he ran her fingerprints through the FBI. It was definitely Jane on that steel table."

"What's this about an old woman telling you that a drug center exists out here?" Tom asked. "Is she credible?"

Tom was an oasis of calm in the eye of Cathy's storm. She was becoming increasingly annoyed with my questions. I really couldn't blame her. After all, my story–how I'd talked to a dead teenager and how an old woman told me about a phantom drug center–must have sounded utterly bizarre. At that point, I didn't want to mention that my source, the old woman, was a drunk being chased by goblins. It certainly would not have helped my credibility.

"Fellas," Tom said, "we'd like to help, but we just don't know what to believe…"

Sol stood. "C'mon, Jimmy. I think we've imposed on these nice people long enough."

I could tell by the tone in his voice that Sol was on to something. Besides, if he wanted more information he wouldn't give a damn about imposing on these people, nice or not. But I had an idea of what was going through his mind. "Yeah, Sol you're right," I said. "Maybe I was mistaken about the girl. I guess she just looked like Jane."

"Sorry, Cathy, Tom," Sol said. "Thanks for your time. We'll be leaving now."

Tom climbed out of his chair and glanced at Cathy. "Honey, wait here. I'll walk these gentlemen to their car."

Cathy eyed him. "What's going on?" When he said nothing, she turned to Sol and me. Distress was evident in her face. "What is it with you two?" She slowly stood; her distress turned to anger. "Who are you people? You come marching in here with some wild tale about Jane–"

"Honey, calm down. They didn't mean any harm."

"Sorry, Cathy," Sol said. "We sincerely apologize for opening old wounds. Let's go, Jimmy."

"I said I'll walk you to your car." Tom's irritation was beginning to show. It was evident that he wanted a minute alone with us without his wife overhearing.

"Bullshit!" Cathy's eyes flashed. "You've got something to say, you say it right here in front of me." She jabbed her finger repeatedly atop the work table.

Sol held his arms out. "Look folks, we didn't come here to dig up old bones, or get you involved in this nasty business, but something stinks in this town. I can smell it. And what I smell is murder."

A chilly silence filled the room, almost as if a dark cloud had settled in above our heads. Sol had a knack, at times, for being blunt and maybe a bit dramatic, but he always said what he thought and what he just said was certainly in the back of my mind. If Cathy and Tom became involved in this affair and started snooping around, they just might end up like Hazel Farris and Robbie's professor, not to mention the man and woman in the newspaper. Someone was killing people, and if the murders were related to the drug center, then Sol and I may have jeopardized these innocent people by the very fact that we brought it to their attention.

Cathy and Tom stared at each other for several moments. Suddenly, Cathy started moving about the room. First she swept up the old newspaper and put it away, then–while forcefully banging the chairs back under the table–she said, "C'mon, Tom, we have things to do."

She turned her lovely face toward Sol and me. "If you'll excuse us, gentlemen, we have a newspaper to get out."

Chapter Nineteen

Sol and I stepped out into the blazing heat with the sun reflecting brightly off the glossy-white exterior wall of the newspaper office we had just left. The glare was intense. Sol whipped out his Ray-Ban sunglasses, the ones with fancy gold frames. I squinted.

Sometimes it was uncanny the way Sol and I clicked, our minds hitting on the same idea at the same time. In the office, as soon as Cathy had mentioned it, we both knew where the teen center could possibly be located. The only logical location, a place sufficiently equipped to house scores of teens, would be the old military base where Jane's father was stationed, Rattlesnake Lake. An obsolete military base, out of the way of prying eyes with built-in security and high fences surrounding it, would be perfect.

The limousine pulled up alongside us. We jumped in, and Sol immediately grabbed the radiotelephone receiver. We waited with the engine idling while Sol made his call. After he hung up he gave detailed driving instructions to his driver. Cubby slammed the limo in gear, roared away from the building in a cloud of dust, and now we were racing along old Route 66 heading to Daggett, a town ten miles east of Barstow.

Sol had phoned a friend in Washington, DC to find out if Rattlesnake Lake Base had been sold or leased to a private entity. Yes, the base had been sold almost immediately after the military had abandoned it. The government had sold it in a sealed bid to an outfit called the Joshobeam Corporation.

The base at Rattlesnake Lake, Sol's friend explained, had been established in the early fifties as an auxiliary emergency landing field when the Air Force started testing the X-series rocket planes at Edwards. The dry, flat alkaline lakebed made for a perfect runway.

Several other small bases, scattered along the experimental aircrafts' flight path, identical in purpose, were built. Most of the bases had been closed at the termination of the X-plane program in the early sixties, but Rattlesnake Lake, the closest emergency base to Barstow, fifty-six miles northeast, was the only one sold.

We raced along the highway going like the wind—and the wind blew about a hundred miles an hour out here. When Sol was on a case he became impatient and darted here and there like a hummingbird on speed. Cubby, his driver, knew to keep the pedal against the firewall. Someone had asked me once how Sol, when roaring around in his beefed up limousine, never seemed to get a speeding ticket. Very simple, I'd answered. He has special license plates on his limo and he also carries an honorary highway patrolman's badge. Both the plates and the badge along with a plaque were given to him by the commissioner of the California Highway Patrol in recognition of his community service; he planted a tree somewhere alongside a new freeway. I didn't mention that I suspected he was given special consideration and the perquisites because of his *anonymous* contribution to the Highway Patrol's widows and orphan fund, ten big ones:, I'd heard.

We sped straight through the tiny community of Daggett and about four miles east of the main shopping area—a gas station and a Chinese restaurant—we turned off the highway, drove along a gravel road for a half-mile, then pulled up in front of a large Quonset hut originally built in the 1930s. Above the arched opening a sign read, 'Welcome to Daggett Airport, Elev. 2000 ft., Unicom 123.0'.

On the eight-minute drive to Daggett, Sol had managed to get in two more phone calls. The first was to Joyce asking her to dig out all the information available on Ben Moran. He also told her that he needed everything she could find out about the

Joshobeam Corporation.

After Sol hung up, he told me that Joyce would have the Silverman team of crack investigators working on it right away. A complete write-up of both Moran and the corporation would be on his desk when he arrived at his office tomorrow morning, right after mid-morning brunch.

The second call he made was to Daggett Flight Service, a charter flight operation located at the airport. Sol had reserved a small plane. He'd asked that a pilot be standing by upon our arrival there in a matter of minutes, said we were in a rush, explained to the dispatcher that the sun was low in the sky and we didn't want darkness interfering with our little sightseeing tour.

The Cessna 182, like an aluminum bird ready to soar, was poised on the tarmac a few feet from where we parked the limo. A guy who must have been the pilot was doing a walk-around inspection of the small, single-engine airplane.

Before Sol and I hopped out of the limo, he told Cubby to head back to Downey, drop the Deacon off at the office, then drive to the airport in Fullerton. "No need for you guys to wait around here. After our little look-see, we'll have the pilot drop us off there," he said. "Faster that way."

The pilot, a lanky guy wearing an orange jumpsuit, ambled over to us. He had a Los Angeles Dodgers baseball cap plopped at a jaunty angle on his head. Tufts of blond hair jutted out beneath the blue cap.

"You the guys that reserved the 182?" the pilot asked.

"Yeah," Sol answered and pointed to the airplane. "Is she ready to go?"

"Just need a credit card or cash deposit."

Sol handed him an American Express gold card.

"You said you'd be doing some sightseeing," the pilot said. "Not much to see out here, just a bunch of rocky canyons and dry lake beds."

The pilot looked at the credit card and started to tuck it

into his side pocket, but he stopped and looked up when Sol said, "Yeah, that's what we want to see, a dry lake. Rattlesnake Lake."

"Oh, hey, I don't know about that," the pilot said. "That's restricted airspace. There's a military base there."

"The base is closed, been closed almost ten years."

"Yeah, but, they never took off the dang restriction. Can't fly closer than fifteen miles to the place."

"Now look here, young fella...by the way what's your name?" Sol stuck out his hand. "Mine's Sol and that's Jimmy over there." He pointed at me.

The pilot pumped Sol's hand. "Name's Del. How ya doin', Sol," He waved to me. "Jimmy."

"Well now, Del," Sol slipped into his backslapping, suede-shoe salesman routine. "Jimmy over there is a lawyer, see." Sol turned to me. "Show Del your card, Jimmy." He put his arm around Del's shoulders and whispered in a conspiratorial voice "Listen, son. Jimmy's going to give you his approval–in writing, mind you. Always get it in writing, my boy."

"I dunno, Sol...." Dodger Del adjusted his baseball cap, tucked his unruly hair back in place. "It's kinda illegal."

"Look, Del..." Sol pulled the kid in closer and leaned into him. "Not only is Jimmy going to give you're a nice letter. I'm going to give you a thousand dollars."

"Well, hell, it ain't that illegal. Let's go!"

Chapter Twenty

The next thing I knew we were in the Cessna screaming down runway 22.

Del, his eyes fixed forward, pulled back on the yoke and the plane lifted off the ground, zooming skyward at 120 miles per hour. A gusty side wind kicked up and the right wing dipped, but Del had it under control; a quick twist of the wheel leveled the plane. I sat next to the pilot up front and Sol had the backseat to himself. He glanced out the side window as we climbed, the ground receding below us.

We both felt it would be a good idea to scope out the base from the air before I went barging in looking for Robbie. Having come this far there was no question about me getting onto the base, if for no other reason than to prove—or disprove, as the case might be—our thought that the base was now, in reality, the teen drug center. A bird's-eye view of their security seemed prudent.

My stomach lurched when the plane nosed over and leveled off at a few hundred feet above the dirt. Because we were now level the Cessna picked up speed rapidly, the airspeed indicator high on its green arch. We flew at thirty degrees on the compass, the town below drifting away behind us. The view ahead was of sweeping flatlands surrounded by jagged mountains and rocky hills, all in various shades of brown and shadowy grays.

Del cranked the wheel to the left. The plane banked at a forty-five degree angle and we shot around the steep slope of a ridge towering in front of us. Another jerk on the wheel, the

Cessna smoothed out, and we raced above a narrow but deep canyon with a dry rocky riverbed snaking through the bottom of it. Del pushed on the control wheel; the airplane dove. Then, a couple hundred feet above the cliff's edge, he pulled back on the yoke. The G-force pinned my butt to the seat for a moment before the plane leveled out again.

The sensation of speed was awesome, the sight of the multi-colored canyon rushing by below us breathtaking. The terrace-cut walls of the ravine were natural frescos etched in the granite, carved by a river that had died a million years ago.

After a few seconds, Del said, "Gotta take her down, fly under the radar."

"Whoa," I said, "down where?" It looked to me like we were skimming the cliff tops as it was. But he didn't say anything, he just pulled back the throttle and pushed on control yoke, and the plane descended fast. I glanced at Sol in the backseat. I thought he'd be worried, but he seemed okay. He was flipping through a *Playboy* magazine that must've been on the seat.

When we got closer to the ground, the apparent velocity increased dramatically, the scorched desert floor rushing by us at an alarming rate. Glancing at Del, I noticed his face streamed with sweat as he twisted, turned, pushed and pulled the controls, maneuvering the small plane through jagged-edged canyons as we raced into and out of one dry lake basin after another. It was hairy and a little frightening, the aircraft jerking and bouncing, and I tensed as the plane veered off to dodge a large boulder that I hadn't seen until it was zooming past my window, missing us by a millimeter.

As I sat there being yanked about like a rag doll in the mouth of an angry pit bull, I grew worried about Sol. I'll admit I was a trifle nervous about the flight myself– having taken a few flying lessons, I knew the stress limits of these types of aircraft–but I figured that Sol, having no experience, would be scared out of his wits by now. Any moment he'd beg to cancel the flight.

Then, suddenly, I smelled smoke.

But after a moment's reflection, I knew nothing was wrong with the plane. The aroma came from the burning of Cuban tobacco. Sol had lit a cigar.

"Hey Del, we must be getting close to the base," Sol shouted in the pilot's ear, leaning forward, cigar in hand. "Can't you get a little lower? Need to get a good look."

"You're the boss!" Del replied, and looked at me. "Don't ya just love it?" He nudged the yoke forward. Down we went, another ninety-nine feet. We couldn't go lower than that. We'd only been about 100 feet above the ground when Sol made the suggestion.

"Yeah, it's terrific," I said, as we swerved to miss a jackrabbit.

The Cessna screamed inches above a dry lake bed, moving like a full blown Indy car going 160 mph. Yet, out here there was no racetrack, and directly in front of us was an ugly ridge of large rocks. The plane nosed up; we climbed, and shot through a narrow saddle-gap between two huge rocky mounds. When we emerged, the ground fell away and the wind-blown desert exploded with life before our eyes. The ex-military base appeared, spread out right below us, filling the front windscreen. A high chain-link fence enclosed several rows of wooden single-story rectangular structures. Guard towers stood at the boundaries of the expanse. With the fence and the towers the place looked like a prison camp. I wondered if the guards were put there to keep people out, or perhaps, once inside, to keep them there.

Beyond the base, outside the fenced-off area, about a mile north of the complex, I saw a ten-thousand-foot runway, scraped flat on the dry alkaline surface of an ancient lakebed. A gravel road ran toward the buildings, a road that came from Barstow about sixty miles behind us. After looping around the outpost buildings it came to a Y. One direction headed to Highway 395 and Calico, an old ghost town turned into a tourist trap by the Knott's Berry Farm people, but the other branch of the road continued on and disappeared into the desolate, rock-strewn mountains a few miles to the west. I wondered where the road ended. There were no towns or settlements beyond those mountains that I knew of.

I leaned closer to Del. "Where's that road lead to, Del? The one going over the mountain out there?" I shouted above the roar of the engine, pointing at the right fork of the Y.

Without taking his attention away from the plane, keeping his eyes fixed forward, Del answered. "Several borax mines, and there's an old ore processing plant out there on the other side of the mountain, as well. Remember the TV show, *Death Valley Days*?"

"Yeah sure, Governor Reagan was the host, I think."

"The show was based loosely on the mines. The way things were back in the 1800s when they flourished. Then a while back the borax ore petered out. But it's rumored that they're working the mines again, and they say the refinery is up and running too. I've never been out there. No reason to go," Del said as he glanced at one of the flight gauges. He tapped it with a finger and the needle jumped. "There, that's better."

We flew above the gravel road at low altitude. Off to our right, half a mile away from the buildings, I saw a large paved yard where numerous pieces of heavy equipment stood. Dump trucks, earthmovers, and enormous Caterpillar tractors were lined up and ready to go, looking as if they could charge out and devour mountains, spitting out boulders like olive pits. Probably had something to do with the old mines.

Del hit the rudder pedal, jerked the wheel to the left, and we pivoted on the wing, the plane tilting at a sixty-degree angle. Almost instantly the Cessna leveled out, and when it did, we were aimed dead center at the cluster of bunkhouse-type buildings. We roared over the compound at rooftop level, the engine howling.

By the time we circled around for a second pass, men had poured out of the structures into the yard. There had to be fifteen or twenty of them, darting around in a wild frenzy, shaking rifles in the air. Even from inside the plane I could see that the guns had the distinctive shape of AK-47s, heavy-duty assault weapons. I was close enough to notice that the mob wasn't made up of teenage boys. These were all full-grown men wearing what appeared to be khaki paramilitary uniforms. I didn't think they wore forest rangers; no trees around here.

The first thing that popped into my mind was that we were buzzing a secret government facility, something like Delta Force, but the men down there were too old and raggedy for that; besides, Sol said the government had sold the base. I wondered what was going on. Could it be a right-wing fringe group that took over the facility? If teenagers were there, none were in sight.

I tried to keep my eyes pinned on the yard, but Del turned the plane and all I saw was blue sky. When the plane flattened out again, I could see that the men on the ground had formed up into military style columns. The first line dropped to their knees, rifles angled ominously toward the sky.

I heard Sol shout from the backseat, "Hey, let's vamoose! It looks like they're getting ready to take potshots at us."

Del jammed the throttle to the wall; the engine changed pitch, and the small plane immediately nosed up into a steep climb. As the base slowly pulled away below us, I turned and glanced over my shoulder. More uniformed men charged out of the barracks, but the military columns were breaking up. They'd fired no shots, and now the men were milling about the grounds. From my birds-eye view, I could tell the base was not a Christian teen drug center, and I was now sure that the khaki-clad goons were just a bunch of sorry-assed, right-wing bozos. It appeared that we might have stumbled upon a clandestine paramilitary group. We would turn the information over to the FBI, of course. But discovering Rattlesnake Lake's secret use wouldn't bring Robbie back, and without Robbie, I'd still be the number one suspect in Hazel Farris's murder.

Sol had to be reading my thoughts. He tapped me on the shoulder and I turned. "Jimmy, I know you wanted to get onto the base and check from the inside out, look around for Robbie and all of that. But now I know it's just too dangerous."

"It may be the only way to tell if he's there, or had been there. I'd like to see if those weekend fascists drive around in black Ford vans."

"Look, we've seen enough to know the base isn't a Christian drug center. All those goons running around with guns…But, I'll tell you what I'm going to do."

"What?"

"Just to be sure. I'm going to alert my friends in the FBI that when they raid the place, to be on the lookout for Robbie."

On the quiet flight back to Fullerton, I worried that I'd never find Robbie, worried about the murder investigation, and wondered what would happen if I never did find him. I also couldn't help but wonder about the teenage girl who called herself Jane.

Chapter Twenty-one

The following morning, a Friday, I walked into the office a little after eight feeling refreshed. I'd thought about my problems before I hit the sack, and had slept well in spite of the trouble swirling around me. I knew that Webster had turned his Section 32 file over to Hammer and his team of homicide detectives, the cops investigating Hazel Farris's murder. And I figured Webster would wait for me to be eliminated as a suspect in the murder investigation before he'd file against me on the section 32 charge.

So I knew I had a little more time to find Robbie. But this morning on my way to the office, I'd seen two hardnosed guys in a plain-jane, a Chevy four-door, trailing me, lurking behind about three car lengths. It had to be a couple of Hammer's detectives. A waste of taxpayer dollars, but I wasn't worried about it. Call me crazy, but I felt that being Hammer's number one suspect wasn't so tough. I was a lawyer and I knew that, without the gun, Hammer had scant evidence to tie me to the murder. Besides, once I found Robbie and brought him in, most of my problems would go away.

But when Hammer finds the real killer and they drop me as a suspect, then if Webster actually charges me with the Section 32 matter, Robbie's escape, I'll just handle the case professionally. At worst, I'll cop a *nolo contendere* plea and pay a fine.

I ducked my head into Rita's office. She sat behind her desk, hands folded politely in front of her. Seated before her was her new client—my old one—the credit card guy charged with fraud. When Rita looked up I mouthed a thank you, referring to the work she did at my apartment. She smiled. I quietly closed the door.

I was making the coffee when Mabel stormed in the door, uncharacteristically late. She shook her head and flashed a cold look, but her language could melt an iceberg.

"Goddamned government, sonofabitch," she said. "I got a goddamn odd-numbered license plate, and it's an even-numbered day. Had to siphon gas from my neighbor's car," she said as she slammed her purse down. "If this keeps up gas will soon be a dollar a gallon, goddamn thieves."

What she said reminded me that I'd have to get gas today for sure. The Yom Kippur War in the Middle East had started a few days before, gas has been in tight supply, and lines were forming at gas stations.

Mabel walked to the coffee bar. "Get out of my way, Jimmy. I'll make the coffee. My mouth still tastes like gasoline. Why make it worse?"

"Hey, my coffee tastes as good as Chevron, maybe not the high-test, but certainly as good as the regular," I said, and in a low voice added, "Sol told me you found a mouse."

"Yeah, and it's gone," Mabel said.

"No one will ever find it?"

"I said it's gone. Don't ask."

"You didn't happen to mentioned finding the gun to Rita, did you?" I asked.

"Nope, and if I were you I'd keep my mouth shut. She doesn't even know the police were here. Why compromise her position?"

"Well, she wants to be my lawyer on this matter–"

"There you go. She doesn't have to turn it over, if what I know about the law is correct."

"Where did you study law?"

"Don't be a smart aleck. I watch Perry Mason."

Just then, Rita and the client emerged from her office. "Danny, say hello to Jimmy O'Brien."

We shook hands. "I'm out of work right now, but I sell aluminum siding."

I shot a quick look at Rita, then turned back to Danny. "Aluminum siding?"

"That's why he needs us, Jimmy," Rita said. "It seems Danny didn't have a job. So he went to one of those seminars. You know the type, 'You-too-can-make-fifty-thousand-per-year-selling-aluminum-siding.' Of course, he believed them. Why would they lie?" she said in a sarcastic tone. "Anyway, he signed up, paid the three-hundred dollar fee, got his sales kit, and left. The next morning, before starting his door-to-door sales calls, Danny stopped at the bank and filled out an application for a credit card. He wrote in fifty thousand dollars as his annual earnings. What the heck, that's what the sleazebags running the scam said he'd make. Unfortunately, it was a bad year for aluminum siding."

"Couldn't pay his credit card bill, and now the bank wants to make an example of him," I said.

"Yeah, owes a thousand. The bank called the FBI."

"That's civil, not criminal," Mabel said.

I glanced at Mabel. "Perry Mason?"

"The bank, Cooperative Purchasers Bank, screamed criminal fraud," Rita said. "They're saying he lied on the credit app."

"That's the same bank that lost a billion on high-interest loans to Brazil, and now wants Uncle Sam to pick up the tab," I said.

"Yep, that's them. They had Danny arrested. Then at the

arraignment, he acted *pro per*." Rita turned to the poor guy standing next to her.

The phone rang. Mabel answered, then handed the receiver to me. "Excuse me a second, Danny." Covering the receiver, I asked Mabel to offer Danny a cup of coffee. His eyes lit up.

The call was from Joyce, Sol's secretary. I put her on hold and went to my office.

A few minutes after I had finished the conversation with Joyce, Rita stepped in and slipped into the client chair next to my desk. "Everything okay, Jimmy?" She crossed her legs and pulled down her skirt. "You look a little down."

I lifted my eyes from her legs. "I…guess so."

We were quiet for a second. "Do you want to tell me?" Rita asked.

I quickly brought her up to speed on my progress, or more accurately my lack thereof. I told her about the Barstow trip, downplaying the scene in the café, at least the rough stuff, but I shared my disappointment at not finding the teen drug center. I also explained Sol's and my theory that the base was now a right-wing compound of some sort. Of course, I didn't mention anything about the cops searching my office, or about Mabel hiding the gun.

"That was Joyce on the phone just now," I added.

"What did she say?"

"Sol is with the FBI right now, telling them what we discovered." I paused for a moment, glanced at the ceiling and gathered a breath. "Joyce said she found out that the Joshobeam Corporation is an offshore company. The owners are hidden, but she's sure the FBI will get to the bottom of it sooner or later."

"What about that guy, Ben Moran?" Rita asked.

"Yeah, it seems Moran is not the penniless old geezer he'd like us to believe. He has extensive mining interests scattered around the Mojave Desert. Could be he owns the old Borax mines the pilot told me about. I don't know if that has anything to do with Robbie, but I did see a lot of earthmoving equipment at the base."

"He must be tied in somehow. I mean to the base."

"Maybe so, but that still doesn't help finding Robbie," I said.

I told Rita that I thought the ex-military base was a dead end but, down deep, I wasn't so sure. There was too much going on at the Bright Spot café to totally ignore the idea that the base somehow figured into Robbie's escape. Moran held mining interests that could've made use of heavy equipment, and there was lots of it at the base. He was obviously the honcho at the café, and he had lied when he said Jane didn't work there. Jane had said she lived at the drug center. She'd called it "the base." All of that tied the café to the base, and I couldn't shake the idea that the base *was* the teen drug center.

It's true the men rushing out of the buildings weren't teens, but they had guns and they could've been holding the youngsters under lock and key. But why would they do that? Is that how a Christian drug rehab center was supposed to work? I didn't think so.

It was thin. Maybe my reasoning was flawed, but with Sol putting pressure on the FBI, I knew they'd raid the place. If Robbie was there, they would find him. I made a mental note to have Sol inform the FBI that I was still Robbie's lawyer that I wanted to be there when the raid went down. I needed to protect my client's interests.

Rita interrupted my thoughts. "Jimmy, you'll find him, I'm sure. By the way, while you were in Barstow I contacted

Webster to officially let him know that I'm now your lawyer. All questions go through me." She paused. "You do want me, don't you, Jimmy? I mean…"

"Of course I want you."

"Maybe you think I'm not experienced enough to be your lawyer at a time like this. Maybe Sol can get you someone better."

Someone better? The thought of Sol's nitwit nephew, Morty, flashed in my mind. But anyway, they'll drop me as a suspect in Hammer's investigation as soon as the FBI raids the base, where I felt in my gut Robbie was hiding. At that point, my need for a lawyer would become doubtful. However, one look at Rita sitting in my client chair, her legs crossed and skirt to mid-thigh, had me convinced. "Rita, yes, I want you to be my lawyer. I need you with me in this."

"Thanks, Jimmy, for the confidence you've placed in me. It means a lot. I'll do everything in my power to…well, you know. But now, I've got to give you my little speech, the speech I give to all my clients."

"Cash up front?"

"Shut up," she said playfully. "It's about trust and being open, telling me everything, even if it's embarrassing." She sat straight, her eyes intent and brimming with sincerity. "Now listen…"

While she talked, the gun matter with Mabel ticked at the periphery of my mind.

Chapter Twenty-two

I jumped on the Freeway and headed north to the San Fernando Valley, ending up at Golden Valley College just off Reseda Boulevard in Van Nuys. I parked in lot A, reserved for the administration staff, and walked onto the campus, following a pathway covered with shiny steel beams. The college was relatively new, built in the fifties, coming to life under Governor Brown's massive higher education program. No ivy walls, trees, or even a blade of grass were in sight. In fact, the architecture–like a lot of stuff built around L.A. at that time–was reminiscent of Disney's Tomorrowland or a chain of modern coffee shops; Googie's came to mind.

I approached a round, metal-clad, futuristic structure that looked more like a large flying saucer than the admissions building. It wouldn't have surprised me to see Michael Rennie, dressed in a pair of shiny coveralls, walk out, stiff legged, his arms in the air, saying, "*Klatuu, Barada, Nikto.*"

Seated at a desk behind the reception counter was a perky young woman with a lot of feathered hair. She wore a fuchsia satin jacket and pink pleated skirt, cinched with some kind of weird belt that had rhinestone monkeys running around on it.

The girl glanced up when she spotted me and laid the book she was reading on the desktop with the title showing: Jean-Paul Sartre's *Existentialism and Human Emotions*, heavy stuff, heavier than the girl.

"Hey, sunshine, what can I do for ya," she asked in a pleasant tone. "My name is Mandy."

"Hi, Mandy. I'm Jimmy O'Brien, a lawyer, and I need some information about Professor Carmichael."

When I mentioned the professor, Mandy's jovial spark

vanished. She turned away, faced her desk and glanced at the book, as if Sartre could bring back her cheerfulness. It was a longshot.

Carmichael was the professor whom Robbie had murdered. Now that the FBI was going to raid the base and perhaps capture Robbie, I felt that I'd better find out all I could about the professor in case my insanity defense fell apart. Maybe Carmichael had a temper and threatened Robbie, maybe it was an accident, or maybe it was something else. Plenty of maybes, plenty of questions, but not many justifiable reasons for one human being to kill another. Then again, all I needed was one.

Mandy turned back and gave me a feeble smile. "The professor was a good guy. I liked him a lot. So did just about everyone else."

"Did he have a temper, anything like that?"

"Oh, no, just the opposite. I mean, like, he was wicked."

"Wicked?"

"Yeah man, you know…like, totally awesome."

"Tubular."

"Yeah, bitchin'."

"A radical dude."

"Mondo primo." Her spark was returning and the smile grew on her pretty face.

Just then, an older guy emerged from an inner office. The guy looked like Mr. Weatherbee, the high school principal from the Archie comics–round, bald with just a tiny tuft of curly hair floating on top. He wore a herringbone suit with a white shirt and a red-checkered vest. His eyes were droopy circles behind pince-nez spectacles pinched high on the bridge of his long nose, and his world-weary countenance was perfect for the role he played, that of a junior college administer. "Mandy, I'll handle this matter," he said, while looking me over. "Mr. O'Brien, I couldn't help but overhear. My name is Gerald Grundy. You are an attorney, is that correct?" His voice had a lyrical but lisping trait to it.

"Call me Jimmy. I'm representing Robbie Farris."

"Yes." Grundy sighed. "I suppose someone must."

He asked me to step into his office. It wasn't much, standard issue government desk, a couple of mismatched filing cabinets, and unlike the building there was nothing *space age* about it, unless you considered the huge computer monitor taking up half of his desk *space age*.

I sat in the uncomfortable chair facing him and asked about the computer.

"Oh...well, we are trying to computerize all of our records, grades, transcripts, that sort of thing."

I didn't say anything, just nodded. I didn't care much about computers, just being polite. Starting out with a little small talk always seemed to take the edge off meetings such as this.

"It will never work," Grundy said. "The machine gave Reggie a full scholarship."

"Reggie?"

"A bulldog, our mascot," Grundy said, nodding with a cheery grin. Had to have been an inside joke, I was sure.

"I see...*hmmm*." I gave him my best knowing smile. "That's rich."

"Now, Mr. O'Brien, what information are you seeking regarding Professor Carmichael? Information that is not in the police report, I presume."

"What kind of a guy was he? I'll bet he could get a little rough, maybe when a student missed an assignment." I smiled wider.

Grundy waved his hands back and forth in front of his face. "Oh, pshaw," he said, but with his lisp it sounded like *thaw*.

"Pshaw? You mean he wasn't a hothead."

"Oh no, not at all. He was a gentle soul. But I know what you are up to." He squinted. "You're looking for mitigating circumstances. Something to justify Mr. Farris's dastardly deed."

First, *pshaw*, and now *dastardly deed*. This guy wasn't Weatherbee, but he talked as if he came from a comic book. Anyway, pshaw, I was striking out with my angry hothead theory. "Maybe you could hit a button on that thing..." I pointed at the computer monitor. "...and tell me about his workload. Anything would help."

Grundy glanced at me for a moment. He pursed his lips and started to say something, but then he leaned over and starting punching keys on the high-tech gizmo that looked like an IBM electric typewriter. After pounding away on it for a while, he looked up at the screen, waited a couple of minutes, and then started again. He typed some more and waited some more and typed again.

I sat there patiently. All of that typing, he could be writing a book. Who knows, maybe he was: *Dastardly Deeds*, a saucy sex thriller, the rhinestone monkey solved the case. Reggie was the culprit.

Finally, after an eternity of this he called out, "Mandy, bring me the Carmichael file."

Instantly Mandy was at the door. Her arms cradled a thick folder pressed against her chest. She toddled over and plopped it on Grundy's desk. He peered inside, then pulled out a huge sheet of paper, the kind from a computer, I presumed. He handed the lined sheet across to me. "Eyes only, I'm afraid, Mr. O'Brien, the report can't leave this building."

Mandy flashed me a quick smile as she left the office.

I scanned the printout quickly. Everything appeared routine, nothing there that would help. Carmichael had been a professor of geology, and had taught several classes, *Geology 104 - Physical Geology and Laboratory, five units*. The geology classes and a couple of lectures had taken most of his time, but he also taught a class that had nothing to do with his chosen field: *Television 022 - Television Production, four units*. It was a night class and it was after this class in the parking lot behind the college's small TV studio that Robbie had murdered him.

I couldn't fathom the connection between geology and television. I looked up from the paper and glanced at Grundy, who sat with his hands clasped, resting on the desk. He was actually twiddling his thumbs.

"The professor taught a TV course?" I asked. The direction of Grundy's rotating thumbs reversed.

"Yes, it started as a hobby. Lately, however, it took practically all his time."

"Teaching a TV course took all his time?"

"No." Grundy shook his head; the hands disappeared beneath the desk. "I meant the time he spent running the studio. He volunteered when no one else would, but as time went on his avocation became much more labyrinthine."

"What do you mean? Like, complicated?"

"Well, certainly more harried than it should have been. KVXR is a PBS station with programming produced here on campus, but for years the station has been losing money. About six months ago the trustees, in their wisdom..." He rolled his eyes. "...had voted to either sell the station or close it down."

"Who'd buy a station that was losing money? Anyway, what does this have to do with Carmichael?" I asked.

"Professor Carmichael, in due course, understood the trustees' position. He finally figured out the station would have to close, and he more or less resigned himself to that fact."

I glanced at my watch and started to fold the printout. "Yeah, I guess that happens," I said, more concerned about the rush hour traffic than Grundy's droning commentary on a small-time college TV station. There was nothing here that would help me with Robbie's defense.

"Until the ten-million dollar offer came in."

I looked up. "What?"

"They offered ten-million dollars."

"Ten million bucks for a losing money station? Who'd

make such a crazy offer?"

"Who, indeed? That's when Dick's.... Ah, Professor Carmichael's nascent hostility materialized. He went on a rampage."

"A rampage?"

"Well, figuratively a rampage. He emphatically fought the sale. Dick was determined that the station would not be sold to the network making the offer. He announced the station's license had been issued for the purpose of broadcasting media developed solely for the collective good of our community. The trustees tried to assuage his concerns, but Carmichael would hear nothing of it." Grundy held his silence for a moment. "Nothing could quell his ardor," he said, then added, "Ironic, isn't it?"

"What's ironic?"

"The station being sold and Dick saying it would only be sold over his dead body."

I dropped the printout. "Who made the offer?" I asked in a quiet voice.

"Why, it was from the Holy Sprit Network. You know, the network owned by J. Billy Bickerton."

Chapter Twenty-three

With traffic, it was late when I arrived back at the office. Mabel and Rita had already left for the day. But a note rested in the center of my desk. The note was from Rita.

I got a continuance for Danny, my other client, and now I'm working full time on your case. Jimmy, I think I've bought us another week. After all, the cops still haven't found the gun, which surprises me. You'd think they'd have searched the office by now. But, anyway, I talked to Webster...

The gun flashed in my mind. I felt a twinge of guilt for not leveling with Rita about Mabel hiding it prior to the cops' search. But, as we had decided at the time, it was better not to compromise Rita's position. I continued reading:

I'm excited. It's just as we discussed. Webster has agreed to drop the Section 32 thing if we could persuade Robbie to turn himself in. Now, that won't stop Hammer's murder investigation of course, but if we bring Robbie in there is no reason to connect you with the murder. The only possible motive goes out the window.

Yeah, Rita that sounds terrific, I mused, all I have to do is find Robbie. But I knew I would. Especially with Sol working on the FBI, getting them to raid the base.

I sat at my desk for a moment, tapping my fingers, and wondered how long it would be before they raided the Rattlesnake Lake compound. Sol had powerful friends and he would light a fire, but there was no telling when the FBI would move. For my sake, it had to go down fast. Rita bought me a week—not much time—and there was nothing I could do but wait.

Rita was now full time on my case, meaning she wouldn't be bringing in any revenue, and Mabel had said we were short on cash again. On top of my own legal problems, I needed clients. I knew if I didn't start looking for new blood right away, I'd be out of business. But how could I show a bright and smiling face, a lawyer with confidence and ability, at the service clubs around town–Kiwanis, Elks, Rotary, and the rest– with a murder rap hanging over my head? I couldn't even troll the court hallways. Everyone knew about the investigation and I'd be like one of Father Damien's outcasts. They'd think being accused of a crime was contagious, like leprosy.

My stomach gave a growl, rumbling about food, so I decided to head to Foxy's Coffee Shop on Paramount. I'd order the burger combo plate with fries. I figured it was about time I had a decent meal; all of those donuts weren't doing anything for my waistline.

I turned out the lights and left the office.

Foxy's was built to look like a ski chalet, an A-frame building with a high peaked ceiling, open exposed wood beams, and a red metal fireplace off in the corner. The architectural style would look great up at Lake Arrowhead, or maybe Big Bear. It would be a warm and inviting place to come in from the snow and sit by the fire with a hot toddy in your hand. But in Downey, on smoggy Paramount Boulevard, it looked like what it was: a burger joint.

I sat at the end of the counter. I liked a little elbow room while dining. Helen, the waitress, whose eyes followed me from the time I walked in the door, had a cup of coffee and a menu in front of me by the time I sat down.

"Good evening, Jimmy. Haven't seen you in a while."

"It hasn't been that long."

Helen, fiftyish, was a little stocky. Her cone-shaped hair, lacquered in place, climbed from the top of her head like a black frizzled beehive. She stood before me with one hand resting on her jutting hip.

"It's been a few months," she said. "Let's see, you were here with your girlfriend, that flight instructor. Susie, wasn't it? Yeah, that's it. You two were dressed up in cowboy outfits. Cute little thing." Helen had the memory of a Univac.

"She liked to square dance. We were going to the Clod Hoppers Promenade Ball, do-si-do, allemande left, and all of that," I said.

I thought back four months earlier. It was the last time I saw Susie. I'd picked her up at her work and took her to my apartment, where we changed into our cowboy costumes. Then we stopped at Foxy's for a bite before we went to the dance. After the ball, we popped into Rocco's for a few more laughs.

I smiled inside and remembered how everyone had howled when we sashayed in, doing a little sidestep, wearing our cowboy and cowgirl outfits. I was dressed up like Hopalong Cassidy and Susie was Annie Oakley. At one point she pulled the gun out of her holster and dazzled the crowd with her tricks. I remembered how pretty she looked when she stood with her legs spread and drew the pistol lightning fast, twirling it around her finger before plopping it back smoothly into its holster. She did it all in a single swift motion. Thank God the gun wasn't loaded; she could have shot someone. Susie was a talented girl: airplane pilot, fast gun artist, and a real spitfire in the lovemaking department. In spite of the square dance, I had a fun time. After we left Rocco's, we'd driven to her place, a condo in Long Beach, where I'd spent the night.

The next morning, Susie was packing her bags. She'd received an early phone call from Piedmont Airlines. They had an immediate right-seat opening and offered the co-pilot job to her if she could report to their eastern headquarters within twenty-four hours. To a young pilot, a call like that was winning the Irish Sweepstakes. A job offer from a real airline was the dream of every flight instructor.

I'd quickly dressed and driven her to the airport. I'd offered to forward her belongings. She thanked me and said the job might not be permanent, but if it turned into a long-term affair, then the airline would take care of the move. I'd kissed her goodbye at the gate. We talked on the phone a few times after that, but I haven't spoken with her since the last call a couple of months ago, when she told me about the new man in her life.

Helen interrupted my thoughts. "Are you ready to order, hon? By the way, are you still seeing the young lady?"

"No, we broke up. Anyway, bring me the burger combo with fries, thousand on the salad."

She scribbled on her pad and without looking up said, "Jimmy, if you took her someplace decent for dinner, instead of this joint, she might not have dumped you."

In a few moments my food arrived. I slipped a greasy limp fry in my mouth and took a bite of my hamburger. As I chewed, my mind drifted to the case. I set the hamburger down, pulled a pen out of my jacket pocket, and jotted a few notes on a paper napkin. I drew a diagram and connected the dots. Robbie was obviously connected to Professor Carmichael and his mother was connected to Elroy Snavley, the pastor of Divine Christ Ministry Church. Elroy Snavley was connected to J. Billy Bickerton, the owner of the Holy Sprit Network, which was buying the TV station at the college. And the professor was killed by Robbie while fighting against the sale. I sat hunched over the counter, my burger getting cold, and appraised my scribbles for a few minutes. A neat little circle, but what did it prove? Nothing.

I wadded up the napkin and tucked it in my hip pocket. The TV station being sold and the professor's prophetic statement would actually hurt my case defending Robbie. His fight to keep the station out of the hands of a religious network could be construed by the D.A. as an excellent motive for the murder. The D.A. would reason that Robbie–religious fanatic that he was–had the notion that the professor was an agnostic, or in Robbie's words, a heathen, and that was why he'd killed him. They would argue that the crime was premeditated, thought out in advance, with laying-in-wait as a kicker. Hardly the work of an insane person. Maybe the work of a religious nut, but not someone legally insane.

But if I didn't come up with something to clear my name fast, I'd be behind bars. Sol's FBI guys had to act fast. They had to raid the base and find him there. I had to show up with Robbie before the cops finally pinned the murder on me, and barring that, before Webster took his file back and charged me with aiding and abetting, the Section 32 thing, helping Robbie flee.

Just as I was about to tuck into my burger again, Helen approached. "You have a call, Jimmy. You can take it in Ted's office. He won't mind, I'm sure." She showed the way to the manager's office, a small cluttered cubical off the hallway leading to the restrooms.

The phone call was from Sol.

"Ah, Jimmy my boy. I knew you'd be there eating alone on a Friday evening. You should have a little *boobele* to take out to dinner."

"Sol, what's up?"

"Hey, I don't wanna butt in. But, you're not getting

younger–"

"Is that why you called? You're a *yenta* now?"

"S'okay, Jimmy my friend. I guess you don't know that *yenta* in Yiddish is–"

"Aw, Sol, for chrissakes, cut it out."

"I got information from my source at the FBI. Information about the old military base, Rattlesnake Lake…but I can talk to you later. I don't want to interrupt your dinner that you are having alone–"

"Sol, Dammit!"

"All right already," he said. "Here's the story. It seems the Feds already knew about the new owners of the base."

"When is the raid going down?" I was practically shouting. "You told them I wanted to be there when they find Robbie, didn't you?"

"There's not going to be any raid. Well, good night, Jimmy."

I sprang from Ted's desk. "Sol, hold on. Did you say *no raid*?"

"No raid. The FBI had already checked them out. The base isn't what we thought. It's not a teen center, and it's not a training camp for a bunch of right-wing whackos playing with guns."

"What do you mean?" I said. "We saw them, AK-47s, everything."

"It's a gun club."

"What!"

"Rattlesnake Lake Sportsmen's Rod and Gun Club, that's what they call themselves. Sounds legit. They have a license and they're members of the CTA," Sol said.

"What's the CTA?"

"I dunno. Something to do with target shooting. Some

kind of trapshooting association."

"*Trapshooting?* That's a crock. What are they doing, standing there in storm trooper outfits blasting away at clay pigeons with semi-auto machine rifles, for chrissake?"

"I said, *sounded* legit. But that don't make it so. Unfortunately, the Feds aren't going to budge. It is out of their hands, they said, unless, of course, we had evidence of wrongdoing—"

"Sol, I've got to get onto the base. Even if I don't find Robbie, that girl I met behind the Harvey House—Jane—works in the kitchen out there. She was going to tell me about him, until the cop showed up and scared her away."

There was a long pause on the line. "No, Jimmy." Sol's voice was serious now. "It's too dangerous for you to go in there. Remember they've got guns, and they didn't seem too friendly. If we can think of a good cover story, I'll send a couple of my men. They're pros—"

"No! It's got to be me. I'm the only one who has seen both Robbie and Jane. Even if I don't find Robbie, maybe I can get her out. She has information and I didn't like the way she said she was going to get a beating. Your men wouldn't recognize them. Plus, they would attract a lot of attention. We have to find a way to get me in there undercover…right away."

"What if he's not there? What if the FBI is right—"

"You know better than that. Help me, Sol. Help me save my neck."

"I don't like it, Jimmy. But, maybe you're right. It has to be you. If Robbie's not there, then we can start looking elsewhere. But first, we've gotta make sure those goons with guns aren't holding teens out there against their will. Give me time and I'll come up with something."

"There *is* no time. We've gotta come up with a plan, and

fast!"

Sol hesitated for a moment. I could almost hear the gears in his head clanking into place. "Now, listen to me, Jimmy. Any kind of scheme to get you in there has to be foolproof and safe. You'll have to have backup..." Sol became quiet again. I knew he was building a plan in his mind. A couple of seconds went by, then he said, "And the plan has to.... Wait a minute! I think I've got the perfect solution to the problem. I'm in the bar at Rocco's. Come on over."

I glanced at Ted's desk: bills and invoices. "You want to see me right now? You have a plan already?"

"Yeah, right now. Yeah, I've got an idea."

"Okay, I'm on my way."

"Get over here quick, before he takes off."

"Who?"

"Your ticket into the Rattlesnake Lake Sportsmen Bullshit Club. That's who."

Chapter Twenty-four

Charlie, the piano player, was pounding out a jazzed-up version of *Blue Moon* when I walked into Rocco's. The guy was awesome. He had been with the Marcels, a Doo-wop group of the fifties. Then in the early sixties, when Doo-wop had faded from the scene, he'd moved up the line, accompanying Frank Sinatra for a while. When André, Rocco's manager and maître d', bragged about signing the guy, I wondered. With those credentials, what was Charlie doing here at Rocco's in Downey of all places? What could he have done that was so terrible? Whatever it was, it must have really pissed Sinatra off.

Elbowing through the crowd, I spotted Sol sitting in the center of the barroom. He sat at a table sagging under heaping plates of hot and cold hors d' oeuvres. Seated with him was Peter Van Hoek, the owner of Sunnyville Farms Dairy, a large milk company located in South Gate, the town just north of Downey. Sol had a drink in one hand and a rib drenched with barbecue sauce in the other. Between bites, he vigorously lectured Van Hoek, but I couldn't make out what they talked about due to all the noise. Just the two of them sat at the table. I wondered where the mysterious stranger was, the guy who was going to get me onto the base. Sol caught my eye and waved me over, and when I moved closer, he jumped up. "Hey, Jimmy, you know my good friend, Peter, don't you?"

Sol had never mentioned that Van Hoek was his friend, much less a good friend. I pulled out a chair and sat, nodding at Van Hoek as I did. Van Hoek remained seated. I had seen him around in the past. He was a big guy. I mean big and bulky and thick and about as tall as Mount Whitney. All that fresh milk, I figured.

"Yeah, sure, I know Peter," I said and shook his hand. "How you doing?"

Van Hoek gawked at me, a befuddled look on his face. "How am I doing? I'll be damned if I know how I'm doing."

"You're doing fine," Sol said, enthusiastically patting Van Hoek on the back. "Everything is going to work out. Don't worry about it."

"Sol, I could lose their business. Hell, it's a good account," Van Hoek said. "And if they're as nasty as you say, I could lose more than that."

I got Sol's attention and mouthed, *What's up?* I didn't want to offend Van Hoek, but I didn't come here to discuss the tribulations of owning a dairy business. I came here to meet the guy who was going to get me onto the base. Maybe I didn't get to Rocco's soon enough; maybe the guy had been here and left.

With a quick shake of his head, Sol indicated that this meeting was more than just small talk. I knew how Sol operated and I knew he was up to something.

"Peter, my friend," he said, "they won't do anything to you. And as far as losing the account, hell, they're going out of business anyway. Ask Jimmy."

I wasn't exactly sure what they were talking about. "Yeah, Peter. Sol's right."

Peter slumped, a beaten man. Sol just had to add the coupe de grace. "Tell you what, Peter, not only will I give you the grand, I'll make sure you get the school contract when it comes up for bid. Now what do you say?"

"Royal Farms has a lock on the schools–" Peter stopped talking when Jeanine hurried over to take my order.

"Coke, Jimmy?" she asked.

"No, sweetheart, bring him a big glass of milk," Sol said. "Sunnyville Farms milk. You know, the milk that I forced André to carry."

Jeanine looked at me. "Coke," I said, but Sol's comment wasn't lost on Van Hoek.

"All right, goddammit, Sol. You got a deal. But I don't like it. If anything happens to my truck—"

"What?" Sol said, his arms out wide. "What could happen, the truck falls off a cliff, maybe? Lighten up, ol' buddy boy."

I was beginning to get the drift of the conversation. Sol was persuading Van Hoek to let us use his truck. That's how I'd get onto the base. Smooth.

Van Hoek looked at me as he stood. "Be at my plant Sunday night at ten o'clock." He spun on his heel and marched off.

Sol flashed a grin and popped an hors d'oeuvre, a cheese puff, into my mouth. Jeanine served my Coke. I took a sip and waited for Sol to explain his plan, but instead he twirled a finger in the air. Charlie, the piano player, caught the gesture and started hammering the keys, pounding out his rendition of Liszt's "Hungarian Rhapsody," the fast part, the part they played in all of those Bugs Bunny cartoons, the background music when Elmer Fudd chased the *wabbit* across the screen.

The barroom exploded with a rousing cheer. Immediately, the bartender lined up glasses and poured drinks as fast as the liquor would flow from the bottle. Jeanine and two other servers hustled to the bar, grabbed the drinks, and rushed to the customers' tables. Sol had a new thing going.

"I've got a theme song now, Jimmy," he shouted above the ruckus. "Classy music, huh?"

Nothing shocked me about Sol's little quirks anymore. It

wouldn't surprise me if he had a brass band waiting in the parking lot. And it was obvious, when Charlie played Sol's new theme song the next round was on him. Crazy guy. "Yeah, Sol, lot of class. But hey, what gives?"

Sol waved his hands in time with the music. "Jimmy, my boy, I caught the double today at Santa Anita. So what the hell, I buy a few drinks. It's only money."

"No, not about the drinks. Tell me about the deal with Van Hoek's truck?"

Sol dropped his hands and beamed. "Aw, *boobee*, your friend Sol is a genius. At times, I even amaze myself."

"Sounds like I'm driving the milk truck onto the base."

"That's right, my boy." Sol leaned into me. "He's got all those little drive-in stores scattered around, but he also sells milk and stuff wholesale, has accounts all over San Berdoo County, where the Mojave desert happens to be, where the Rattlesnake Lake Gun Club just happens to be. Get my drift?"

"The *gun club* is one of his customers."

"It's perfect," Sol said in a loud voice, just as the music abruptly stopped. Charlie, thinking that Sol was talking to him, got up and gave us a bow. Everyone in the place raised their glasses to our table. Sol jumped up. "Play it, Charlie!" A cheer erupted again, more earsplitting than before. Elmer Fudd was on another wild dash.

I knew better than to interrupt Sol when he was having fun. So I just sat back and laughed with the crowd. But when the laughing stopped and the music finally wound down, Sol continued talking about his plan.

"You'll pick up the truck at Sunnyville Farms Sunday night—"

"And I'm going to deliver the milk order to the base. Drive right through the gate."

"You got it! You'll be the new temporary driver, dressed as a Sunnyville Farms delivery man. Simple and elegant. You'll take the milk and eggs and stuff to the commissary. While you're unloading the truck, you make up an excuse–I dunno, maybe, something like you have to use the potty–then you get lost and wander around. What do you think?"

"Sol, you're a genius. It's perfect! If they're holding teens captive, then you can go back to the FBI–"

"Yeah, but it's dangerous, it's gotta look real. You gotta physically unload the milk yourself, and the gun club wants their stuff delivered at six a.m. Monday morning, sharp. You can't be late."

"Hey, I'll be there on time–"

"Listen, Jimmy, you'll have backup. My technical guy will hook up a radio direction finder on the delivery truck, and me and my boys will be in a car behind you. We'll pick you up when you get close to the base. We'll follow, but not close enough to be obvious." Sol searched my eyes. "Think you can handle it?"

"Hey, I used to be a cop. One of L.A.'s finest, remember? But, I got one question."

"Shoot."

"If they want their milk order delivered at six o'clock Monday morning, why do I have to be at the dairy at ten Sunday night? It's only a three-hour drive."

"It's part of the deal," Sol said. "You've gotta make all the dairy's delivery stops along the route, of course."

"Of course." I groaned.

Chapter Twenty-five

It was late when I left Rocco's Restaurant, and actually, in spite of everything, I had a good time. With Sol buying the drinks and the thirsty crowd lapping them up like desert rats at an oasis, what had started out as a simple meeting with Van Hoek had turned into a bacchanal bash. Jokes I hadn't heard in years were flying, music with a wild beat and loud shouting and louder singing reverberated. At two a.m., Joey the bartender came around the bar and had locked the doors, closing the place with all of us still inside. Sol hollered, "One more round."

"Hungarian Rhapsody," the cartoon music, filled the air and the merrymaking had continued.

Later, Jeanine, who'd also been sipping a few, jumped up on a table next to the piano, and as Charlie pounded out a halfway decent version of David Rose's *The Stripper*, she treated us to a tarty morsel of bump and grind. The party ended when Scooter, Jeanine's boy friend, who was there waiting for her to get off work, but encouraging the impromptu act along with the rest of us, popped Judge Frisco in the nose when he made a lewd remark concerning Jeanine's left boob, which had slipped out of her low-cut uniform during the provocative exhibition.

It was about three a.m. when I took the last sip of my Coke, said goodbye to Sol, and left the bar. Gravel crunched beneath my feet as I walked to my Corvette, parked in Rocco's gritty lot behind the restaurant. Nobody liked the dirty parking lot and tonight was no exception. It was dark, dusty and practically deserted. I spotted only two cars, mine and a sedan parked at the edge of the lot by the rear fence. Sol's limo awaited him in front at the curb, where most of the customers parked.

I slipped my key into the Corvette door lock, jumping a little when I heard the grinding sound of another motor starting up. My eyes swept the lot. An almost imperceptible movement of the dark sedan parked by the fence and the vapor billowing from the exhaust told me that I wasn't alone in the lot. Someone else was heading home, but it was strange; I hadn't seen anyone leave Rocco's when I left.

After cranking the Vette to life and driving out of the lot onto Florence, I looked in the rearview mirror and noticed that the dark car had waited until I'd turned onto the street before it pulled out. The sedan was now following me.

It was too dark to make out what the people in the car looked like, but two of them sat in the front seat. I could see their heads backlit from the headlights behind. They had to be Detective Hammer's men. It seemed like a waste of taxpayers' money, cops following me around. What was Hammer thinking? Did he think I'd stop somewhere and check my gun just to make sure it was still snug where I supposedly hid it?

The hell with the cops, I wasn't going to let them get under my skin and destroy my weekend. I turned on the radio and punched in KHJ. They had a new night guy I liked, Machine Gun Kelly. I chuckled, he was a straight shooter–*groan*–but he played a lot of Buddy Holly and Elvis stuff. I liked that, although I frowned when Machine Gun put on the next oldie, "Jail House Rock."

As soon as I parked my Vette in the carport at the rear of the apartment building and climbed out, I knew it was trouble.

The dark sedan had followed me to my spot and wedged in behind me.

Two goons jumped out. These guys weren't cops.

The first guy out was big—King Kong in a suit. And his temperament suggested that someone had just stolen his banana.

This was going to be trouble.

"You O'Brien?"

Before I could answer, he came at me and tried to take my head off with a solid right. I ducked, and he got a knee in the groin for his trouble. He doubled over. I felt something hard slam across my back. I let out a yell and spun around. The second guy had a baseball bat, a Louisville slugger, the gangster's choice. Autographed by Al Capone, no doubt.

He wasn't out to kill me. He could have done that with one blow to the head, but he wanted me to hurt, really hurt. He wanted me to remember this night.

He swung again, aiming for my midsection, and connected. I went down, gasping for air. I rolled, skittered to my feet, the adrenalin pumping, and charged the guy before he could wind up again. I smashed my fist into his nose and watched it shatter, blood gushing. He dropped the bat and covered his face with his hands. I stood and watched him for a second…a second too long.

The first guy, now recovered, pounded the back of my head with something hard. Lightning exploded in my brain, a whiteness that blotted out the night. I staggered, but didn't go down. In slow motion, his fist came at me like a fright train, looming larger as it approached my face. Instantly, real time came back. The blow connected, knocking me off my feet.

I looked up to see the guy with the broken nose standing over me. He started to plant his boot into my solar plexus, hard.

I tried to turn away, and as I twisted, I vaguely felt the other guy kicking my side. Through a foggy gaze I saw one of them pick up the bat. Then it stopped. The world turned out the lights and closed up for the night.

Sunlight flooded my eyes, but all I saw was a yellow sheet of paper. I was lying on my back, still in the carport behind my apartment. And the yellow piece of paper was covering my face. I tried to move my arm. I couldn't; the pain. I went out again, but came back. Saturday morning, but what time was it? It must be early; no one was around, messing with their cars. Even Quinn, who went to early mass every day, hadn't left yet. Muscles and bones hurt, everything hurt, even my hair hurt. I felt like roadkill. With great effort, I reached up and grabbed the paper off of my face. The sun almost blinded me.

I turned onto my side, tucked the paper in my pants pocket, and tried again to move. I was able to crawl. The door to my Vette was open and it was right above me now. I pulled myself up and managed to climb into the bucket seat. I glanced down at my shirt. It was covered in blood. I rubbed my hands over my face and examined them. I wasn't bleeding. The blood must have been from the guy I hit. I sat there for a moment not knowing exactly what to do. The thought of negotiating the stairs to my apartment on the second floor was too much to bear. Fishing around in my pocket, I found the car keys. My hand shook, but I managed to start the Corvette. Pain ran up my spine like a jolt of electricity, a thousand-volt charge, when I turned and glanced over my shoulder as I backed out of the carport.

I'm not sure how I did it, but I survived the short drive to Downey Memorial, all the while trying to figure out why they jumped me. My wallet was still tucked in my back pocket, empty as it was, and nothing in my car was disturbed. No, it wasn't a mugging. Those guys were pros, professional leg-breakers. And I was their target—one guy called me by my name. I wondered if it had to do with Robbie Farris. Maybe I was getting close to something hot, maybe I just got burned.

I bumped the curb in front of the hospital's main entrance trying to park, and slumped forward in the seat. I must have passed out again, but I woke with the sound of my car horn blaring. I untangled my arm from the steering wheel and the horn stopped.

I leaned back. The next thing I knew, some guy in white was tapping on the driver's side window.

"Hey, buddy, the party's over. Sober up and go home. This is a hospital district; you're making a lot of noise."

I slowly turned my head his way and started to roll down the window. He gasped when he saw my face. A shudder ran through me when I realized that his look of horror was because of my appearance. I must've looked like a freak.

"Oh, my God. Are you all right? Jesus." He opened the door. "Wait here, I'll get help."

"No, it's okay. I just need a doc to check me out. I think I can walk." I started to climb out of the car. Suddenly, a wave of dizziness swept over me, my legs gave out, and I fell back into the seat. "Go get someone," I said to the guy in white.

Chapter Twenty-six

The bright lights, the cold antiseptic air, and the noise–lots of noise–were not calming me down at all. I thought hospitals were supposed to be quiet. Guess they make exceptions in the emergency room. The doctor who leaned over me, raising my eyelid and peering into my pupil with his little light thing, had to be about ninety. I doubted if he actually went to medical school, probably learned medicine reading by the light of a fireplace. He kept asking questions, always wiping his mouth first with a small cloth he held, then he'd hesitate and say something like, "Aw...aw...Mr. O'Brien, do you know what day of the week this is?"

At the same time a middle-aged woman wearing white, clipboard in hand, stood next to me while I lay on the gurney. She asked questions as well: "Can I have your name, please?"

I felt like saying, *no*, it's mine, but I meekly answered, "O'Brien."

At that point the doctor, said, "Aw...aw.... Not your name, the day of the week."

"Saturday."

"What kind of name is that?" The woman in white asked.

"No, it's not Saturday–"

It went like that for a while, the doctor asking me stuff and the woman in white getting frustrated when I turned to answer him. But the question that tore it apart was when the woman in white asked: "What's the name of your insurance provider?"

Insurance, I thought. "I don't have any." As soon as the words were out of my mouth, the room got quiet. It was like a freeze-frame in the movies, like time itself had stopped. The air conditioner stopped humming and even the guy in the next gurney quit screaming. In fact, he raised his bleeding head and gawked at me in a silent, slack-jawed stare. It was as if I were a hardened criminal and had just committed a vicious crime– *Jimmy O'Brien, the mad dog, went into a hospital, just strolled in and asked for treatment, my God, without insurance.*

"Well, Mr. O'Brien, it appears you might have a concussion, and a bad cut on the top of your forehead, but I don't see any reason to keep you here," the old doctor said. "Go home and take–"

"I know, two aspirins, and call in the morning," I said, finishing his sentence.

"No, you don't have to call. Good day, Mr. O'Brien." The old-timer turned his attention to the guy on the gurney.

As much as they wanted me out of there, they wouldn't let me leave without someone driving me home. Liability, no doubt. So, after thinking it over for a moment, I called Rita.

I wasn't keen to tell her about the dustup with the goons, but I knew it'd come out sooner or later. One look at me and she'd know that I'd been in a fight.

She picked me up, and after several *oh my Gods and egads,* drove me to my apartment. On the way there, I told her a white lie. Although I was now sure the beating had something to do with the Farris case, I lied when I explained that it was a simple mugging. I knew she'd worry, so why frighten her?

Rita helped me hobble to the living room couch. Then she darted out, heading to Foxy's. She said she'd be back with chicken soup. To Rita, every malady was curable with chicken soup, even a black eye and a throbbing headache. Who was I to argue? Besides, I was hungry and Foxy's made good soup.

She returned and was in the kitchenette putting the soup in a bowl when it hit me. I was watching a rerun of *Dragnet*, not really following the plot line, but when one of the bad guys was being fingerprinted the light bulb above my head lit up. I struggled off the couch just as Rita walked in the living room carrying a bowl of soup, the steam wafting.

She stopped. "Jimmy, what are you doing? You should stay down."

"I've gotta get to the phone."

"Why?"

"Gotta make a call."

"To who?"

When I didn't say anything, she went back into the kitchenette with the soup and returned carrying the phone, the long black cord snaking behind her.

I pointed to my dinette sitting in the alcove next to the kitchenette. "Set it on the table."

She put the phone down, went to the kitchenette, and returned with the soup. I sat down and Rita placed the bowl next to me. When she left to tidy up, I pulled a pen from my pocket. Then I dialed information, and while waiting for the operator to come on the line, I reached into my pocket again and found a piece of paper.

"Oh, my God," I mumbled when I glanced at the yellow-lined paper in my hand, the paper that had covered my face when I came to after the fight. The note was written in red crayon, a threat, just more crap. Not worth thinking about.

"Number please."

I turned the paper over and wrote the phone number I'd asked for on the back of it. Rita returned and stood next to me as I dialed the number.

The *Barstow Sun's* phone rang. I knew someone would be there, even on Saturday. Small business owners didn't work forty-hour weeks. On the fifth ring, Tom picked up. After identifying myself, I asked if I could have a word with his wife.

He remembered me, of course, and at first was reluctant to bring Cathy to the telephone. He indicated she was still upset over our visit.

I explained how important it was for me to speak with her. After all, didn't they want to be sure about Jane? Didn't they want to know if she was truly dead and buried, or conversely, wouldn't they want to know that some goons weren't holding her captive in a supposed teen drug center? I also promised that if I were on the wrong track, I wouldn't brother them anymore. But, I told him, there was one thing I had to clarify, something Cathy had said about identifying the body.

Tom sighed and finally relented. A moment later Cathy was on the line.

"I'm sorry to keep dredging up memories, but I have a question. Was Jane ever in trouble, arrested, anything like that?"

"No, of course not. She was a good girl, and besides, she was only a child. What is this all about?" Her tone still held a touch of hostility.

"You said that when you identified the body, the chief told you that he had confirmed Jane's fingerprints with the FBI."

"Yes, he said that."

"But why would that matter? Why would he mention fingerprints if you saw her body and were sure it was Jane?"

Cathy hesitated a moment. She had to know what I was getting at. "I didn't see her face.... Burt Krause, he's the chief of police. He's been the chief forever, even back then.... He said the shotgun blew her face away. Oh, God...Burt didn't want me to see her in that state."

"So you didn't actually *see* her–"

"Oh, I saw her all right. But a sheet covered her body and her face. And then Burt told me about her fingerprints–" Her voice broke off.

"Cathy, this is important." I paused for a moment to let the woman gather her wits. "If she had never been arrested, the FBI wouldn't have her fingerprints on file. Burt was lying."

"I don't believe it."

"Listen to me," I said. "The girl I saw behind the Harvey House was real. She told me her name was Jane. Cathy, the teenager I met looked just like the girl's mother in the photo. The police lied to you about her prints.... You didn't actually see Jane's face. You didn't actually identify the body, did you?"

There was a long silence on the other end of the line. I could hear her breathing. I let her mull over what I'd said and didn't interrupt her thoughts. Finally, in a quiet voice she asked, "But whose body was on the table?"

"I dunno and we may never find out. I have a hunch what's going on, and it's ugly. But I know now Jane is alive—"

I didn't finish the sentence. Cathy let out a whimper and I heard the phone receiver thump as it hit a hard surface.

Tom spoke up. He had been listening on the extension. "Oh, my God, Mr. O'Brien." An agonized sound crept into his voice. "What can we do to help get to the bottom of this?"

"Tom, listen to me. Your safety is at stake. It is extremely important that you two keep quiet about this. Sol and I are working feverishly to get a handle on the situation. But these monsters will stop at nothing. They have already murdered several people. I'll keep you informed, but please—"

"Say, no more. I understand."

I hung up the phone. Rita stared at me, her eyes wide. "Oh, Jimmy, I'm frightened."

"It's scary, that's for sure." I looked down at the yellow piece of paper on the table.

"What are we going to do?" Rita pushed the yellow paper aside and picked up the telephone receiver. "Jimmy, we have to call the FBI, right now!"

"Put the phone down. Sol already did that. They won't listen. They said they've checked on those people and they said the base is legitimate, some kind of a gun club."

"But with new evidence, won't they take another look?"

I leaned forward, took a sip of chicken soup, and tried to figure out where I was going with this. Other than sore ribs, a headache, and the nagging tick in my brain, I was feeling better. The soup went down smoothly, stayed down, and tasted good. After considering the facts at hand, I knew it would be hopeless to go to the authorities with what we suspected.

"What evidence, Rita?" I ate some more and put the spoon down. "You're a lawyer." I leaned back in the chair. "You know how facts can be twisted. What do we really have? Think about it. Some guy–a murder suspect–claims he saw a dead girl. A woman who identified her body eight years ago now changes her mind. And to top it off, the chief of police is a crook working with a thug who owns a bunch of mines in the desert. C'mon, Rita. The cops hear that they'll think *I'm* the one going for an insanity defense."

"What about Robbie and the teen drug center?" She glanced at the yellow paper next to the phone. "They'd know you didn't make that up."

"What drug center? It's a gun club. And what does Robbie have to do with something that happened years ago in Barstow? Hazel Farris is my only link between the drug center and Robbie…and she's dead."

"Jimmy, we can't just sit here." Rita turned the paper over. "We have to do something."

I shrugged. "Sol and I will get to the bottom of this and when we have tangible evidence we'll bring in the authorities."

"What's this?"

"What?"

"This note." She picked up the paper. "It's hand printed and the guy used a crayon. Here's what it says, '*First warning. Quit snooping around. Next time you're dead.*'"

"Lemme see."

She handed me the paper. Just as Rita had said, the writer used a red crayon when he printed the note in block letters. A popular mystery novelist, in one of her books, postulated that an expert couldn't authenticate the handwriting if the ransom or threatening notes were written with a crayon. I didn't know if that were true, and until now I had never heard of such a note written in crayon. Maybe Ben Moran read mystery novels. Maybe his thugs read coloring books.

Rita put her hand to her mouth. "Oh, my God!"

"It's a prank. The paper was on my face when I woke up after the fight," I said.

Her back stiffened. "You lied to me."

"What? Why would you say that?"

"It wasn't a mugging. You knew all along who attacked you, didn't you? You knew it had to do with the case, with Robbie Farris. You got beat up and you didn't tell me why."

"Let's not jump to conclusions."

Rita stood there glaring at me, doing a slow burn.

"Rita, even if it was them, do you think I'd just quit and walk away–"

"You lied to me."

She silenced me with a stare chiseled in granite. There was nothing more I could say. Rita was right. I'd lied to her and she knew it. After what seemed like a long time, she turned and started for the door. Halfway across the room she stopped and said, "Gimme your car keys. I'll get someone to help me bring it back. I'll leave it in the carport. Your keys will be under the seat"

I tossed her the keys. "Listen, Rita–"

Her eyes cut deep. "Don't ever, *ever* lie to me again," she said and walked out the door.

I sat at the table and stared at the cold soup. What she said had hurt. It felt like my blood had turned to dust, like somewhere along the line it became easier to lie than face the truth. I knew I'd have to face up to it and come clean with Rita about the gun Mabel had stashed, and I'd have to let her know about me sneaking onto the base; after all, she is my lawyer now. I'd sat there and listened to her little lawyer speech about being totally open and had agreed with her terms. Anyway, I just didn't want to lie anymore. But right now my mind had only room for one thought: find Robbie and bring him back.

After she left, I made two phone calls. The first one was to Sol. I wanted to let him know of my suspicion that the chief of police was in cahoots with the gang at the base. He wasn't in, so I left a message with Silvia, his wife. I told her I had new information, but it would keep until I met him at the dairy tomorrow night.

I made my next call to Mabel at her home and told her briefly about the fight. Then I told her I wouldn't be in Monday, but would clue her in on what I was up to when I returned to the office on Tuesday.

What she told me put a chill up my spine. "Jimmy, the police are talking to all our neighbors, even friends of mine. And guess what? The phone isn't ringing. People are not going to hire a lawyer who the cops think is a murderer." Mabel sighed. "In their predicaments, I can't say that I blame 'em. The people who call us are crooks, for chrissakes. They don't want to have anything to do with the police snooping around."

"Yeah, they wouldn't like that."

"I was going to tell you about this yesterday, but I didn't want to spoil your weekend. What the hell, seeing as how your weekend is ruined anyway, I suppose it's okay to mention it."

Burning acid churned in my stomach and welled up in my throat. "Hey, we get most of our business from the county, and Rita's got a few clients, doesn't she?"

"Just one, and if he doesn't sell any aluminum siding soon he won't be able to pay his bill. Anyway, she got a continuance for the guy and isn't taking on anyone new. She said that she needs to work on your case full time. I'm sorry about your problems, Jimmy, but now Rita won't be bringing in any cash either."

"Mabel, don't worry about it. Things will get better soon." I tried to keep the anxiety out of my voice. "Forget about the cops. They'll go away soon. They're just harassing me. Cops and defense lawyers are natural foes, like a fox and a rabbit. I'm the fox." I tossed out a chuckle. Mabel didn't catch it.

"I don't think so, Mr. Fox. The cops told the travel agent next door that you're gonna be arrested any time now."

"Bye, Mabel." I hung up the phone.

Chapter Twenty-seven

The smog blanketing the L.A. basin couldn't be seen in the dark of night, but it was evident in the tinge of the burnt-orange gibbous moon drifting above the horizon in the east. At a little before ten o'clock Sunday night the streets were deserted as I drove along Atlantic Avenue in South Gate, heading to Van Hoek's milk bottling plant. From three blocks away, the tall Sunnyville Farms stainless steel milk tank gleamed in the sky. The huge, shiny tank was lit from the ground by beacons spotlighting a twenty-foot rendering–painted high on the side– of a fat cow grazing in front of a red barn, the dairy company's logo.

Though early, everyone was there waiting for me. Sol and his men Cubby and the Deacon, and Peter Van Hoek were gathered in a circle on the loading dock at the rear of the plant. A couple of guys in white uniforms rolled two-wheeled dollies stacked with cartons of milk toward a refrigerated truck backed in against the dock. I scrambled up a ramp, waved at Sol, and shouted lightheartedly, "Hey, where're the cows?"

Van Hoek heard my question. "In Chino," he said. "Used to keep them across the street." He pointed in the general direction of Atlantic Avenue. "Had two thousand head over there, but the city finally forced us out. Moved 'em to a new farm in Chino."

"Yeah, and made a few million on the real estate when you sold the land," Sol said.

"That was my dad. But he didn't leave me none of it, blew it all on gambling, booze and broads. The old snollygoster." A big grin spread across his face. "What a guy," Van Hoek said, the admiration evident in the tone of his gravelly voice.

Sol, with a nod of his head, indicated for me to follow him. We walked along the dock, a few paces away from the others.

"Okay, Jimmy, what gives?"

I knew what he was referring to. The jagged scar on my forehead wasn't exactly a poster for *Healthy Living* magazine. "Got in a little tumble, that's all."

I didn't want to mention the yellow paper with the warning on it. Knowing Sol, he'd call off the plan. He'd be concerned about my safety.

"Look, Jimmy, don't feed me a line, I've been around. Somebody worked you over. It has to do with this case. A professional bone crusher, a strong-arm guy jumped you. Didn't he?"

"No."

Sol held his silence, waiting.

"There were two guys."

He continued to wait, his eyes boring into me.

"Yeah, I guess they were trying to scare me off," I said.

"Look, Jimmy, maybe we'd better call this off. I know it was my idea, but it's a longshot, and it probably won't work, anyway–"

"Hang on, Sol."

He stood there with an eyebrow raised.

I glanced around, looking up and down the dock. "Sol, listen to me." I wanted him to understand exactly how I felt. "There's a lot going on here. It's not just Webster's threats, charging me with the Section 32 thing, or Hammer's murder investigation that worries me the most. If that's all there were to this, I'd quit now and fight them in court and I'd win.

But there's more to it than that. There are madmen out there killing people, and the bastards are locking up kids in a bogus drug center. Don't forget, Robbie's still my client. He could be at the base. He could be in danger, and anyway, he still needs a lawyer. And what about Jane..." I paused, letting my words sink in. "I can't get her out of mind. A dead girl shows up alive and now, because she talked to me, she's going to get a beating. Christ, she could be killed. Murdered, just because she talked to me! We can't let that go. Can we Sol?"

"Jimmy, I'm more concerned about *your* safety. What kind of lawyer are you going to be for Robbie if you're dead?"

"Better than most."

Sol laughed. "You crazy idiot. Okay, you win. You'd probably go anyway, but you're going to carry protection." He reached under his suit coat and brought out a 45 automatic. "You're gonna take this with you."

I didn't argue. "Put it in the truck. I'll keep it with me, just in case."

He nodded. "Yeah, just in case. By the way, the gun has no serial numbers anymore. It's not traceable." He walked back to his men.

After putting on a milkman's cap, which would cover the scar on my forehead, I changed into a white uniform that I grabbed from an employee's locker–'Chip' was the name embroidered above the left breast pocket–then I got a knockdown on the peculiarities of the route from the regular driver, Roger. I asked him if he saw teenagers being mistreated at the base. He said he saw youngsters working in the commissary, but he didn't know if anyone mistreated them. He figured they just worked there, like kids work at McDonalds. He had never been beyond the commissary, though. The commissary building was close to the main gate and the security was tight: men in uniforms with guns. They would only let him out of the truck to unload his order. Roger wished me luck; he was happy to have the day off.

I'd be Chip for the day and I'd be working Roger's route. I'd have to make ten stops before the last one, Rattlesnake Lake Sportsmen's Rod and Gun Club. The milk order seemed fairly large for a gun club. More than most of the other restaurant stops that I was supposed to make. They had to be feeding a lot of people out there at Rattlesnake Lake, and I hoped Robbie was one of them.

I walked back to the dock and met up with Sol and his men. Van Hoek had left, allowing us the privacy we needed to plan our strategy. The Deacon, Cubby, and I huddled at the cab of the large bobtail truck and, of course, Sol took charge.

"Chip," he said, noticing my nametag. "I don't want you to worry about a thing. Just go along on the route like you do every day–"

"Sol, I'm a lawyer, not a truck driver."

"See, goddamn it, that's what I mean. You've gotta get into the role. Forget about being a goddamn lawyer. You've gotta make sure those hooligans out there think you're the goddamn milkman, or you're gonna be a goddamn goner."

"Thought I wasn't supposed to worry."

Sol let out an exaggerated sigh. "Shut up, Jimmy. Now where was I? Oh yeah…. Cubby, show Jimmy the gizmo."

Cubby held up a rectangular gadget. It was black, about the size and shape of a pack of cigarettes, and appeared to be made of metal.

"It's a beauty, military issue, the latest technology," he said.

"Tell, him how it works."

"It's magnetized and sticks to steel–"

"He knows a magnet sticks to steel, for chrissake," Sol said. "Tell him what it is."

"It's a radio tracking transmitter. We'll hide it on the truck and we'll be able to follow you in the limo."

Cubby pointed to Sol's tricked-out black limousine parked close by. After Sol had seen his first James Bond movie and saw how Q had rigged Bond's cars, he'd outfitted his fleet of company limos with the latest available spy doohickeys. He also installed a couple of doohickeys that weren't so available. He had sources.

"The device transmits on an FM frequency," Cubby continued. "And the signal can be picked up within a half-mile of the subject vehicle. We have a direction finder in the limo."

"Yeah, it's an XB-7, special issue, terrific." Sol beamed. "Anyone with an FM radio can get the signal, but unless you have the corresponding direction finder, you're out of luck. We'll be right behind you the whole time, but we'll be out of sight. Tell him about the panic button, Cubby."

"Okay. The gizmo broadcasts on 106.7 FM and normally sends out a beep like this." He licked his lips. "Beep...beep...beep." He articulated the beeping sound in a slow steady manner. "But if you flip the switch we've hooked to the dash on the truck..." He pointed out a small toggle switch screwed under the dashboard in the cab of the milk truck. "...the receiver in the limo will hear a signal like this, beep-beep, beep-beep." He sounded like the Roadrunner. "So, if you need help, flip the panic switch and we'll close the gap."

"Yeah, you flip that switch, buddy boy, and we'll be there, guns blazing," the Deacon said, a big grin spreading across his face.

Sol shot a glance at the Deacon, whose eyes fell. He then looked at me. "Well, what do you think, Jimmy, I mean about the tracking thing?"

"Provocative."

I climbed in the cab of the bobtail. A clipboard with the route customers and instructions lay on the seat. The .45 rested on top of it. I quickly shoved the gun under the seat.

Sol climbed on the running board and leaned in through the open door. "Don't forget, Jimmy, in and out. If you spot Robbie, snatch him. It's legal–he's an escaped fugitive–but Jane's another story. If she doesn't want to go, leave her there."

We had assumed Jane Simon would be working in the kitchen where I was to unload the milk order. I might spot her even without snooping around the base. Nonetheless, if I grabbed her, and she didn't want to leave with me, then I could be nailed with an additional kidnapping charge on top of the Section 32 thing and the murder rap.

I sat there looking out the front windshield, my hands tightly gripping the steering wheel. "I won't be stupid. I'm no hero, Sol."

He didn't say anything, just studied me for a moment. He didn't have to say a word; I knew what he was thinking. Friends know things like that about each other.

Finally, he hopped down from the running board and turned back to Cubby and the Deacon. "We all know you're not a hero, don't we, boys?"

The men nodded in unison. Sol turned back to me, smiling. "But I'm a little worried about the stupid part." He laughed. Then he suddenly grew serious. "Be careful, my boy, and remember, we'll be right behind you, unseen, but we'll be there."

Four hours later I was over the hill, down the mountain, and cruising east on the new I-15 freeway heading deeper into the Antelope Valley. My ribs hurt, my head throbbed and, after unloading dozens of cases of milk at several convenience stores and restaurants in San Bernardino, I felt like a punch-drunk fighter making his last stand.

The next stop on my way to Rattlesnake Lake, according to the sheet on the clipboard, was a roadside café/gas station called Twin Oaks. It stood on a lonely stretch of Stoddard Wells Road five miles outside of Victorville. The instructions said the place would be closed for the night, but I was supposed to pull around to the back of the café where the cleanup man would let me in to unload the order.

I slowed when I saw the old rusty Twin Oaks sign swinging in the breeze out front of the gas pumps. Slowing some more, I turned the big steering wheel and pulled the truck around to the back of the café, an archaic building made of natural stones, which I assumed were gathered from the desolate landscape around here.

As the truck's headlights swung through their arch, a tall lanky guy wearing a white T-shirt and apron cinched over his Levi's bolted from the back door of the café. He stumbled into the gravel lot waving his arms frantically. I slammed on the brakes, just missed the guy, and after jerking out the emergency brake handle I jumped out of the cab.

"Did you see them? Are we under attack?" he shouted, hopping around.

I took a quick look about the area and saw nothing but the dark, quiet desert and a few overgrown weed stalks casting a dim shadow on the side of the building next to four overflowing trashcans. "Who's attacking?" I asked.

"Rooskies! Martians! Hell, I don't know. The radio is sending out a warning signal," he hollered, running away.

"The radio? What are they saying?" I shouted to his back.

"Nothing, I was listening to KROQ, you know, Humble Harve, the rock 'n roll guy, and suddenly, the radio starts beeping." The cleanup guy was now hiding behind the truck, peering out from behind the refrigerator van. "You know, the worldwide warning system. They didn't say it was a test or nothin' just, beep…beep…beep."

Oh, Christ, Sol's gizmo was broadcasting a worldwide alert–or at least a half-mile alert–as I drove along. "What's the station frequency?" I shouted to the guy.

"L.A rocks with K-rock, one-oh-six-point-seven on your dial." The guy shouted the station's jingle in a singsong voice.

"C'mon, fella, I think the radio is just broken or something. Why don't we go inside and try another station?"

The poor guy. It was obvious: his bag of marbles had a hole in it.

Chapter Twenty-eight

Back on the road there was nothing as I drove through the night, my eyes focused ahead at the endless ribbon of black. Nothing except a pair of headlights following in the distance; Sol's limo, I assumed. I thought about pulling over to the side of the road where I'd wait for Sol to come up behind me. I wanted to tell him that everyone was hearing the beeps coming from the truck. I glanced around some more. There was no one on the highway–except Sol–and just a few shacks were off in the distance, so unless jackrabbits had transistor radios there was hardly a soul out there for miles who could hear my worldwide alert. Even when I got to Barstow, I'd be through the town so fast no one would notice a couple of beeps coming from their radios.

Sol was a little wild, but he was my friend, a simple declarative sentence that said it all. I smiled, thinking of the stuff he comes up with: a tracking beeper on the truck, James Bond spy limos, and now he and a couple of his tough guys are following me in the desert? What next? Pearl handled revolvers and maybe a tank division or two to help out when needed? I loved the guy.

I glanced at the headlights behind me in the distance and remembered back to the beginning of our friendship. It started when I was a member of the Los Angeles Police Force. Christ, it's been well over ten years. What happen to the time? It was 1962, Kennedy was president, Marilyn was still alive, but by then Rock 'n Roll had faded out with a whimper. Chuck Berry and Fats Domino were nowhere to be seen or heard. Buddy

Holly had been killed in a plane crash a few years earlier, Elvis was making one-note movies, and the British invasion had yet to happen. That year's mega-star was Frankie Avalon, for chrissakes.

In 1962 I was a rookie cop, still in my probationary period, a Police Officer status 1, cruising in a one-man black-and-white working the first watch, nights, starting at eleven p.m. My turf was out of the Newton Street Division.

Although Newton had been known as one of the toughest divisions in Los Angeles, most nights it was calm, boring actually. On other nights–nights when I earned my keep–it could be a war zone, but on that particular night there wasn't much going on, just a few radio calls coming in. I was drinking a lot of coffee trying to stay awake.

At about two A.M. I was parked at the curb on Central Avenue, sipping hot coffee with one hand and writing up crime reports with the other when, suddenly, this big Cadillac came barreling around the corner at Vernon Avenue. It skidded thorough the intersection and ended up on Central going north at a thousand miles per hour.

I lit up the flashers and started the motor. I was getting set to give chase when the Caddie's taillights vanished around the corner at the next intersection. I stomped it.

My unit's wheels burned rubber. I was halfway out onto the street when, suddenly, another Cadillac, bigger than the first, shot out from around the same corner behind me. It roared onto Central in hot pursuit of the first guy.

"What the hell," I said out loud and cranked the wheel. When I glanced back, I saw that the second guy was zooming right at me, on a collision course. He was going to broadside me.

I hit the brakes–hard.

At the last second, he swerved. The Cadillac fishtailed as it flew past me, just missing by a millimeter. It spun around, rolled to one side, up on two wheels, and slammed down, totally out of control. The big boat did a brodie, sideways, and smashed into a solid-steel light pole. It instantly burst into flames.

My car was five feet away, skidding wildly, heading directly for the ball of fire. I stood on the brake pedal and stopped inches from the smashup. I could see a man inside the burning wreck scraping at the window in a vain effort to get free.

Instinctively, I tore the riot gun from its bracket and bolted out of the patrol car. With the butt of the gun I smashed the Caddie's window, reached into the flames and yanked the guy free.

I didn't know my strength, but I dragged him away just as the automobile exploded.

The percussion knocked us both to the ground. I stayed there a moment, panting. Then I crawled over to the guy, who was lying on his back, motionless, two feet away. I did a quick inventory of his body parts. He seemed to be all there, and he seemed to be coming around.

He sat up and shook his big head. With his wiry hair still smoldering, he focused on me.

The guy blinked a couple of times and said, "Hey there, buddy. How ya doing? Sol's my name." He held out his right hand. "What's yours?"

There was something about the guy–it wasn't the way he looked, bitty little legs, a huge barrel chest, and a round smiling face–that made me laugh. No, that wasn't it at all. It was his attitude, *How ya doing, buddy*. The guy was just in a horrible smashup, his car on fire, a total loss, and he had almost been killed. His hair was still smoking, for chrissakes, and he asks me how I'm doing!

I started to laugh, and so did he. In fact, we laughed all the way to Downey as I drove him home. Being a cop, I was supposed to have taken him in and booked him on a dozen violations of the California Vehicle Code, but I didn't do that. I did what he asked me to do, just drove him home.

The next day, after drawing a thirty-day suspension, I went to my place to sulk, and when I got there I found a brand new color TV resting on my front step. There was no note. But it had a big red ribbon around it with a tag that said, "For Officer O'Brien."

I knew I could keep it, and I knew it was a gift from Sol. I had his address, so it was a simple matter of getting his phone number. I called. He wouldn't admit that he sent the TV, but he invited me to lunch. I don't know why, but I accepted.

We hit it off big time. There was something genuine about him. For one thing, he cared about people, had sincere compassion for those of us who were less fortunate, but he still had a sense of justice and wanted to take down the bad guys. Couple that with a razor-sharp wit, mind-boggling intelligence, and an *I don't give a damn* attitude, and you have an idea who and what Sol Silverman was.

That day at lunch I knew I'd found a friend, a friend forever. Of course, he bragged to everyone in sight how I had saved his life, pulled him to safety just seconds before his car blew up. He went on and on about my bravery. I didn't mention that I wasn't aware the car was about to explode. Hell, I wouldn't have gotten near the thing if I'd thought it was about to blow up. At least, I didn't think I would have. It's funny, I never did find out why he was chasing that other Cadillac around South Central L.A. that night.

But all of that was over ten years ago. In the intervening decade, I watched Sol's investigation business grow. It went from a one-man operation to being one of the largest security firms in the state with dozens of operatives and a support staff that the federal government would've loved to have if they had the money.

And during that same ten-year period I had lost my job with the police force, became a drunk, and when Barbara sued for divorce, I almost gave up. But with Sol's help–he browbeat me until I'd do anything just to get him off my back–I took the AA cure, went to night law school, and when I passed the bar exams I hung out a sign: Jimmy O'Brien, Lawyer.

Now when Sol and I are out somewhere having fun and there is a lot of drinking going on, someone invariably asks why I'm not imbibing. And when that happens, Sol always says, "Jimmy quit. He wasn't a drunk or anything. It's just that when he went out for a cool one, he'd be gone for days at a time. He'd pass out, and maybe wake up in Mexico...at a dogfight." Sol would laugh, then continue, "...in the ring on all fours, snarling at a pit bull."

"I rarely won," I always added.

Seven hours after pulling away from the dairy company's loading dock I blew through Barstow. I didn't stop at the Bright Spot. When I turned off the highway onto the dirt road leading to the base, morning sunlight was creeping over the mountain ridge in the east, casting the wide sky in an endless expanse of burnished turquoise streaked with wispy, pink clouds. The promise of dawn, a new day.

I thought of a painting I'd once seen at the L.A. County Art Museum years ago when my mother dragged me there. It was a Monet, and the sky this morning reminded me of the one in that painting. It's funny what you think about at a time like this, things like paintings and new beginnings, but I guess it's better than dwelling on the misery likely caused by the thugs running the base at Rattlesnake Lake.

After an hour of kicking up spirals of dust in my wake, I drove through the rocky pass and down into the small valley. I could see the base ahead. From the distance, the *base* or *gun club* or *teen drug center* or whatever it was looked like a fortress. A high fence surrounded the camp with gun towers at the corners. Stanchions running the perimeter stood like giant sentries; their lights, mounted high, bathed the grounds in an eerie bluish hue. The road led directly to the main entrance. Outside the barricaded gate stood a guard shack, and like a military bunker it was made of solid concrete. Cut into the side was a metal door, with a slit just wide enough for the guard inside to peer out as the enemy approached.

I'd been told to be there at six, but it was past 6:30 when I pulled up to the gate. I was nervous about being recognized, and drawing attention to myself by being late didn't help matters. But remembering what the blind hustler at the court had said: *workers in uniform going about their business are not noticed*, gave me some comfort. I would just have to be cautious, that's all. I'd keep my head down and act unobtrusive. I tugged at the bill of my milkman's hat, shading my eyes and covering the scar on my forehead. I patted the name stitched above my left shirt pocket. We can we pull this off, Chip...can't we?

A man in a camouflage-brown shirt wearing a fatigue hat, like the Marines wore, emerged from a steel door and moved over to my truck. Stitched above the bill of the cap, instead of the USMC emblem, was a bizarre logo. It appeared to be a snake impaled upon a cross. I had no idea what that was all about and right then wasn't the time to discuss it.

He had a buzz cut, a pock-marked face, and a crescent-shaped, jagged scar, a serrated scythe that ran down from under his right eye and followed the contour of his angular face: a face of hard edges that matched his hard-edged swagger. He had a sidearm holstered at his hip and his hand rested on the butt of the gun.

I rolled down the window. Why didn't he just open the gate and wave me through, as the real driver, Roger, had said he would? I glanced in the rearview mirror: no sign of Sol's limo.

"Hey, you." The guard jumped up on the running board and stuck his head inside the cab, giving me the once-over. I glanced at his hands gripping the edge of the window. His knuckles were heavy with scar tissue. He had been a fighter in his day, maybe still was.

"What's the holdup? I'm late on my route."

"Where's Roger?"

"Sick."

The guard scowled. "You got a radio in this rig?"

The thump I heard was my heart dropping to my socks. *Sol and his damn beeper.* They nailed me, even before I got through the gate, I thought. I'll be lucky if the guy doesn't shoot me. "What radio?"

He pointed. "The one on the dashboard. What else?"

"Oh, yeah…" I felt a wave of relief. "What about it?" I leaned over and twisted the knob, turning on the truck's AM/FM broadcast radio, a Motorola. Static came through the speakers. "Can't get much way out here."

"Tune in 106.7."

"Why?" The pain in my side kicked in. Did everyone in the Mojave listen to 106.7?

"My radio inside," he nodded toward the guard shack, "is beeping like crazy."

I dialed in 106.7 as instructed and the beeping came through, loud. "Mine beeps, too. Must be the station," I said and turned off the radio. "I hope it goes away by the time I leave. I want to listen to Humble Harve on the drive back."

"It's not the station," he said coldly.

"What do you mean? It's beeping on my radio, too."

"You got a problem, buddy." His right hand shifted from the edge of the driver's window. Was he reaching for his gun? My back stiffened and my ribs felt like a boil on a carbuncle. I slipped my hand low, under the dash, ready to flip the panic switch.

"What kind of problem?"

"You got an FM transmitter, a tracker, planted on your vehicle."

It took a moment for his words to register, then the thought of the .45 automatic under the seat crossed my mind. I wouldn't go for it unless he brought his gun out first.

"What are you talking about?" I tried to act dumb, but I knew the plan was over. They were on to me now. My cover was blown. I couldn't blame Sol, though. I had brought it on myself. Why did I think no one would notice me sneaking onto the base? The thugs who attacked me had called me by name and, by now, everyone had to know about me, including the guard, the angry guy with a gun standing two feet away from me. Yet, there I was, driving through the night with the truck beeping like crazy, broadcasting a worldwide alert–*hey, are the Russians coming? No, run for cover, it's Jimmy O'Brien in a milk truck*–God, am I a schmuck, or what?

"They think you're a thief. Are you a thief, Mr. Milkman?"

What was this guy talking about? If someone warned him

about me, then he knew I wasn't here to steal anything. He'd know I was a lawyer. But, then again, maybe he couldn't make the distinction. "A thief? I'm not a thief."

"The beeper's probably under the bumper, stuck on by a magnet. Your boss is tracking you. They don't trust you. "

"Hey, I'm new. I think they do that with all the new guys." I knew I'd just dodged a bullet.... Ooh, bad choice of words.

"Okay, I'm going to let you in, but I'm going to call the commissary, tell them to keep an eye on you."

The guard turned and went into the shack. In a moment, the gate swung open. I put the truck in gear, drove through it and continued on, following the road to the commissary. By the time I pulled up to the loading dock I was sweating, and I hadn't even unloaded the milk order yet. I made it this far and felt exhilarated, but at the same time I was scared out of my wits.

At the end of the dock was a metal rollup door. It clanked open a moment after I banged on it with my fist. Inside, a man dressed in white stood at a tall desk; the receiving clerk, I presumed. He looked to be in his mid-thirties, and had a three-day growth of heavy stubble and a thick dark head of hair, the color of which matched his eyes. He glanced up at me for a second and then shifted his gaze back to the desk, jotting something on a pad.

"You're late," he said. "They're getting ready to serve breakfast, no milk. Unload your truck and hurry it up."

I took a quick peek beyond the guy into the kitchen area. The room was bright, well lit with fluorescent tubes in the ceiling. The walls were yellow ceramic tile, the floor red cement squares, and the equipment all shiny steel. The area was about the size of a small college or large restaurant commercial kitchen.

Teenaged boys and girls were busy working, some at the prep tables, while others scurried about with trays in their hands. I estimated that ten or twelve kids silently prepared the morning meal. If there was that many kids just fixing breakfast, how many people resided on the base?

A large TV, mounted high in one of the corners, beamed down a flickering image of a women's choral group. The group contained half a dozen members or so–each wearing a white surplice over a delphinium-blue gown. Even with the noise of clattering pans and pots, I could tell that the music was religious in nature. The kitchen staff ignored the TV. I didn't blame them; when I was a teen I liked rock 'n roll, still do.

I hadn't expected to see Robbie, but I thought Jane might be working in the kitchen because of what she'd said at the Harvey House. I quickly scanned the area, but she was nowhere in sight either.

"Hey, Mac, I told you to move it." The receiving clerk made a sweeping motion with his hand like I was an insignificant piece of rubbish, something easily brushed away. But I kept my cool; to this guy I was just a uniform.

"Sorry, I'm new on the route."

"Yeah, that's what the gate guard said. Now, dammit, Chip, go get the milk."

I started to turn, but took one more glimpse inside. The choral group on the TV was gone, replaced by a familiar figure, the guy I'd met at Hazel Farris's church, J. Billy Bickerton, the part-time preacher and owner of the Holy Spirit Network. He was pacing back and forth across the stage, his hand clutching the mike. He whipped the cord around behind him until it became a skinny black snake that followed in his steps, ready to jump up and bite him on the ass. The teens in the kitchen turned and gazed at the screen. They stood mesmerized, listening intently to Bickerton's bombastic sermon. I couldn't make out what he was shouting about but, of course, I didn't care. I turned and hurried back to my truck.

Since this was the last stop on the route, I didn't have to check the order sheet. I just loaded everything remaining in the truck on the dolly and wheeled it over to the receiving clerk.

Clipboard in hand, he checked the order. "Hey, are you trying to pad your commission?"

"No, why?"

"You got an extra case of butter here. We ain't paying for butter we didn't order."

"Got a new promotional deal. Fourth Monday of the month, free case of butter."

"It's only the third Monday."

"Our mistake, take the butter."

I was eager to get inside the commissary. I wanted to poke around while unloading the order. If I spotted Jane, I'd have to figure out how to get her aside and explain the plan I'd worked out in my mind, the plan to get her off the base, the plan where I'd rescue her without getting shot. The plan was a simple one. I'd somehow hide her in the truck and drive through the gate. I had everything worked out—everything but the details.

The receiving clerk gave me a look but stepped aside. I pushed the dolly past him into the kitchen. The TV was still going full blast, but some guy standing in front of a lectern pounding a bible had replaced Bickerton.

My eyes combed the room studying faces: blank faces, faces of kids without passion or vivacity. These kids moved and acted like zombies, like the walking dead I'd seen in the B-movies of the '50s at the Gage Drive-in Theater when I was a teen, *I Was a Teenage Deadhead*, or something.

"Over there," someone said. A teenaged boy with blond

hair cut short, wearing a rubber apron, leaned listlessly against a washing sink. He pointed to the walk-in refrigerator door cut into the wall beyond a bank of several mixing machines.

"Thanks buddy." I started maneuvering the dolly through the tables. "Give me a hand, okay? I got a sore back." My ribs were sore, but that's not why I asked for help. I wanted him to move close to me, close enough so I could quietly ask about Robbie and Jane.

The kid ambled over to the cooler. He grabbed the latch and yanked the door open. "In here," he said in a flat voice. "I'll unload the stuff."

When I got to the door, he took the dolly from me and I followed him into the cold, darkly lit room. The kid bent and lifted the cartons. Shelves lined the walls behind him.

"Do you know Robbie Farris, a kid who lived out here for a while?" I said in a low voice.

He wagged his head from side to side and kept on working.

"How about Jane Simon?"

The kid stopped in mid turn, stood stark still for a moment, then slowly turned to me. His face was white.

"Who are you?" he asked.

Chapter Twenty-nine

From the look on his face I knew he didn't believe I was the milkman, so I took a chance. "I'm here to help her. My name's Jimmy."

The kid set the crate down. "She told me you were going to save her. She said you were coming for her."

"What? How did she know that?"

"You're her guardian angel, aren't you? She said you were."

"I'm just a guy who wants to help her...and maybe she can help me too."

"Hey, I've never heard of an angel named Jimmy."

"Look, kid, I'm not an angel—guardian, cherubim, seraphim, or even an L.A. Angel."

I sensed a presence and glanced over my shoulder. The receiving clerk, hands in his pockets, stood braced against the freezer door jamb. I didn't know what he'd heard. I stiffened up. The kid went back to stacking the milk crates.

"Hey, Saint Butterfat, what's going on? The dishes are stacking up, and you're jawboning with my dishwasher about angels. The Reverend gives the sermons around here." He waved a hand. "Get back to the sink, Ariel. You know better than to talk to this guy. Angel Gabriel here is paid to unload his own stuff."

The guy had obviously heard the part about angels, but it seemed he hadn't overheard me asking about Jane.

The kid fled into the kitchen. I made a move to stack the remaining crates, but as the clerk started to turn away I said,

"Gotta use the restroom." I didn't know how much time I had here before they suspected I wasn't really the milkman. I felt this might be the only chance I'd have to take a look around the building.

"All right, but make it snappy. Go out through the kitchen to the hall. Turn right. Men's room is three doors down."

I dropped the milk crate and dashed to the door that led from the kitchen into the depths of the building. Instead of turning right I went left, figuring I'd get a better picture of the place, and if I it was my lucky day I might spot Jane. But as I jogged along, it dawned on me that I had no clue where I was heading or where she could be.

I paused for a second and glanced around. The hallway, a narrow well-lit corridor, had a cracked, speckled linoleum floor. The walls were plain, covered with a putrid yellow tinge that might've originally been painted white but had long aged. Unmarked doors—all of them closed—ran the length of the hall. Scattered at intervals, mounted high on the walls, were more of the TV sets like those I had seen in the kitchen, only smaller. They showed the well-groomed image of Bickerton again booming dire warnings, predictions of eternal torture waiting those who doubted the word of the Lord. Running to the end where the hallway formed a T, I turned left again.

More unmarked doors, more TVs, and another hall at the end of this one. I turned right this time and kept running. Not a soul was in sight. I tried a doorknob: locked. A few more: they were all locked.

What the hell was I doing here? Jane was supposed to be working in the kitchen. She wasn't there; the plan was tanking. I'd never find her running through hallways, rattling doors. This hallway alone had a dozen of them, the building had hallways going off in all directions, and there had to be half a dozen buildings in the compound.

A guy could get lost charging around these hallways, all of which were identical, nothing to show me the way back. Maybe I should drop a few bread crumbs, like Hansel and Gretel, but look what happened to them.

All of the doors were locked. But what if one wasn't? If I opened it, did I expect to see Jane standing there? Am I being foolish, or what? I had to get back to the commissary. The receiving clerk seemed suspicious to begin with and if I wasn't back soon...well, I didn't want to think about that.

I raced to the end of the hall, hung a right, and skidded around the corner. More of the same; just putrid yellow walls and closed doors.

I kept running and thinking. Maybe behind these locked doors were bedrooms like in a college dorm. Or maybe they were like prison cells. Maybe they all held teens, boys like Robbie and girls like Jane, young kids all locked up in these little cubicles. How many kids were held here? Where did they all come from and what were they doing on this base named after a serpent? Was Bickerton the head snake, or did they just pipe in his verbose diatribes to grant comic relief to the inhabitants? My thoughts whirled as I ran.

More doors, more running, more hallways. *Quit thinking O'Brien.* Get back to the kitchen fast before you're spotted dashing around these halls like a lunatic turned loose in a maze. I stopped, bent forward at the waist, and placed my hands on my knees, gulping air. But how do I get back to the kitchen? Which hallway?

Hold on, if there's a kitchen here, then there has to be a dining room or mess hall close to it. I should have turned right when I left the kitchen, just as the receiving clerk had said. Sure, that's it. What's the matter with me? The restrooms would be located next to the mess hall and Jane would be working there, serving the food or cleaning tables just as she'd been doing at the Bright Spot café.

I turned and ran back down the length of the corridor.

Stopping at the end of the hall I tried to think: left or right? I wasn't sure, but I took a left and raced to the end of the hallway where it dead-ended at a door with a small window cut into it. I hadn't gone through any doors to get where I was, so I turned around and headed back.

About halfway down, one of the doors swung open and a boy with a mop and pail emerged. I was moving fast and damn near ran him down, but stopped before we collided. He had on khaki work clothes and appeared to be about sixteen. Now less than a foot away, he jumped when he saw me. Then he gave me a strange look, eyes wide with the brows riding high on his forehead. He eyed me as if I were some kind of alien being.

"Sorry, fella," I said. "I'm the milk delivery guy and I'm lost. Which way is the dining room?"

He didn't answer. He just stood there, stiff, holding the mop in one hand and the pail in the other.

"C'mon, guy, where is it? I kinda lost my way," I chuckled, a little levity, laughing at my foolishness.

He turned and pointed, shook his finger once or twice, then angled his hand and pointed to the left. *Down the hall, then turn left* was what he said with his finger.

"What's the matter? You can't speak?" I asked.

The kid shook his head and put his finger over his mouth.

"They won't let you talk around here, is that it?"

He nodded and silently ambled away, head hung. I stared at his back as he made his way down the corridor. My God, what kind of weird place is this? Supposed to be a gun club; that's a laugh. What kind of gun and target shooting club has facilities this huge, sermons blaring from every nook and cranny, and teenaged kids working there who moved like zombies? The kids weren't even allowed to talk. Teenagers in the L. A. County juvenile hall have fewer restrictions than the kids have in this loony bin.

In spite of the sermons blaring from the closed circuit TVs, I was sure this place wasn't a Christian drug rehab center. Real Christians don't treat people like slaves and they don't have gun turrets on the premises. I jogged to the end of the hall and rounded the corner in the direction the kid had indicated.

I stopped dead my tracks.

Three men were walking toward me, the two thugs who had attached me at my carport, and the redneck brute I'd seen sitting with Ben Moran at the Bright Spot Café. Moran had called him Buddy; I'd call him the Bear. They were talking to one another and hadn't noticed me yet, but I figured if the Bear recognized me, he'd do more than just give me a growl.

I spun on my heel and scurried back to where I had just come from. I turned the corner and kept walking, stiff legged, down the corridor. They'd seen me, I was sure, but I didn't think they recognized me and silently prayed that they'd turn the opposite way when they reached the T. Was the blind guy correct when he said people didn't notice guys in uniforms while going about their tasks?

A voice shouted, "Hey, you! You in the white uniform, what are you doing here? This area is off limits." Nope, the blind guy was full of crap; they noticed me.

The three guys turned toward me. I knew this was going to be trouble.

"You deaf, or what? Stop, I'm talking to you." I pretended not to hear Buddy Bear's angry demand and kept walking.

I picked up my pace some more and marched with alacrity

straight down the hall. If they decided to push it, where could I go from here?

"Get him, boys!"

They decided to push it so I ran.

I rounded the first corner I came to and heard the pounding of my pursuers' boots hammering the floor. Buddy Bear's voice echoed behind me: "Give it up, O'Brien. Yeah, we know who you are. You'll never get outta here."

I shot a quick glance over my shoulder. The goons appeared to be gaining.

"Last chance, asshole," one of them shouted.

Head down, legs pumping, fight or flight...I choose *flight*. How do you fight an army of gun-toting bastards on their own turf? I ran with adrenaline valves wide open, the energy coursing through my system.

I slipped and skidded around another turn, then made a mad dash for the end of the hallway. Unmarked doors flickered past as I continued to run flat out. In a few seconds I reached the end of the corridor and turned right. I didn't look behind me. I didn't want to waste the energy, but I sensed that they were getting closer.

A shot rang out!

"Jesus Christ!" I cried as the slug whizzed by my head and slammed into the wall.

Faster legs, faster, let's move it. These sons-of-bitches mean business.

Another shot. The explosion reverberated in my skull.

If only I could find an exit somewhere and get outside of the building, out into the open, I might be able to make it to the truck and hit Sol's panic switch, the one on that stupid beeper. But what could Sol do with only two of his men? What chance would we have against an unknown number of armed hoodlums?

The blasts were deafening; two more quick bursts, this time from an automatic weapon. The slugs ricocheted off the walls and buzzed around me like angry bees as I ran a zigzag pattern, racing for the hallway intersection. One more gunshot. Everything slowed. My legs were iron stumps. I moved dreamlike, reaching out for the next corner in this labyrinth of mindless hallways.

I made it to an intersection and drifted left this time. Real time came flashing back, and the certainty of my fate knocked at my consciousness: nowhere to run, nowhere to hide. Enough! I stood flat, hard against a wall. Looking down I noticed blood splatter, droplets gathering around my feet. I had been hit, and suddenly I felt a searing pain on my right side just below the ribcage. I ripped open my shirt. The wound was a deep gash. The slug hadn't hit anything important, just tissue. The seepage was already diminishing, but the pain wasn't. I'd live, this time.

I clenched my fist into a tight steel hammer, my knuckles protruding like solid ball bearings. The first guy to show his head was going to get slammed in the face. I might connect and get one guy down before another one shot me. But then again, I might not be so lucky.

I waited, sweat gushing from every pore, gulping down oxygen as if I were a drowning man. The seconds ticked away, the clock in my brain running on frenzied, disjointed gears. I stood there with every muscle quivering. "C'mon, you rotten bustards, lets get this over with."

The footfalls retreated, and as time crept by it became apparent that someone had called off the storm troopers. They must have reverted to plan B, seal off the corridors and gradually close in on me from all directions.

What could I do—nothing, just stand there and wait for the inevitable. It became very quiet…

I almost jumped out of my skin. A voice was calling me, a small lyrical voice, one that I recognized. I cranked my head to the left and saw her standing next to an open doorway a few yards down the hall. Jane was beckoning to me.

Chapter Thirty

"Jimmy, don't be frightened. Come this way."

I quickly scurried to her side. "Jane! I've been looking for you, but you found me."

"Ariel told me you were here. Now look, there's no time. Come this way, hurry. If they catch you they will kill you."

She turned and led me through the doorway, into another narrow passage, at the end of which was an opening that led to the yard outside of the building. Okay, I'd still be on the base, but they at least they wouldn't corner me in these hallways. I might have a chance in the yard. "This is where they let the dogs in at night," she said.

"Dogs?"

"Guard dogs, they unleash them and the dogs roam the halls at night."

"Why?"

"So the kids won't leave their dorms after lockdown. Won't wander in the halls and try to leave this place. That's why they couldn't turn the dogs loose on you, they'd go after the kids working in the building, too." She pushed the door open. "The kennels are on the left, so go right and you won't disturb them. The barking will bring the guards."

I peered out into the yard. The sunlight was intense. Heat waves shimmered above the blacktop in the distance. I could see the kennel she was referring to, about a hundred feet to the left. A dozen or so Dobermans lolled in the heat, protected by an open front lean-to inside a wire mesh fence.

"Will you come with me?" I said to Jane. "If we can get to

my truck–" I was about to tell her how I could ram the gate, and about the panic switch and how Sol would, somehow, help get us out of here, but she cut me off in mid sentence.

"No."

"Why?"

"Because they'll catch you unless I draw them off. I'll go and disturb the dogs. Their barking will bring the guards. Keep down and crawl to the right, around to the front of building. As soon as you hear the dogs, make a run for it. Maybe you'll have a chance."

"What about you? I can't let you get caught helping me."

"I'll be gone by the time they get there. Don't worry, they won't see me."

"Tell me about Robbie," I said.

"He's not here. They've taken him away. Now, hurry. Go!"

She took off running, and glanced back once. Our eyes locked for a moment before she disappeared around the corner of the building.

I took a quick look in both directions and saw no guards, just a couple of teenage girls listlessly sweeping the yard. They seemed oblivious to what was going on.

I crept, crab-like, along the length of the building, keeping below the line of barred windows lining the wall. When I reached the northwest corner, I stopped and peeked around the edge. The milk truck was still parked there, backed up to the loading dock, about fifty yards away, exactly where I had left it.

Half a dozen men milled around in front of it. They wore the same paramilitary uniforms as the gate guard, and each had an automatic rifle slung over his shoulder. While I waited for the dogs to bark, I glanced back and noticed that I'd left a trail of blood droplets behind me. The wound still bled, but I was more concerned about being spotted than I was about the pain. One nice thing about having a bleeding gash in my side was that I didn't notice the pain from my cracked ribs. If caught, I wondered if they'd give me a couple of aspirins before they shot me.

Suddenly the dogs let loose, barking, snarling and making a general nuisance of themselves. The guards perked up, looked around in all directions, then—just as if they were all wired together—charged off toward the kennel in the opposite direction from where I was hunkered down. I sprang from my crouch and made a wild dash for the truck.

I calculated that it would take me six seconds to reach the truck. Five seconds into my race for it I heard a man shout, "Halt! Stop right there." Then the sound of rapid gunfire filled the air, bullets dancing at my feet.

Without looking, I lunged for the truck and grabbed at the driver's side door handle as I fell to the ground. The door flew open. The gunshots continued, bullets slamming into the passenger side.

The truck would offer only a modicum of protection. But now I had to get this big milk wagon started. Then I could ram the gate and drive this thing the hell outta here. I clambered into the cab, keeping my head down.

My getaway plan showed promise but had one tiny flaw: no ignition keys! I hadn't taken them with me. They snatched them. Mabel was right; I never lock anything. Damn!

An old wheezy voice I recognized shouted out. His words cut like a knife. "Give it up, O'Brien. You're surrounded. Take a look-see."

Peering over the dash, I looked out through the front windshield. Yeah, it was Ben Moran. He stood, hands on his hips, in front of about a dozen soldiers. They had formed up into a semi-circle in front of the truck. Their automatic weapons were on a dead aim for my head.

"Hands in the air, and climb out slow-like. Don't bother looking under the seat. Your gun ain't there. Move it!"

I thought of a line from Carroll's *Through the Looking-Glass*: *"I'm very brave generally, only today I happen to have a headache."* I was scared shitless.

My left hand inched to the dashboard. I flipped Sol's panic switch.

Chapter Thirty-one

"Time's up! Get out of the truck, now!"

I opened the door slowly. Holding my arms high, I climbed down from the cab. As soon as my shoes hit the ground, the guards closed in. I stood in the middle of a tight ring of thugs, their AK-47s pointed at my gut.

Ben Moran, a malicious scowl on his face, cut his way through the guards. At his side dangled a .45 semi-auto, his finger hooked through the trigger guard. He carefully dropped it in the pocket of his bib coveralls. I figured it was the gun Sol wanted me to bring along for protection. The gun I shoved under the front seat of the truck.

The wind was right and I could smell his stench. He smelled like evil, like the decay of a dead rat. "O'Brien, I want information," he said. "You play ball and you won't suffer."

"Hey," I said, lowering my arms. "I'm just helping a friend. The guy took sick and asked me to take his route."

The back of Moran's hand flew at my face. I blocked it with my forearm, and got a rifle barrel jabbed in my gut. I doubled over, and a guard pounded my back with the butt of his weapon. I yelled as I dropped to the tarmac.

Moran snarled, looking down at me. "You were warned, but you had to press on. Didn't you?" His voice matched his face: ugly. "Straighten up, act like a man."

I hunched up onto my knees, bent over like an animal with my hands planted on the blacktop. Nauseous and woozy, I shook my head as if the movement would cast out the pain and restore my vigor. It didn't.

"You're not so tough. Without that Jew bastard, Silverman, and his boys around you're nothing."

That's me. Jimmy O'Brien, wimpy lawyer. Cracked ribs, a

bleeding gash in my side...and I hollered when the guy whacked me with his gun. What a softy. But now, I was starting to get irked.

I stood, a little wobbly on my feet, and got right into his face. "Listen, you miserable excuse for a human piece of crap. I came out here to get my client. You murdered his mother, and then grabbed him at the court. I want him back."

"Is that so?"

"Where is he?"

"Now, you listen to me, you miserable excuse for a lawyer. First of all, I'd nothin' to do with his ma's death. Anyways, Robbie Farris came here of his own free will. He was a messed-up heathen just like you and we taught him respect for the Lord; put the fear of God in that boy. That's what we do around here. We redeem lost children."

"Yeah? Well, he stabbed his professor twenty-seven times. Murdered him. So what does that say about your concentration camp redemption tactics?"

"Enough of this! Tell me what you think you know about me and our little gun club."

"I'm not going to tell you squat."

He slapped me across the face. I winced, but it didn't hurt that much.

"Ah, hell, you don't know nothin', or you wouldn't be snooping around like a damned fool, all dressed up in a milkman's outfit." He turned to the guards. "Get *Mr. O'Brien* out of my sight. I don't want to see him again."

Moran started to walk away, but he stopped and came back.

Then he did something weird. He raised his hands high above his head. While looking at the sky he turned his body slowly in a circle and in a deep booming voice, chanted, "*If I whet my glittering sword, and mine hand take hold on judgment; I will render vengeance unto mine enemies.*" He stopped for a moment, and then, with eyes blazing, he rushed at me, shouting. "I will make mine arrows drunk with blood, and my sword shall devour flesh."

I didn't know what to make of it. That is, until I thought about what he was saying: some kind of bible quote, a passage that somehow justified capital punishment.... *My God, was the son-of-a-bitch going to have me executed?*

"The Lord has spoken. Take him away." Moran lumbered off, dusting his hands.

His words hung in the air, frozen, then shattered and fell to the ground when I realized that the madman was going to kill me.

I couldn't die today!

With a strength that I didn't know existed in my wounded body, I grabbed one guard and flung him to the ground, smashed another in the face, and stove off blows from the remaining guards, but they kept coming at me. The momentary adrenaline rush was waning fast. I had to hold up. I had to get free somehow.

I fought and struggled against my captors, but there were so many of them. Finally, it was over. My arms gave out and the last of my energy drained away. Two men grabbed me under my arms, holding me erect, while the rest formed up in two columns, one on each side of me. Cradling their guns across their chests, they started marching me away.

"We'll take him to the back wall, drag him if we have to," one of them said.

One guy poked me in the ribs with the muzzle of his gun, and I yelped.

"Hey buddy, don't worry, your hurt will be gone in a few minutes." The guards laughed.

"Yeah, we got a sure remedy for those nagging aches and pains, "They laughed some more.

I tried digging my feet into the hard surface, but the more I resisted, the harder they pulled on my arms. We were still in the front area of the camp, about fifty yards from the main gate.

The guard indicated that the wall was in the rear. They'd have to carry me there. I wasn't going to make it easy for them. I jabbed an elbow into the gut of the guard on my left. He flinched. I came across at him with a right fist to his jaw. It connected and he went down. A flurry of fists and rifle butts slammed into me, and I went limp. The world was turning white and I knew I couldn't hold on much longer. But, I kept at it, hanging in there by sheer determination. At one point I got my hands on a guard's weapon and almost wrenched it away before he twisted it out of my grip. A rifle butt flashed past, then more fists, a club…. The sky tilted. I started to drop. *But I can't. I have to get free, survive, resist and fight back…*

I had to keep fighting. Oh, God…

A crash echoed across the grounds. The air vibrated with ear-cracking bursts of heavy-duty, military machine gun fire. A riot had erupted.

Shouts and curses from the guards next to me pounded in my ears. I looked up. Sol's black, armor-plated limo had crashed through the gate. The big limousine was roaring straight toward me, trailing a voluminous cloud of white smoke. The horrific gunfire was coming from the car.

Some guards dropped to the ground and covered their heads; others ran seeking protection from the blazing machine guns. I stood, dazed. It's funny, I didn't see any slugs hitting the ground and I knew Sol didn't have any machine guns. The limo skidded to a stop right next to me. A door flew open. A hand reached out and yanked me into the back seat. We roared away in the smokescreen Sol had laid out. Three seconds later we were through the gate–the gate guard dropped his gun and ran for his life–and out of the compound racing toward Barstow on the dirt road that led into the base. The limo's machine guns were still blasting away.

"Turn off those goddamn guns," Sol hollered above the din to Cubby the driver.

The noise instantly stopped.

"It a tape recording, hooked up to a speaker system under the car," Sol said. "The smoke's real, though." A huge grin surfaced on his face. I didn't know if he was grinning because I was safe now, or because he had a chance to play with his tricked-out limo spy stuff.

"What took you so long?" I asked and managed a smile.

"Hey, we were having lunch in the car, waiting. When the beeper thing went off, I had a bottle of '62 Mouton Rothschild open. I didn't want to spill it. I had to re-cork it perfectly or it would've oxidized."

"Yeah?" I said. "When James Bond rescued Ursula Andress from Dr. No, he didn't give a damn about spilling a little wine."

"Hey, buddy, you ain't no Ursula Andress," he said, and we all laughed. We laughed real hard, and the laughter helped the pain go away.

Chapter Thirty-two

The long thin stretch of concrete spooled out in front of us as we drove through the sun-baked desert heading back to Downey. The Deacon patched my gunshot wound using a serious first aid kit, which I figured was *de rigueur* on all spy limos. I declined the proffered shot of morphine.

I quickly took Sol through my ordeal and described the base layout, the bunkhouse, the maze of locked cubicles, and how Jane had helped in my escape effort. I also told him what she'd said about the kids being locked in their rooms at night and about Robbie not being on the base, that they'd taken him away. We agreed that we were back at square one when it came to finding Robbie, but now we knew for sure that Moran was the head honcho at the Rattlesnake Lake base and heavily involved in exploiting vulnerable teenagers. We figured he worked with unsuspecting church groups that sent the troubled or abandoned kids to his so-called "Christian redemption center." His motives for this escaped us, but we knew his intentions were more than just saving their souls.

Neither of us mentioned what a failure the day had been.

I glanced at Sol, who sat quietly with a chilled gin martini in his hand. "Sol, this whole affair borders on the absurd. A religious nut in cahoots with a gang of neo-Nazi thugs imprisoning teenaged kids in the middle of the Mojave Desert."

"Aw, Jimmy," he said, and took a small sip of his drink. "Realism and absurdity are often similar in the lives of overzealous true believers, but Moran is more than that. He's a smart son of a bitch and he's got some kind of scheme working. But now we've forced his hand. Moran is not going to sit on his ass while you run around looking for Robbie. He's gonna act, you can bet on it. We've gotta come up with a new approach."

I didn't like the sound of that. "What do you mean?"

"Don't worry about it, my boy. We'll think of something."

I thought about the dairy truck still backed up to the dock, riddled with bullets. "Van Hoek is going to be pissed," I said.

"Who gives a damn about the truck? Van Hoek will send somebody to get it." Sol paused, then added ominously, "But I *am* concerned about the gun."

"Steve at Matthew's Gun Shop always gave me a good deal when I was a cop. I'll get you a new one."

"Damn it, that's not the point. The bad guys have the gun now. It's not registered, can't be traced, but I'm trying to remember if you handled it."

I stared out the window, watching the Joshua Trees that grew by the thousands on the bleak wasteland drifting by. The Mormons named the species *Joshua* because they thought the cactus mimicked the Old Testament prophet waving them on toward the Promised Land. They gestured at me now, but they weren't guiding me to any Promised Land. They waved and laughed. *You're an idiot, Jimmy. First that ridiculous milkman routine and now the gun with your fingerprints all over it.* Shimmering in the desert heat, a vivid image formed. Ben Moran came to life holding Sol's .45 by the trigger guard. I knew for a fact I hadn't seen or heard the last of him or the last of the gun that he'd dropped into the pocket of his bib overalls.

Earlier, as the Deacon tended my wounds, Sol had insisted that when we get back to Downey he was going to have a doctor check me out. I told him I'd be fine, that I was tired of doctors. I just needed some rest.

"No way," he said. "Forget about the bruises, but the bullet wound…you could get an infection. I would've stopped at the emergency room in Barstow, but the doc there would have reported it to the police, and from what you tell me, the chief is involved up to his fat ass with Moran and the Rattlesnake Gun and Torture Club." He paused, lit a cigar, and continued: "I'm taking you to my guy, a doc who owes me. He won't report a thing."

"Sol, maybe it's time we turn it over to the state police."

"Are you crazy? You're still not off the hook for Hazel Farris's murder. Nobody would believe you. Besides what do we have? The FBI cleared the gun club. It would be your word against the chief of police. And besides, how long do you think Jane would live if the word got out about a police investigation? Let's wait 'til we have absolute proof. Then somehow we'll take them down."

"I see your point. But what are we going to do?"

"We'll figure it out...later. After you've rested, after the doc gets through with you."

"What kind of doc is this guy, anyway?" I asked.

"He's good," Sol said. "He's got penicillin and everything,"

"Sol, what kind of doctor is he?"

"A vet. So what? If he can stitch up a snarling Rottweiler, he ought to be able to handle you. Do me a favor, though..."

"Yeah, I know. Don't bite the guy."

It wasn't long before we arrived at Doc Tully's Animal Clinic in Pico Rivera. I stripped out of the bloodstained milkman uniform, put on one of the doc's lab coats, and sat on a stainless steel table, holding my arm above my head, while the doc finished his Frankenstein stitch job.

When Tully was through, he gave me a handful of pink pills that looked as if they could choke a horse. Maybe they could, but he explained how I was supposed to break them up and take a quarter of one every six hours. I put the pills in my pocket. I'd take the first dose after I had my oats.

By the time we left his office, I was starting to feel weak again. I wondered if I'd ever get out of this mess. But all I wanted at that moment was to get to my apartment and ask Rita to bring me some of Foxy's therapeutic chicken soup.

The Deacon and Cubby practically carried me back to the limo. Sol was talking on his mobile radiophone when Cubby opened the passenger door and I slid into the backseat.

Sol said, "Ten-four" and cradled the receiver. He turned to me. "Jimmy, we're taking you to a safe house. Don't argue, because it won't do any good. I don't want to take any chances. No telling about Moran and his goons."

I was too beat to argue. I didn't care where he took me, all I wanted was to eat and lie down. "Okay, Sol." I glanced at my watch: just after four in the afternoon. Rita would still be at the office. She could bring the soup to the safe house.

"Sol, can you get my office on the horn, please?"

He didn't respond. Cubby started the car and we drove out of the parking lot, heading south on Rosemead.

"Sol, I've gotta call the office. I want to talk to Rita."

He just glanced at the floor of the limo. "Don't push it, Jimmy–"

My pulse quickened. "Sol, something is wrong!"

"Calm down, my boy, it's nothing like that."

"What's the matter? Damn it, Sol, I'm talking to you."

"Don't get hot. Rita's a...trifle upset, that's all." A crooked grin appeared on his face. "You know how women can get."

"What do you mean a trifle upset?"

"Well, Mabel said she just quit. She doesn't want to have anything to do with you."

"What the–"

"She said she can't be your lawyer anymore. Can't trust you. Mabel told her you got worked over out at the base."

"Goddammit, how'd Mabel know?"

He shrugged. "Ah...I might have said something." Then he perked up. "Hey, you want I should get Morty to take your case?"

"Oh Christ, Sol. Call my office."

The limo turned left onto Artesia Boulevard and soon we were in Dairy Valley, a city of milk barns and cow shit. The smell complemented my mood.

Chapter Thirty-three

Sol's safe house wasn't a house at all, but a barn. To be precise, it was a one-bedroom suite–kitchenette, small bedroom, sitting room with an old-fashioned console TV built into the middle of a milk barn. Long rows of stalls, each a rectangle four feet by eight feet and each loaded with a Holstein cow, hid the entrance to the suite. Hooked up to the cows were milking machines with suction nozzles and long hoses, contraptions that made loud slurping and clanking noises, a mechanical cacophony mingled with the occasional moo.

Sol ran around the suite like a bellboy, opening doors, adjusting the thermostat; he even turned on the TV. "Welcome to the Holstein Hilton, Jimmy."

"Yeah, rooms with a moo."

"A Guernsey getaway."

"No bull."

I agreed to stay in the so-called safe house until I felt better, a couple of days at most. Sol's men would secure my apartment, setting up an alarm system and attaching profession deadbolt locks on my door. Who knew–Moran might attempt to follow through on his *sentence of death*. As Sol had said, "He's a real badass, makes Attila the Hun look like a nun. His boys might try something rash."

The barn stood on Herman Van den Berg's farm in the community of Dairy Valley, twenty miles east of downtown L.A. The town, established by milk farmers, was set up to protect their lands against the encroachment of urban sprawl.

But the sprawl went on unabated, devouring everything in its path like molten lava, an eruption of tract houses and strip malls. Now it had already been decided that the dairies would be closed, the cows hauled to Chino, joining others, which had been relocated from South Gate, Norwalk, and Downey years earlier. Dairy Valley would then be a memory, and what was left of the community would be merged into the city of Cerritos, its nearest neighbor to the north.

I crashed on a ratty Naugahyde sofa, a piece of furniture straight out of a '50s TV sit-com. *The Honeymooners* came to mind. Cubby ambled into the kitchenette to warm up a can of Campbell's Chicken Noodle.

Sol left and returned a few minutes later with Herman Van den Berg. Herman was a big-boned, gangly man of about sixty with a tangled mess of burnt-orange hair, which crowned his thin, pinched face. His round blue eyes were close set, separated by a spider-veined, misshapen nose. The eyes seemed to be asking a question, but I didn't know what it was and Herman didn't say. He might've been asking something like, *what in the hell is this guy doing sprawled on my Ralph Kramden couch?* What could I tell him? Could I tell him a bible-thumping monster was out to get me? He'd probably say aren't they all.

Could it be that everyone in the dairy business was named *Van* something or other? Van Hoek at Sunnyville Farms, and now Van den Berg out here. When Sol introduced us, he said that the name meant *from the mountains* in Dutch.

After mulling it over for a moment, I realized there weren't any mountains in Holland. That is, unless they were referring to the mountains of Holstein dung at all those diaries there. So, I reckoned, loosely translated, his name meant *Herman, who came from a pile of shit*. His body odor confirmed my reasoning.

"Jimmy," Sol said. "Herman here was gracious enough to let us use his hideaway for a few days until you're better."

I waved. "Thanks, Herman."

"Yaw, Immy. I help Sol. He's my friend," Herman replied in a heavy Dutch accent.

Herman explained how, sometime ago, he had a problem and Sol had helped him out of a serious jam. It seems that Herman had a fire on his farm. A year's supply of baled hay—worth thousands of dollars—had caught fire and burned up. The hay had been insured of course, and at first the insurance company disavowed the resulting claim when it was discovered that the fire had been purposely set. But when Sol had proved that a fanatic animal rights activist had hired an arsonist to start the fire, the insurance company promptly cut the check.

Herman had built the bedroom suite inside his milk barn as living quarters for his foreman, who had later married and moved away. As a gesture of his appreciation for Sol's efforts in the insurance matter—along with a sizeable check—Herman granted the use of the suite whenever Sol needed to stash someone out of sight for a few days.

Everyone cleared out as soon as the soup was served. I took a few spoonfuls, but my appetite was gone and the soup was terrible. It wasn't just because it was canned; Cubby had decided to spice it up and dumped in about a gallon of Tabasco. I liked Tabasco, but give me a break. Making my way to the bedroom, I stretched out on top of the covers. I stared at the ceiling and thought about Rita. Maybe I should've just leveled with her from the beginning; then, if she didn't want to be my lawyer, so be it. At least I wouldn't be a liar in her eyes.

She was gone by the time I'd called the office from Sol's limo. Would she come back? Would she stay on with our little law firm? She wouldn't for sure if she found out about the gun that Mabel had hidden.

Chapter Thirty-four

I must have dozed for a couple of hours, because when I awoke sunlight was no longer filtering thought the thin cloth curtain covering the window. I glanced at my watch: almost seven o'clock. I carefully made my way into the bathroom and winced as I examined my image in the mirror. I looked like hell, about the same as I felt. The guy who stared back at me wore an animal doctor's lab coat, had bloodshot eyes and a three-day growth of stubble. I looked more like the Wolf Man than a criminal lawyer. Some people said criminal lawyer *were* monsters, and my appearance tonight would certainly reinforce that. I leaned in closer to the mirror and flinched when I lightly touched the blue and yellow puffiness growing just below my left eye. The bruise was as big as a tomato; I figured it would get as big as a rutabaga before it healed.

I opened the medicine cabinet. It was fully stocked, filled with shaving gear, a couple of new toothbrushes, toothpaste, and a large economy-size bottle of aspirin.

A fresh terrycloth robe hung from a hook on the door. I slipped out of the lab coat, turned on the water in the shower, and brushed and shaved while I waited for the water to get hot.

While in the shower I was careful not to disturb the bandages covering my gunshot wound, and when I was through, I shrugged into the robe and wandered back into the sitting room.

I stood in the center of the room and stared at the phone. Should I call her? It was seven-thirty; she'd be home by now.

I made a couple of calls to Rita's apartment, and each time

when the answering machine came on, I hung up without leaving a message.

Turning on the TV, I sprawled on the sofa and flipped through the channels with the clicker. *Mannix, a private peeper, with not a hair out of place beat up the bad guys without breaking a sweat*...click.... *The FBI*.... click.... A live variety show, fresh-faced youngsters dancing and singing. Some kind of oddball disco thing, like disco as performed by Lawrence Welk. It was a pop religious number, young women telling viewers, "...*let's get down and funky with Jesus*..." Wait, the reverend leading them was the guy I'd met with Bickerton at his White Front church. Snavley, Hazel Farris's pastor, the guy who told her about the teen drug center...the one who told her to send Robbie out to the base at Rattlesnake Lake.

I noted the station. The live broadcast originated from the school in the valley where Robbie had killed his professor, Golden Valley College. When the dance number ended, Bickerton walked out on stage and introduced the audience to Reverend Elroy Snavley and his dancers, *J.C. and the Sunshine Singers*–The J.C. of the group being there in spirit only.

Flashing on the screen while Bickerton pranced around the stage booming his sermon was a phone number. Words scrolled by under the number saying something to the effect that if you were a teen in trouble, had a drug problem and nowhere to turn, call this number, that angels were standing by the phones with help.

Snavley handed all of the young dancers a white lily, saying the flower was a symbol of virginity, female purity, or something like that.

I leaned back and pondered; the college station must have been sold to Bickerton's network after all. Sold, as the college administrator had said, *over Professor Carmichael's dead body...*

I grabbed the phone again–couldn't just sit here while this was going on–and dialed Sol's home number. "Hey Sol, send someone to get my car, will you? I left it at Sunnyville Farms when I took the milk truck. I have a hunch."

"Go to bed, Jimmy. You need your strength. We have to figure out a way to get Robbie back. We'll talk about your hunch in the morning. I'll pick you up early tomorrow–"

"Sol, I need my car!"

There was silence on the line. "Sol–"

"Listen, Jimmy, ah…. There's a little problem."

"What do you mean?"

"Don't get upset," Sol said. "I'm working on it."

"Working on what."

"Well, Van Hoek, the owner of Sunnyville, is a little pissed. Can't blame him. After all, we didn't return his truck now, did we?"

"Sol, you said he'd send someone. What are you saying now?"

"He's holding your car hostage. But, hey, it's just until he gets his truck back."

"Oh, Christ–"

"It might be a little touchy at the moment trying to get the truck out of the Rattlesnake base, know what I mean? But don't worry, I'm working on that too. Good night, Jimmy."

"Sol–" He hung up the phone. I stood there with the receiver in my hand feeling like a fool. Why did I let him talk me into this?

While wondering what to do next, I heard a knock at the door. I answered it. Framed in the doorway stood a woman who appeared to be in her late fifties. She was squarely built, with wide shoulders and thick arms, and there was no visible waist hidden under the flower-print housedress she wore. Her face, which once, long ago, might have been pretty, had a look of grief about it now. Her hair, once blond, was mostly gray, and the blond strands that remained weren't really blond but were the yellowish color of old paper stored in a musty attic. Folded over her arm was a pair of pressed Levis and a checkered shirt.

"Hello, Jimmy. I am Betje, Herman's wife. I brought you some fresh garments. Socks and underwear are in the drawer in the small bedroom."

After thanking her I stepped aside, and Betje Van den Berg entered, draping the clothes over the back of the sofa.

She turned and studied me intently for a moment. "Yes," she said. "Herman told me you looked like him...same size.... My God, you have the same blue eyes. Herman was right."

"Who, Mrs. Van den Berg? Who do I look like?"

"Oh, my goodness," she said and covered her mouth. Finally, after a few seconds, she dropped her hands and said, "You sound like him too. You could be brothers."

"Who, Mrs. Van den Berg–"

"You call me Betje, yaw? I'll call you Jimmy."

"Okay, Betje."

"You are exactly like our son, Joris. Herman told me, but I had to see for myself."

"Does your son live with you?" As soon as I asked the question, I knew what the answer would be. It was etched in her face.

She turned and fussed with the clothes, straightening the shirt, refolding the jeans. When she turned back to me, there were no tears in her eyes. They had dried long ago, I could tell, but the hurt was still there. "Viet Nam," She said. "Joris was the commander of a little boat, patrolled the rivers in the jungle. They told us–Herman and me–when they give us his medal…. They told us Joris was very brave, saved his men at the cost of his own life."

"I'm so sorry, Betje," I said, and after a moment added, "your son died a hero."

"Yes." Her voice trailed off and she made a move for the door. When her hand touched the knob, she paused and turned back. "This country is wonderful. When Herman and I moved here from Friesland–you know Friesland?" I nodded. "When we came here, we had nothing, not even one cow. Now we have many…America gave us everything, and we gave America everything back when we gave our son. We still have the cows, though."

We stood motionless without saying a word, letting the silence wash over us and soothe our wounds, mine superficial and visible, hers deep and raw, and not at all superficial.

Finally, she said in a soft voice, "Are you a hero, Jimmy? You've been hurt. Herman told me you were hurt trying to save a boy who had lost his soul."

"No, ma'am, I'm not a hero and I'm not really hurt. What pain I'm feeling now will pass and I'll be fine."

"No, you are having pain, real pain. But you must fight. Don't let what you are fighting for slip away. Do you understand?"

I glanced at the phone, then back at Betje. "Could I borrow a car? There is something I must do."

"Herman took our sedan to a city council meeting, but you can use the El Camino." She tucked her hand into a big pocket on her housedress and pulled out a set of keys.

Chapter Thirty-five

My plan was to catch Bickerton at the college where the broadcast originated and lay it on the line; browbeat him until he came clean about his involvement with Moran and the Rattlesnake Lake base.

The idea flashed in my mind as soon as I saw the TV show. Moran and Bickerton were working together. The more I thought about it, the more certain I was right; it all fit together. It had to. I figured that Bickerton, through his Holy Spirit Network, recruited the troubled teens, snagged them with the funky entertainment, then pitched the drug program and captured them with his religious mumbo-jumbo, like the Pied Piper had mesmerized kids with his magic flute. And what about Robbie killing the professor–the man who was dead set against the sale of the college station? Could he have been a pawn, brainwashed by Bickerton or Moran and sent out to deliberately eliminate the only obstacle standing in their way? Perhaps I was overreaching, seeing conspiracies where none existed. Yet I couldn't stay cooped up in the dairy barn and do nothing until Hammer pinned a murder charge on me.

Before I asked Betje to loan me a car I thought about calling Sol back, but I knew he'd try to talk me out of going to see Bickerton. He wouldn't feel as strongly about my hunch as I did. And even if he did he'd want to wait until morning, he'd want to have backup, pack a lunch…Christ, he'd want to make a production of it. No, if my plan had a shot at all, I'd have to catch Bickerton by surprise tonight while he was off guard.

But, I also realized I was being optimistic. Bickerton wouldn't want to talk to me. At first he'd deny any suggestion that he was involved with Moran, of course. But I'd keep pressing. I'd pound it into him that Sol and I knew the whole story, had the evidence–I'd make that part up–and I'd tell him how if he didn't cooperate, he'd be indicted for murder. Even if he didn't participate in the activity at the base, or in the professor's homicide, I'd explain how he'd be indicted anyway for conspiracy, which in the eyes of the law is the same as if he'd wielded the knife himself. And as a kicker, I'd offer him a deal. TV stations had recording equipment. He could record his testimony, then I'd give him twenty-four.... No, make it forty-eight hours to get out of the country, time enough to grab some cash and flee, before I'd turn the tape over to the authorities.

If he was as smart as I thought he was, he'd take the deal. But the truth was, down deep, I doubted that I could pull it off. My chances of succeeding were about a billion to one. But I knew I had to try. Betje said to keep fighting and that's all I could do.

I fired up the Chevy El Camino and charged out of the dairy, heading north on Artesia Boulevard. I'd have to hold the sporty pickup to the speed limit; God forbid, I didn't need some cop pulling me over. But I'd have to hurry. I figured I had a couple of hours to catch Bickerton there. The TV show had just started and would be on the air for at least an hour. Then it would take another hour or so for the dancers to shed their makeup and costumes and change into street clothes before Snavley locked up. I wondered if Bickerton would stick around that long. My guess was that he would. He seemed to be a control freak; I doubted that he'd leave Snavley in charge of his big musical extravaganza.

Golden Valley College looked just as it had before–no ivy covered walls, or gray stone Gothic structures–all space-age, tarted up architecture and rolling acres of blacktop, an homage to the gods of functionality. Except now it was nighttime. But the darkness didn't help; they had floods everywhere.

I slowed on Reseda Boulevard to make the turn into the

parking lot, and suddenly a black Mercedes 600 limousine darted out directly in front of me. It missed the El Camino's right front fender by inches. It was Bickerton, the back of his huge leonine head prominent through the limo's rear window. In an instant the traffic subsided and the limousine pulled away, its bright red taillights growing dim as it receded in the distance.

I was too late. I was always too late. I slid down in the seat and stared straight ahead, fuming. I'd never catch him now; the limo was moving fast and I'd have to punch it. The cops would pull me over for sure. I was devastated; I'd never get another chance like this. By tomorrow morning, Moran will have clued him in about my foray onto the base and Bickerton will put up his guard. I wouldn't be able to crack him now, damn. He'll barricade himself inside a fortress of silence as thick and impenetrable as the concrete bunkers on Normandy Beach.

I continued into the school parking lot, needing space to turn around. As the headlight beams swung slowly through the wide circle, a flicker of light reflected off the chrome trim of a lone car parked way down at the end of the lot. I drove forward toward it. The small sedan rested in the shadows along the wall of the building that housed the TV station, approximately the same spot where Robbie had murdered Professor Carmichael.

A man emerged from a door cut into the building, hurriedly locked it behind him, and dashed to the parked car. He stood by the driver's side, saw my lights coming toward him, looked up and stared at me, wide eyed like a startled fawn. I pulled forward and stopped, all the while gazing into the frightened face of Reverend Elroy Snavley.

As soon as he recognized me when I climbed out of the El Camino and walked closer, he began to shout, "What do you want? Why are you pestering me?"

"Let's talk."

He stood facing me, illuminated in the pickup's headlights "Here? Right here in the parking lot?"

"Yeah, right here, right now."

"I have nothing to say to you. I didn't do anything. I'm not guilt–"

He stopped in mid-sentence and turned back to the car, jangling his keys nervously. It's been my experience that when someone protests his innocence before being accused, he's usually guilty of something. "Hey, Elroy, I didn't say you were. I wanted to talk to Bickerton, but you know what's going on and you and I are going to discuss it." I grabbed his shoulder.

"Don't hurt me!"

The guy was stressing out. His body stiffened. It was like he slipped into a trance, catatonic like a spiny-tailed lizard. I could feel his muscles tighten and let go. "I'm not going to hurt you. That is, if you come clean with me." I wasn't going to hurt him anyway. That's not the way I operated, but I'd keep that to myself for now. "Tell me about Moran and Bickerton."

His face went blank. "Who's Moran? I don't know anyone by that name." He loosened up now; in fact, he became quite animated, waving his arms. "Why are you threatening me? Why are you gonna beat me up about someone I don't even know?"

He stood in the light quivering. It was strange: he didn't appear to be lying about not knowing Moran. Maybe he *didn't* know him. Moran kept a low profile, but Snavley knew Bickerton and he definitely knew about the base. That's where he told Hazel Farris to send Robbie. He couldn't deny that. "What about Rattlesnake Lake? It was your idea to send the Farris kid there."

Snavley froze up again. His mouth became a tight thin line and he moved his head from side to side.

"C'mon, Snavley, talk to me. Do I have to get rough?"

"I can't talk about that. Don't you understand?"

"No, I don't."

"I'll get fired if I tell you anything."

"Fired! You're in deep legal trouble and you're worried

about getting fired?"

"You can't prove nothing. But, if I talk about the drug center Mr. Bickerton will fire me. He's my boss, you know. I'm not supposed to talk about that either, about him owning the church. But he let it slip when you were here before."

"I don't give a damn who owns the church, and I don't care if he's your boss or any of that crap. I just want to know about those kids at the base. What's going on out there; and I want to know about Bickerton's involvement with Moran."

"I told you I don't know any Moran. I don't know anything. I was just trying to save a few poor, wretched souls. I do the Lord's work." He paused and looked up at the sky. "Oh, Lord, help me. *Please*. I know I'm a sinner, but I've changed." He kept at it, praying to the Lord, and the harsh timbre of his voice spoke of a certain agony that gripped *his* soul. "I promised I'd atone..." He stopped. His mouth hung open; his body stiffened again, and he stared straight into the bright headlights of the pickup truck. "Go ahead, Mr. O'Brien, hurt me if you will. But you not so tough, big shot lawyer–that's a laugh–sitting behind that cheap metal desk all day waiting for clients to show. Besides, there's nothing you can do that will cause me more pain than the pain that's already ripping me apart."

A breeze kicked up. A fast-food wrapper fluttered in front of the El Camino's headlights, momentarily casting flickering shadows across Snavley's face.

A sharp voice resonated behind me: "Hey! What's going on down there? What are you guys doing here?"

I spun around and saw the beam of a flashlight dance across the lot. A man in a uniform held the light. "What's that pickup truck doing here?"

"It's me Charlie, Reverend Elroy. And this gentleman was

just leaving." Snavley turned to me and in a hushed voice said, "Aren't you?"

"Oh, it's you Reverend. Just checking, you know. It's my job." The security guard stopped and leaned against the El Camino's hood. He gave me a probing look, tapping the flashlight against his leg. I felt I'd get no more out of Snavley tonight. But he was as fragile as a porcelain teacup and I knew he'd crack once I could get him alone, someplace where I could bounce him off the walls if I had to.

"I'm not through, Snavley. We'll be in touch." I walked to the pickup and slid into the front seat.

It was nearly midnight when I turned off the Santa Ana Freeway onto Paramount Boulevard. The traffic was light all the way back from Van Nuys to Downey, where I planned to stop at my apartment to check my answering machine. I was dying inside. Rita had walked out on me, pulled a stunt like that–not only quitting, but dropping me as a client–without telling me in person; highly unprofessional. If she had any class at all, she'd at least have left a message. But who was I kidding? I'd known her too long and I thought we were friends…maybe close friends. No, it wasn't like her to do that. There had to be something, a critical fact that I should have seen.

Though upset about Rita, and just missing Bickerton at the college, I felt good about bumping into Snavley. I figured he knew that something horrible was going on at the base and he was keeping quiet about it. I couldn't fathom why–maybe he was afraid–but whatever his reasons, it was chewing him up. And I knew it was only a matter of time before he'd come clean. A man like him couldn't keep that kind of information bottled up inside forever. He'd explode; already the fissures were starting to show.

I turned onto Cecilia a couple of blocks from my apartment. My head swiveled as I rolled along the dark street, checking for cars, especially ones that held some ugly bruisers. A few cars lined the curbs; they were empty.

Sol always said I was a little reckless–stupid? –but I didn't think the bad guys would stake out my place and wait for me to show up. They'd know there were too many neighbors with prying eyes who'd spot them–suspicious mugs lurking in the shadows–and call the law. If they were truly after me, they'd cruise the street a few times, and when they noticed a light in my window or saw the Corvette, then they might try something. The goons would not place themselves at serious risk. Hit and run was the style of all the leg-breakers I'd heard about. Besides, they wouldn't expect me to be driving an El Camino.

I pulled up to the curb in front, slipped out of the pickup, and dashed upstairs to my apartment on the second floor. The red light on the answering machine wasn't blinking. Damn, no message from Rita. After I picked up the receiver to see if the phone was working–it was–I grabbed a few things–a book, a change of clothes–and was out the door in a matter of minutes.

Arms filled, I stayed in the shadows and peered around the corner of building. Seeing nothing out of the ordinary I made a run for the El Camino. As I struggled with the junk, trying to open the driver's side door, I sensed someone near. I was about to turn when a man slipped up behind me. Suddenly, I felt a sharp pain in my sore ribs: no doubt the hard jab of a gun barrel.

I dropped the stuff and instinctively raised my arms.

"Hold it right there, O'Brien. Don't move."

The voice was familiar, too familiar. But it was a relief. A cop, Hammer; it wasn't one of Moran's thugs that held the gun. Over my shoulder I said, "What is this, Hammer? Gonna give me a ticket?" I looked down at my belongings in the street. "Littering?"

"What are you doing here, wise guy?"

"I *live* here, for chrissakes."

"Yeah, looks like you're moving out. Trying to escape. Where you get the El Camino? Steal it?"

Lowering my hands, I turned until we were face to face. I could smell whiskey on his stale breath. "Are you charging me with–"

"Keep you arms up, or I'll drop you where you stand!"

"Cool it, Hammer. I'm not armed."

"Oh yeah, not armed? What's this here?" He opened the front of his jacket. Tucked in his belt was a snub-nosed automatic. I knew what this was. I'd been a cop. The gun was a thrown-down piece, probably lifted from some street hood, untraceable, of course. He could shoot me, plant the piece in my cold, dead hand and claim self defense.

My stomach churned. He'd get away with it.

"Turn around," he said.

I started to talk fast: "Look Hammer, I know you think I'm guilty of killing the old lady, and all the talk in the world won't convince you otherwise, but until I prove differently–"

"Cut the bullshit. You're guilty, and if I could prove it, you'd be a goner right now. But I'm not through with you." He paused for a moment. "You're still breathing, but that doesn't mean you're not dead." He turned and disappeared into the darkness.

Chapter Thirty-six

I pulled away from curb, and as I did I saw the detective's unmarked car make a U-turn and drive away in the opposite direction. I breathed a sigh of relief. Hammer had been drinking, and I noticed that he hadn't written down the plate number of the El Camino. And now it didn't seem as if he was following me, but despite that I took a roundabout way back to the dairy, checking my rearview mirror every three seconds. When I felt sure that no one had tailed me, I turned on Artesia and headed straight for the dairy.

Bellowing cows, and grunts and shouts from dairy workers, woke me up. My noisy bovine neighbors filled the milk barn just on the other side of the wall. The morning milking ritual was in full swing. I stumbled out of my bed in the Holstein Hilton and made my way into the kitchenette to put on a pot of coffee. The clock above the sink read 8:10.

After I got out of the shower and into my clothes, I poured my first cup of the day. I sat at the little table, hands ringing the warm mug, and let my thoughts wander. What was I going to do now? Especially about Hammer waiting for me to make one small mistake? Of course, he'd been drinking but I felt as if he'd shoot me on sight with the slightest provocation. I'd have to be extra careful with him lurking in the shadows.

And what about Rita? Would she come back? I was carrying a ton of guilt. I should've come clean with her from the start. I should've trusted her, trusted her ability. If she did return, I'd lay it all out. Let her know why I did what I did, why

I went to the base, and I'd tell her about the gun too. I shouldn't have let Mabel get rid of it to begin with; stupid thing to do. After all, it was the murder weapon, a serious piece of evidence, and maybe the real killer left his prints or something. It was a longshot but the gun might have proven my innocence. Now the only way to clear my name would be to get Robbie back.

I took another sip. The coffee tasted bitter.

Suddenly the door burst open.

Sol's voice boomed, "Jimmy, turn on the TV! Quick, Channel nine."

I didn't like the sound of this. "Sol, what's going on?"

"Turn on the goddamn TV!"

"*Why?*"

Sol grabbed the remote, and clicked on the set. "Christ, you've done it now," he said as the television warmed up. "It's been all over the news this morning."

"Done what? I just went to see Bickerton."

"You went *where?*"

"Went to see Bickerton. I had a hunch and thought…. Sol, I missed Bickerton out there, but I had a powwow with Snavley–"

"*…And now the local news…*"

"Shut up, Jimmy. This is it."

A talking head filled the screen and a chill crawled up my spine. "*…the young victim, identified as Robbie Farris, a client of the suspect, attorney James O'Brien, was discovered by L.A. County Sheriff's deputies. The body was sprawled in the back of an abandoned milk truck parked on a side street just off of the Pomona Freeway in a remote area of San Dimas. Farris had been shot to death with a .45 semi-automatic pistol. According to police, the victim had died last night sometime* *before eight p. m., and O'Brien's fingerprints were found on the murder weapon as well as the milk truck. O'Brien, also a suspect in the murder of the victim's mother, is considered armed and dangerous. An all out search is underway for the missing Downey attorney..."*

The newsman went on to say that the police had already talked to Peter Van Hoek. He denied knowledge of how I happened to have the truck. The film cut to Van Hoek standing in his lot pointing at rows of identical delivery trucks. "I've got a hundred of 'em. Can't keep track of all of them, can I?"

"Van Hoek doesn't want the cops *or* the bad guys to know he was involved." Sol clicked off the set.

There was a big empty hole where my soul had been. Robbie was dead, and so was I. There was no hope now. I slumped to the couch and stared at my shoes, trying to concentrate on what I'd just seen, failing to make sense of it all. Hammer had seen me at my apartment at around midnight, plenty of time to shoot Robbie, snatch an El Camino somewhere, and get back to Downey. He saw me with my arms full of clothing, like I was taking it on the run. It would look bad for him if word got out that he had me in his clutches, then let me, a murderer, walk away like that. One thing was for sure: the next time he saw me he'd shoot to kill.

Cubby, Sol's driver, barged in. "Boss, the office patched a call through to the limo. Rita wants to talk to O'Brien." He glanced at me.

"Rita?" I asked.

"Yeah. Says it's important. Says she has an idea."

Chapter Thirty-seven

I bolted from the room and raced to the black limousine. The smell of cow manure wafting from the dairy corrals hung in the warm air and black flies buzzed in lazy circles as I slid into the driver's seat and grabbed the receiver.

"Jimmy, I heard the news–" Rita began.

"Why'd you run out on me?"

"What are you talking about? I didn't run out on you."

"Mabel said…"

I glanced up. Sol was standing next to the open door. "Be careful what you say. Calls on a mobile phone can't be traced, but they're sent out over the airwaves, and anyone can listen."

"I don't give a damn what Mabel said." Rita's voice had an edge. "I wouldn't run out on you just because you're a jerk."

I nodded to Sol and continued my conversation. "She said you stormed out of the office."

"I was tired of you getting beat up and decided to do something about it. That's why I left in a hurry. And now with the new developments–Robbie being dead–I'm glad I did."

"Listen, Rita. I've got to tell you about the gun behind the file cabinet–"

"Jimmy, I know all about it. Remember, I'm the one who wanted to get rid of it in the first place. I figured you came to your senses and saw it my way. Now keep your mouth shut about that. We're on the radio phone."

"Okay, but…. Well, we can get into that later."

"Shut up and listen. I'm on to something, can't talk about it now, but remember you told me Carmichael was a geology professor and Moran had mines out in the desert?"

"Yeah," I said.

"Well, yesterday when I left the office I shot straight to the college where Carmichael taught, talked to a Mr. Grundy. When Robbie killed him, the professor was working on a story for the college TV station. Now, I'm going to follow a lead."

"Rita, what in the hell are you talking about?"

"Uh-uh, I'm not getting into it now."

"Rita–"

"Hang in there, Jimmy; I'm with you no matter what. You should've known that. Bye."

She hung up. I sat there and stared at the phone in my hand. I wasn't exactly sure what she had in mind. I felt a tremendous relief knowing she was on my side, but I wondered what she meant when she said that she was going to follow up on a lead. What kind of lead?

Sol interrupted my thoughts. "Get back inside, Jimmy. Cubby and I have to get going."

"Hey Sol, I can't stay here while all of this is going on. I've gotta do something. I've got to go with you."

"Go where? What's the matter with you? If you're spotted, no telling what could happen. Didn't you hear what they said on TV? *Armed and dangerous*, means they shoot first–"

"I *gotta* do something."

Sol rested his hand on my shoulder. "Look, Jimmy, I've clued Herman in. We don't want him accused of harboring a fugitive, so if anything happens, he doesn't know you're here. You broke in, got that?"

"Yeah."

"Now, you just go back inside and relax until you hear from me."

"Are you nuts? *Relax*?"

"Bad choice of words, but listen. I've got an angle that I've been working on. Bickerton's the key to this whole affair. That's why you went to see him. He's the guy who's been recruiting the kids, sending them out to Rattlesnake Lake, telling them on his TV show that it's a drug rehab center. Right?"

"Yeah, but so what? Things have changed. Moran or his thugs killed Robbie. That's what I've got to prove. Who cares about Bickerton now?"

"Goddammit, get out of the car and go back inside. I haven't got time for this." He turned to Cubby. "C'mon, let's hit the road." Sol yanked my arm.

"Hey, ease up. Okay, I'll go, but I'm not going to wait forever." I climbed out of the limo and trudged back to the milk barn.

Rattling around in the *suite*, I paced the living room floor, moved into the kitchen, and sat at the table for a while. Then I got up and moseyed into the living room again. Before long I walked back to the table and sat some more. At one point I picked up the book I'd brought from my apartment, an old Raymond Chandler mystery, *Trouble Is My Business*. I stopped at a line that seemed to reflect my mood: *"I felt like an amputated leg."*

I put the book down and suddenly realized what Rita was talking about. She said she was onto something.... *Going to follow a lead*. Something about Carmichael being a geology professor. I made a beeline for the phone but stopped short of picking it up. My office phone would be tapped by now. Hammer would've gotten a warrant within five minutes of the cops discovering my prints on the gun that killed Robbie.

I had to get to a phone. Mabel would know what Rita was up to. She had to know; she knew everything that went on in the office. But I couldn't call her from the dairy; the cops would trace the call.

I ran from the suite, then stopped and realized the only car available was the El Camino. Hammer had seen me in it. He didn't take down the plates, but by now the cops would be on the lookout for anyone driving a blue '63 El Camino. I stood there and stared at the car. Wait, maybe Hammer didn't mention the El Camino to the brass hats after all. I'd been a cop and knew how they thought. Everyone would be pointing fingers and Hammer would be in trouble if he told his superiors that he had me at gunpoint and then let me go.

I didn't have any choice. I'd have to take the chance. I jumped in the El Camino and peeled out of the dairy onto Artesia. I had to get to a phone.

Slow down, Jimmy. Play it cool. Let's not wave any red flags. Let's not get a goddamned speeding ticket on top of everything else.

I drove three miles before I pulled into a Union Oil gas station and stopped next to a phone booth. I dug into my pocket. Damn, I had a few bills but no coins. The attendant was waiting on a car, checking the tires. It would take him forever, and I didn't have the time to wait.

Another block and I saw a bar, a drinker's bar. The kind bikers loved–a run-down joint with a beat-up pool table in the center of the dingy room and a small screen TV mounted in the corner. The TV was on, a soap, but no one was paying attention. I threw down a dollar bill. The barman gave me a withering look when I asked for change for the phone.

"Gonna buy something, a beer?" he asked.

"Nah, just change."

A weepy-eyed stiff at the end of the counter, clutching a glass, raised his head.

The bartender tossed the coins down. "Sure you don't want a beer?"

I made my way around the pool table, brushed by two Asian guys, built like sumo wrestlers, playing eight-ball, and moved to the old-fashioned wooden phone booth at the rear of the room. As I pulled open the squeaky door and stepped in, I glanced up at the TV. A choker close-up of my face flickered. The announcer was somber: "*The manhunt continues, but so far the police are having no luck tracking down attorney James O'Brien, the man suspected of the killings. Anyone with information should immediately contact the Los Angeles County Sheriff's department.*"

Not looking at the bartender or his customers, I quietly closed the phone booth door and covered my mouth with a handkerchief–like I'd seen gangsters do in the movies. After dropping a dime in the slot, I dialed. Mabel picked up on the first ring. "Don't say anything. Just tell me what you know about Rita's hunch," I said.

"I don't know anything and she's not here. I don't know where she went."

Cold fear gripped my heart. I had a gut feeling Rita would try to confront Moran. She must have figured that the professor was tied in somehow. "Did she say anything about Moran or Professor Carmichael?"

"No, but she called Sol's secretary, then left in a hurry."

"I gotta go." Hanging up, I quickly dialed Sol's office. I didn't think the cops were listening in on his phones. A judge would never grant a warrant to tap an innocent civilian's line.

It took forever for Joyce to come to the phone. I glanced back at the barroom. The heavies at the pool table were pinning me hard, steely eyed, like they were about to break out the long knives.

Finally, Joyce's voice: "Oh, Jimmy, we're all so worried–"

"Joyce, quick, what did Rita talk about when she called this morning?"

"She asked about the information Sol had me dig up on Moran, stuff about him owning those mines and the ore processing plant out there in the Mojave."

"Damn, what is Rita doing?"

"Said, she gonna serve them a writ or something, interrogatory, I dunno."

"My God, a writ?"

"Yeah, she called about ten, fifteen minutes ago…and Jimmy, she especially asked about Moran's borax works, the ore refining plant. Why, what's this about?"

"Asked about the borax works?"

"Yeah, she wanted to know how to get there."

Chapter Thirty-eight

I stood there in the sweltering phone booth trembling, staring at the receiver in my hand. I should've leveled with Rita from the beginning, let her know just how dangerous Moran and his band of religious whackos were. She hadn't gotten the whole story. She wasn't aware that he was a stone-cold killer. She didn't know he'd shoot her and watch her die just for the fun of it. I should've forced her to give it up, hang back and let Sol and me work this out. Gonna serve a writ! Oh, Rita! Gonna walk right into a den of deadly vipers and hand them a writ, for chrissakes. I had to stop her. I had to get to the borax works before she did. Maybe I could block the road or something. I slammed the receiver down and elbowed out of the booth.

My photo still flashed on the TV screen, and from the way those Chinese King Kongs at the pool table were giving me the eye when I left the bar, I thought I was going to have to fight my way out. But they gave me a wide berth, and even the bartender seemed to shrink when I rushed by him. It pays to be famous; still, I doubted the Chinese guys recognized me. We all look the same to them.

Before we hung up, I'd asked Joyce to get a message to Sol. "Tell him I'm going to try to head off Rita. Send help," I'd said.

Rita had a fifteen-minute head start, but she'd take the 605 and I'd be heading out on the 91 Freeway. If I hurried I might beat her there.

Leaving Dairy Valley, I held the El Camino close to the speed limit when in traffic–constantly watching for Chippies in their black-and white cruisers–but when alone I opened it up, pushing ninety.

Swerving off Highway 58, I bounced onto old Badwater Road, bypassing Barstow. I took a shortcut directly to the borax works, one that wouldn't pass in front of the Rattlesnake Lake base. Once on the dirt road, I floored it. Now, with pistons hammering and the wind rushing by like the roar of a jet and trailing a tornado of dust in my wake, I screamed along Badwater Road in a frenzied rush.

I was flying low on the deserted, gravel surface about ten miles from Moran's complex, zeroed in on his borax works. Yeah, I was provoked.

I hadn't taken the time to listen to Joyce's detailed explanation of what she'd said to Rita. But before hanging up, I caught enough of it to give me a picture. She told Rita that the prior owners had abandoned the borax works before World War II, but Moran bought the plant and the mines that fed the ore to it fifteen years ago, roughly at the same time that the government sold Rattlesnake Base to the Jeroboam Corporation, which we now knew he also owned.

I knew how Rita's mind worked. I could almost see the thoughts forming. She figured these guys were businessmen, that legal documents would bring them to their knees. Christ, a *writ*. How could I let this happen?

Couldn't this damned El Camino go any faster? I twisted the wheel to miss a jackrabbit, skidded and almost lost control. Then I stood on the gas pedal and kept the mass of metal bouncing forward.

I shot over a rise and sped down a long incline aiming for the small desolate valley below. Serrated peaks of hostile mountains off in the distance surrounded the desert floor, and laid out in the center of it was a long forgotten industrial complex. But now, twin smokestacks towering amid a gathering of old stone buildings belched swirling clouds of soot and smoke.

I slowed. Still a few hundred yards away from the works, I saw an area devoid of brush and rocks, where I pulled off the road and parked. I couldn't let anyone at the borax works see me out here.

I crept away from the El Camino and moved a hundred yards closer. On a high mound, at the road's edge, I hid behind a cluster of tall sagebrush. I shaded my eyes from the mid-day sun, and with one sweep I scanned the whole complex. Looking down from the vantage point, I saw dump trucks unloading their cargo of rocks and dirt, skip loaders, operated by kids, scooping the stuff up and moving it about, and forklifts, also driven by teens, racing in and out of the smokestack building, which had to be where the ore was processed. The guards slouched in the shade watching as the kids, in the sun-blinding yard, formed up into a line, lifting and hauling heavy bags to waiting trucks. A small kid stumbled when a large sack came at him too fast. One of the bastards ambled over and gave him a whack, grabbed him and slapped him around before shoving him back into the bag line.

As I watched, the shrill whine of a whistle filled the air and the activity slowed. I glanced at my Timex: noon. Must be lunch hour. Another short blast sounded and instantly a scratchy recording of Bickerton's voice reverberated from loudspeakers: "*Behold, the scripture saith, how good and how joyous it is for brethren to labor together in unity…*" His voice droned on and on, extolling the virtues of hard work. Asshole.

In a matter of minutes, gun-toting guards escorted several rows of weary teenagers out of the smokestack building. Boys and girls marched like the dead across the yard to a smaller structure close by. Had to be the mess hall.

A low-rise clapboard building, probably the office, stood closer to the road. Behind the wooden structure, a small landing strip ran north for a couple of thousand feet. Adjacent to the office was a vacant pad; must be the airplane parking ramp. Beyond that, disappearing into the distance, was a dirt road on which a couple of empty dump trucks rambled away from the works, probably going to one of the mines to load up on more ore.

Parked in front of the office building were six or seven cars and a few black Ford passenger vans. But Rita's yellow Datsun was nowhere in sight. I must've beaten her here. I gulped a deep breath and exhaled slowly. Thank God for that! But wait, maybe she wasn't coming out here after all. Yeah, that's it, if she really was going to serve papers on these guys she'd use a process server. What's the matter with me? Always dashing off half-cocked. Maybe Sol was right. He said I was impulsive. But what could I do? I couldn't take any chances. Goddammit, not with Rita's life.

But standing there watching the cruelty, seeing all those kids work until they dropped made my stomach churn. Bile welled in my throat.

It didn't take a lightning bolt for me to realize what was going out here in this desolate place. Moran, under the guise of rehabilitating lost kids, was exploiting them. He turned them into his slaves. He housed the teenagers at the base, then worked them like dray animals at his plant and at the borax mines. Obviously, he controlled them by using the time-worn techniques of brutality, fear, and religious brainwashing.

It all fit. When the borax ore yields dropped and the mines had failed to produce a profit, due to the high cost of labor, the original owners ceased operations and abandoned them along with the plant that the mines supported. But Moran—with a bit of entrepreneurial flair—was able to overcome that trivial labor matter and make them profitable again.

I had to find out more. Creeping closer to the facility, I saw a big man in bib overalls amble out of the mess hall. It was the guy I'd seen with Moran, the guy who almost killed me at the base, Buddy the bear. He stretched, yawned and rolled a cigarette, licking the paper with his tongue. He took a few puffs and dropped the butt on the ground. A moment later a young black kid—couldn't have been more than eleven or twelve—came out of the same building. Head down, he walked past Buddy the bear. The psychopath grabbed the kid by the scruff of his neck, backhanded him across the face and jabbed his finger in the direction of the cigarette butt on the ground. The kid bent to pick it up and Buddy planted a boot in his backside. He sprawled flat. Buddy belched, laughed and swaggered off. If the world ended today and the only things left on the planet were the cockroaches, Buddy would be crawling around in the slime with the rest of his kind.

If only I had a movie camera, I'd have all the proof needed to show probable cause. Enough for the FBI to conduct an investigation.

I wasn't being naïve. Now that Robbie was dead, an investigation wouldn't get me off the hook with the DA. But if the authorities raided Moran's operations, his whole scheme would unravel. Maybe one or two of the kids—teens that hadn't been totally brainwashed—might know who actually murdered Robbie and maybe, just maybe, one of them would talk. But even if they didn't, I'd have enough to show reasonable doubt at my murder trial.

But regardless of what happened to me, with the movie

plainly illustrating the brutality, the kids would get their freedom.

I had to get to a telephone fast, call Sol on his radiophone and tell him to bring a 16 millimeter movie camera with a telescopic lens. We were going to make a horror flick.

I looked at the pebbly ground. All of the pain and misery happening out here caused my heart to ache, but soon it'd be over and the kids would be free.

And for me, I was beginning to see a way out of the horrible mess, and it felt good. I got to my feet and for the first time in days I was able to stand in the sun and breathe the air and feel alive again. It felt as if fate had finally turned my way.

But five seconds later, I saw how absolutely wrong I was.

Edging out from behind the scrub, I turned back toward the road just as cloud of dust appeared. Rita's Datsun came out of nowhere, went zooming by, and headed straight for the borax works.

Chapter Thirty-nine

I froze, an immovable object, a ton of lead. *This can't be happening.* But it was. Rita's Datsun zoomed right by me, heading right for the facility. I raced to the center of the road and hurried after her, eating the dust of her receding car, waving my arms wildly, and shouting.

The dust cleared a bit, and in the distance, down at the bottom of the sloping road, I saw the yellow Datsun pull up to the clapboard office. Rita parked and went inside. *Damn!*

I stopped a hundred yards short of the borax works when a couple of guards, weapons slung from their shoulders, came out of the mess hall and milled around.

Standing on the high ground, gazing at the complex, I wondered how I'd get her out of there without us both getting shot. Moran had already issued my death sentence, and his number one honcho, Buddy, was only too happy to carry it out.

I heard a noise. A car. I spun around. It skidded to a stop.

Two men jumped out.

Oh, God!

I stared at the gun pointed at my face, the gun held by Sergeant Joe Hammer.

"Move and you're dead," the cop said.

"What the hell–"

"We tailed her, figured she'd lead us to you. She did." Hammer nodded to the other cop. "Hook him up, Butch." Then to me: "Don't even think about it."

"Hammer, you've got to help! *Rita's in danger*!" I pointed toward the works. "She's at the borax plant down the road–!"

Butch grabbed my arms and snapped the cuffs on.

"Hammer, you gotta listen to me! They'll see us–"

"You're under arrest. Put him in the unit, Butch."

The cop shoved me toward the unmarked vehicle. "Goddamn, Hammer, they've got guns, *assault weapons*."

The plant's whistle let out a long blast.

Hammer peered at the complex as teens filed out of the mess hall, nudged by guards jabbing them with automatic rifles. The kids paraded back toward the main building.

"Hammer, you gotta believe me!"

Butch pushed my head down, trying to get me in the backseat. I banged him with my shoulder. He cocked a fist.

"Hold it a second," Hammer holstered his gun and, without taking his eyes off the borax works, gestured for Butch to cool it.

One of the guards looked up. He saw us standing out here on the road. Nudging the man next to him, he pointed at us and shouted. "Hey! Who are you guys?"

"Police, official business," Hammer shouted back.

The second guy started to raise his assault rifle.

"Good Christ," Hammer said. "What are they doing?"

"Move! They are going to kill us."

Butch shoved me aside, jumped in the cop car and grabbed the radio mike. Then he dropped it. "Goddamn radio, too far out, can't raise anyone–"

A rifle shot banged in my ear. Butch's head exploded.

"They're firing!" Hammer exclaimed. We jumped behind an outgrowth of rocks at the edge of the road. Three more rapid gunshots; the bullets buzzed over our heads.

"We got to get out of here," Hammer said as he peered over the rocks. "We're outnumbered–" Then he saw Butch's body lying in the dirt. "Oh, Jesus…Jesus Mary Joseph, oh God…Goddammit!" Sliding down below the rock's edge, he fell silent. He bowed his head and his body deflated slowly, like his soul was leaking out. Maybe it was.

I raised my head until I could barely see over the top of the rocks. Buddy barged out of the office. "What the fuck–"

The guards huddled with him, pointing in our direction.

"Go get 'em. Shoot the bastards," Buddy roared. His voice carried across the valley.

I ducked down.

"Let's go, O'Brien, move it!" Hammer grabbed my arm.

"Listen to me! We can't leave. We've got to save Rita."

He gave me a blank look. "What?"

"Rita's down there. She's in the office. They'll kill her!"

"There's nothing we can do. We got to get to the car." He started to crawl away. A bullet almost took off of his head. He jerked back. "Must be eight or nine of them. They're moving out. *Shit, man*, let's go. They're coming after us!"

I thrust my bound wrists at him. "Here, dammit, unhook me. I didn't kill Robbie, they did."

He grabbed a key from his pocket and unlocked the cuffs. Then he snatched a gun from his ankle holster. "I don't know if you murdered anybody or not, but you used to be a cop. Here, use this. We'll lay down some fire and then make a dash for the car." He handed me a small automatic, a Beretta, not exactly police issue, and not much of a weapon.

He pulled another gun, a big revolver, from his shoulder holster, checked the cylinder, and snapped it closed. With a determined look on his face, he said, "I'll go first. You follow. Barstow's down the road and—"

I shook my head. "Forget Barstow, the chief's one of them."

"Are you sure?"

"*Dead sure.*"

"Aw shit...maybe I can flag a Chippie on Highway 58. We'll take the cutoff road. Don't worry. We'll come back for your secretary. Now, let's go!"

No, I was staying. I held the small pistol and thought, how am I going to hold off nine guys firing AK-47s with this peashooter until he returns with the 7th Cavalry?

I took a deep breath and let the air escape from my lungs. I figured I might not make it, but I couldn't leave without Rita.

Raising my head, I peered over the edge. Hammer was right. The men were coming, crouching military style, creeping forward cautiously. They couldn't know how many of us were out here. Maybe I could spook them.

I got off three quick rounds. The guards scrambled.

Buddy stood defiantly in the middle of the gravel road and shouted, "Hey, we just want to talk. No sense in gunplay. Come on out with your hands in the air. I'll hold my men back till I count to three. If you don't come out, then we'll be comin' for ya. And I'm afraid we'll have to kill you."

I took a shot and missed by a mile. He dropped to the ground and looked around. When he saw one of his men he raised his hand and tossed a signal, his finger stopping when it was pointed right at me. The guard swung the weapon around.

Adrenalin coursing, I dove down next to Hammer. A heavy barrage of gunfire ensued. The rapid fire rattled my teeth. Slugs bounced off the granite in front of us, rock shards flying.

I tried to burrow deeper into the dirt.

An eerie stillness suddenly filled the air. I glanced at the red ants crawling up my arms, gnawing my flesh, and waited for the bullets to start flying again. I could hear my heart banging against my ribs.

Hammer said, "There's a riot gun in the unit. You'll ride shotgun..." He paused, seemingly appraising me. "You ready, O'Brien?"

"Not going."

"You crazy bastard–" He started to say something else, but didn't. "It's your funeral."

Buddy's voice rang out: "Okay, I'm countin'." He paused for a second. "*One...*"

Hammer's eyes locked on mine. "Cover me."

"*Two...*"

Rita's image flashed in my mind. Hammer *had* to get help.

I rolled sideways, out from behind the rocks, sprang to my feet. "Three! You son-of-a-bitch," I shouted. Then I fired.

All hell broke loose.

I got off two more fast rounds. The shots missed, but Buddy's men scattered.

I darted to my right, dropped, rolled, and shot again.

Buddy shouted at his men as they scattered. "Goddammit, get back here." He swung around, drew a pistol, and fired two quick shots over their heads. They stopped and turned. "Shoot that cocksucker! Now goddammit." He pointed right at me. The men raised their guns.

My heart raced.

Suddenly, to my left, a series of huge blasts sounded. Hammer, gripping the riot gun, stood next to the police car, pumping rounds into the line of guards.

I looked back. One guy went down, screaming, "I'm hit!"

Another guy dropped like a sack of rotten tomatoes. That left seven. Too many.

Buddy pointed at Hammer. "*Kill him!*" The men swung their rifles toward Hammer.

He lunged behind the car just as the AK-47s exploded.

I ran a zigzag pattern, sprinting through the scrub. Tripping over a rock, I struggled to my feet and got up running. I tore along the ground racing closer to the works. Stopping halfway there, I slid behind a large yucca tree, gulping air.

I heard Hammer call out, "I'll be back, O'Brien!"

Maybe he would. It was my only chance.

I raised my gun, squeezed the trigger and drew their fire, then jerked back behind the yucca. Almost instantly slugs from the AK-47s peppered the tree trunk and whizzed by on both sides. Peering out, I saw Hammer leap into the cop car. Wheels spinning, the car zoomed backward and disappeared beyond the hump in the road. Some of the guards were still shooting at the fleeing car. Others continued to shoot at me.

I wouldn't be safe here for long. Any more of this and the

slugs would chop the tree in two, or they would rush me and I'd be one dead lawyer.

I checked the Beretta's clip: one round. I jammed the gun in my belt, crouched down, and looked out from behind the tree. The shooting had stopped, and I knew why.

The kids at the borax plant had scattered in all directions. Buddy turned and pointed. Some of the guards took off to chase them, scurrying like rats across the desert. I bolted, moving five yards closer.

Buddy immediately turned back. He stood in the road with two of his men. They searched intently for me, gazing out at the scrub. I'd have to get past them to reach Rita.

I crept toward the office, moving quietly from one thicket of sagebrush to another. Most of the guards would be busy for a while, I figured. I had to find Rita and get her out of this place. But first I had to sneak past Buddy and his goons.

He continued to scan, his eyes sweeping from side to side. He signaled his men to fan out; one marched off my left, the other to the right. They'd circle around and come up behind me. Then he must've thought he saw something. He shot three times at a dense cluster of cholla cacti ten feet away from me. Some cactus wrens fluttered and took flight.

Buddy was alone now, but didn't budge from his spot. I had to make my move. If I waited too long, I'd be so outnumbered that I'd never get Rita out of here. I had one bullet left. If I shot at Buddy and missed…. Well, I didn't want to think about that. Besides, I'd need that round in case anyone was guarding Rita.

On my belly, I slithered out from behind the bushes and inched closer. I scooted forward, moving at a deliberate pace. I thought of the old World War II movies, thought about how John Wayne would handle this. He'd throw a rock off somewhere, drawing the bad guy's attention, and then he'd jump up, rush the guy, take his rifle, and gut him with the bayonet. I couldn't do that; Buddy didn't have a bayonet.

Chapter Forty

A dry breeze stirred, and the scent of coal tar pitch from the creosote bush I hid behind filled my nostrils as the sun continued to beat down on me. The unblinking reptilian orb of a fat chuckwalla, inches from my face, pinned me eyeball to eyeball like in a kid's game of chicken. I wanted to smash the goddamn lizard with a rock.

I lay sweating, waiting for Buddy to move from his spot and come look for me, to move away from the road long enough for me to circle around him. I was only ten yards from where he stood, and another ten yards behind him was the entrance to the borax works. I figured they had Rita in the small office, which was located in the middle of the facility next to a towering crane and surrounded on three sides by piles of slag. Used equipment and rusty junk were scattered on the grounds, heaped among a number of old stone buildings.

Shifting my eyes, I could see the two guards advancing through the scrub on either side. In a few moments they'd be behind me.

I didn't have a second to lose; I had to make my move *now*. The guards who'd been chasing the kids were starting to return, dragging them by the scruffs of their necks, and soon they, too, would be looking for me.

Scrunched over, I moved out from behind the bush and scuttled closer. If Buddy turned his head in the slightest he'd see me. But I kept crawling through the undergrowth, purposeful and silent, like a cat after its prey. Five more yards and I'd be close enough to get the jump on him, take his gun and put it to his head. Then I'd force him to release Rita.

A thousand to one shot, maybe ten thousand, but it *was* a shot.

Suddenly, he turned. I leaped back behind a tall bush and dropped to the ground. Shots rang out; two slugs hit the dirt next to me. "Hey, O'Brien. Get out here. The next one's gonn–"

A police siren pierced the air. *What the hell...?*

Buddy lowered the gun to his side, shaded his eyes and peered out at the road in front of him. He continued to stare.

I took a quick look around. The guards had also stopped and now glanced up the road. A fast-moving black and white cruiser, its red lights flashing, drifted over the hump trailing a thick cloud of dust. The car grew ominously larger as it sped closer to the works, the resounding wail of its siren reverberating in the valley. Buddy obviously knew who drove the vehicle. He stepped casually to the side of the road and waited. The police car zoomed right on past me and slammed to a stop next to him.

Burt Krause, chief of Barstow's finest, leaned out of the driver's side window and spoke to Buddy. I couldn't hear what they talked about, but Buddy looked pissed. Sitting stoically in the passenger seat, staring straight ahead, was Ben Moran.

A few seconds passed. The cop car pulled away and drove up to the front of the office. The men climbed out and rushed inside.

Buddy shouted and waved his arm, signaling for the two guards to return. They conferred with him for a few seconds before he stormed off in the direction of the office.

The guards glanced out at the scrub once more, then trailed in Buddy's wake and took up a position in front of the door holding their rifles across their chests. No one seemed to be looking for me now. Why'd they stop?

I had no idea what was going on in the little building, but I grabbed at the chance to move. I jumped up, veered right, and made a beeline for one of the slag piles close to the rear of the office. I covered the distance in three seconds flat and hid behind the small mound.

Two more guards appeared, patrolling the area between me and the clapboard building. Turning, I glanced at the area behind me. I looked out beyond a five-foot-high stack of old wooden beams and a huge pile of rusting metal, way out to a landing strip. I relaxed for a few beats. No one was watching. I turned back and peered around the slag pile. The guards moved cautiously, their weapons extended in front of them. When they came to the far edge of the office, they turned toward the front and disappeared around the corner. They'd be back soon.

I dashed to the rear of the building and flattened my body against the wall. Without looking down I fingered the automatic in my belt, a reassuring gesture...though not *too* reassuring with only one cartridge in the clip. I pulled the gun out. My hand trembled in fear–or maybe anger–as I chambered the round and tucked it back in my belt. Taking a deep breath and exhaling slowly, I slid along the wall toward a dirty window in the center of the building next to a closed door.

Ducking down, I crossed under the window and put my hand on the rusty knob. I twisted it, and the door opened a crack. With every instinct in my body telling me to retreat, I ventured into the building. I stood in a dim utility room, where I saw a door cut into the opposite wall. It was slightly ajar; a sliver of light spilled through and fanned out as it fell across the floor.

I tiptoed to the door and peered through the opening. My knees buckled. Rita sat there, tied to a chair at the far end of the vintage office. A strip of duct tape covered her mouth. It took all my willpower to stop from barging in and shooting Moran where he stood, but I only had one bullet and Krause wore two big revolvers on his hip. He'd shoot us both if I tried anything.

Krause and Buddy were talking at once. Moran, holding a large shoulder pouch, stood ramrod straight next to an old cabinet safe.

"Shut up, goddammit," he bellowed. "It's all over. O'Brien's pal, that P.I. bastard Silverman, talked to Bickerton. Must've scared him good. The snake oil preacher told him everything."

I froze at the mention of Sol's name. What did he have to do with this?

"What could Bickerton tell him?" Buddy asked. "He don't know shit about what we do out here."

Krause jumped in. "That tax-exempt asshole told Silverman that Ben here gives him kickbacks to send his recruits, the druggies, to the rehab center at Rattlesnake Lake."

"So what?" Buddy said. "Everybody gives kickbacks, even the legit drug centers."

"Go ahead, might as well tell him rest, Burt," Moran said.

"That Jew bastard figured out Moran doesn't have a state license to operate a rehabilitation center. Rattlesnake Lake's cover has always been that it's a gun club, right?"

Sol had told me he was working on something. But why was he worried about Moran's damn licenses? God almighty, they're turning kids into slaves!

"That goddamned Silverman," Moran said, "had his buddies, brass from the San Berdoo County Sheriff's Department, raid the base. That son-of-a-bitch used that license bullshit as an excuse. He's there now with the cops. They're talking to the kids, for chrissakes. I was in the café when Burt got the call. He came in and got me and we rushed out here."

"The FBI will be out there soon," Krause added.

Oh Sol! You lunatic. You wonderful crazy human being. Who'd think of taking down a group of hardened mad dog killers with a simple license code violation? If you were here, I think I'd kiss you...nah, but I'd say something nice.

"What about, O'Brien?" Buddy asked. "He's out there in the bushes–"

"Forget O'Brien. You idiot, it's over. As soon as that damn plane gets here, I'm gone."

"*Wait a minute.* You're just gonna leave?" Buddy said.

"I knew it'd come to this one day. I've got my goods and I'm gonna haul ass. The plane will be here any minute."

My mind swirled. Sol knew I was heading for the borax works; Joyce must have told him. He'd bring the cops here for sure. I just had to wait it out. Hang on without getting caught until they arrived. It wasn't my job to capture Moran, so why take any risks now? I'd just have to play it cool. Moran would get away, but so what? Rita would be safe. And that's what mattered. I shook my hands at my sides and did a couple of neck rolls, trying to loosen up.

I heard the drone of a small plane. It would touch down on the little runway at any moment. Then Moran would take off. Buddy and Krause would leave as well. They'd have to if they wanted to save their necks. I waited and listened.

"You've got what, ten, twelve million in uncut diamonds stashed in that pouch, Moran?" Buddy asked.

"Suppose you tell me what's on your mind," Moran said.

"Suppose I tell you I want my share!"

"Take it easy, Buddy," Burt Krause said. "Ben's taken good care of us–"

A gunshot exploded. I nearly jumped out of my skin.

I spun around and peered in. My eyes swept the room.

Rita, wide eyed, squirmed in her chair, scared out of her wits, but okay. Buddy was sprawled on the floor, blood oozing from a third eye in the center of his forehead. Moran stood in front of the open safe still holding the black pouch in one hand; in the other he held a smoking gun.

"Christ, Ben! I could've talked him out of it!" Krause exclaimed.

"He had it coming. You got a problem, too?"

"*Hell no*! You did fine by me. I've got plenty stashed. You're right, he had it coming. But hey, I gotta get outta here too, before the authorities show up."

I ducked back and crossed the room. Glancing out, I saw the plane sitting on the runway. *Damn*, the pilot was headed this way, coming to get Moran. He'd walk in the door and spot me. I darted back, desperately looking for a place to hide. Nope, nowhere.

Moran's voice came from the other room: "The plane should be here by now. So long, Burt."

Any second Moran would come through the office door and the pilot would walk in through the back door. I'd be caught in the middle.

But wait, the pilot was farther away, and Moran was just on the other side of the door. He'd get here first, before the pilot could warn him, then I'd have the drop on him. I held my breath and drew my gun. I'd jam it in his face and force him to release Rita. I stood at the edge of the doorway. My heart did a rumba in my chest as I waited. But Moran didn't appear. He was still talking in the other room.

"Hold it a minute," Krause said.

"What, goddammit?"

Too long. The pilot would be here any second. He could be armed. I'd be in the middle of them. They'd all draw their guns and it'd be over.

Hurry up, Moran. Goddammit! Get in here.

"O'Brien's still out there," Krause said. "Could be hiding on the other side of that wall, for all we know."

"Yeah, you could be right."

Oh, mother of God! They figured I might be here. My pulse raced. My plan was going down in flames. I'd be nailed after all.

"Get the guards," Moran said. "I'll need an escort. I'll take the girl too. She'll make a good hostage. I'll eliminate her in Mexico."

Christ! If he came though the door with a gun on Rita we'd never make it. Think, Jimmy, goddammit. *Think*!

All of a sudden, rapid gunfire from outside shook the room. An instant later the pilot staggered in, blood pouring from his chest. The guards had shot him. Must have thought the guy was me. In the dim light, our eyes locked. He fell on his face at my feet. I recoiled and flattened myself against the wall.

"*What the hell*." Moran appeared in the doorway, holding Rita in front of him, twisting her arm behind her back. A cocked gun was in his other hand, pressed against her ribcage. One twitch of his finger and she'd be dead. The black pouch hung on his shoulder. Moran didn't see me standing in the shadows.

"*Aw shit*!" he shouted. "Someone shot the goddamn pilot. Stupid fucking guards! How in the hell am I gonna to get outta here now!"

He shoved Rita farther into the dim room. She struggled, kicking and thrashing, her cries muffled by the tape across her mouth. He stared down at the dead pilot.

Krause shouted from the office, "I think the cops are here! All the guards took off, shooting it out with the cops. I hear gunshots coming from the road. I gotta move!"

Sol's troops were coming. They'd be here any minute, firing their weapons. Moran would use Rita's body as a shield. She'd be killed for sure.

I tucked the Berretta in my belt under my jacket and stepped out of the shadows.

"I'll fly you out," I said. "Just let her go."

Chapter Forty-one

Moran swung his revolver around. "I don't trust you. The girl goes with us."

At first Rita was shocked at seeing me, but now the shock had turned to anger. She shook her head violently and stomped her foot. The words couldn't escape the tape that covered her mouth, but I knew what she was trying to say. She didn't want me to fly Moran out. She knew he'd kill me when we landed somewhere; I figured the same thing. But she didn't know that I had a little surprise in mind for him once we got into the air. I had to stall, though; my plan didn't include taking Rita along.

"You've got two seconds–"

"I said I'd fly you out of here," I interrupted. "But damn it! Let her stay–"

"Shut up. We're taking her. If she's in the plane you won't try anything."

I heard gunfire in the distance. The police were still shooting it out with the guards. They'd shoot their way back here any minute, firing their riot guns.

I gestured for Rita to cool it. She understood, but shook her head and glared at me. I had no choice. All three of us would be in that airplane.

Moran stuck his cannon in my face. "*Move.* If we're not off the ground before the cops get back here, I'll kill you both."

He meant it; he had nothing to lose. "Okay, Moran. Let's go, but be careful with that gun. Anything happens to her, and I swear..." There was no need to finish the statement; he knew what I meant. But with the .38 magnum in his hand, he probably figured it was a paper threat.

We hurried to the Cessna. Moran frogmarched Rita behind me, the gun in her back, as I moved fast around the slag piles and junk.

After I climbed in the plane, Moran shoved Rita into the backseat. She sat directly behind me. He got in next to her, keeping the gun pointed at her the whole time. He had the hammer cocked, holding it with his thumb. Even if I could draw my weapon, aim, and somehow hit him, his reflexive action would cause his gun to fire, killing Rita.

I cranked the engine to life and eased in the throttle; the Cessna moved forward. Moments later I was gazing down the length of a short dirt runway. I wasn't much of a pilot. I'd had a few lessons. Susie taught me enough to get the plane off the ground, and how to control it in the air, but I was never any good at short field landings and had tried it only twice. Both times she had to take over the controls at the last minute and bring the plane down safely. I would've crashed the damn thing.

I felt the gun barrel tap the back of my head and jammed the throttle to the wall.

The engine howled. The plane raced down the runway. Fifty on the airspeed indicator, then sixty. A building loomed ahead. I pulled back on the yoke. The wheels lifted, but then hit the ground again. The plane bounced, and we were airborne.

Moran shouted, "I thought you said you could fly this thing."

"Screw you, Moran. We're in the air aren't we? Be careful with that gun; ease back on the hammer. It could get bumpy. And if she gets shot, I'm going to fly this thing into a goddamn mountain. I mean it!"

He fully cocked the gun, locking the hammer. The barrel

was still pressed against Rita, but at least it wouldn't go off accidentally. "Just do as I say and no one gets hurt."

Yeah sure…. I glanced at the flight gauges; they were bouncing around, telling me nothing. I hauled the yoke back some more.

The nose shot up, the airspeed fell, the planes shimmied—*stall*! The warning horn blared. Forward on the yoke until we were level. The right wing dipped, but I brought it back with the aileron control.

Sweat gushed from every pore. I fought the plane and wondered how long I was going to be able to keep it in the air. But then I figured as long as I was flying it, Moran couldn't shoot me. I took comfort in that thought.

I felt Moran's breath next to my ear. "Take a compass heading of 180 degrees," he said.

I glanced at the compass above the windshield. It was tumbling and spinning. But 180 degrees was south, and I was heading north. I pressed the left rudder and turned the wheel in the same direction. The nose of the aircraft veered, the plane rolled through an arch. I stopped the turn when we were pointed in the opposite direction, toward the northern slope of the Calico Mountains off in the distance.

I seemed to have the airplane under control. At least I could keep it in the air. The technique was coming back to me. But navigation was always a mystery, a lot of jargon about bearings, headings, and lines of azimuth and altimeter settings, Zulu this and Zulu that; it made no sense. The wings were level and we continued soaring toward the mountains.

"Are we at 180 degrees now?" Moran asked.

I had *no* idea what the heading was. The compass bounced and bobbed, impossible to read. "Yeah, we're flying at exactly 180. Now what?"

"Tell me when we reach the Mexican border. I'll give you a new heading then."

What did Moran think, that there'd be a big white line painted on the ground, one side saying "America," the other "Mexico" in big bold letters? It's all desert out here. How in hell would I know when we crossed the border? But one thing was certain: Moran knew less about navigation than I did. He couldn't read the compass either.

"No tricks. If we're not in Mexico in an hour, your cute little partner is going to be a dead little partner." Cocky old bastard; the gun that he held against Rita's side gave him a sense of control.

Fishing around in a pouch attached to the door, I found an aeronautical chart. I unfolded it and held it up with one hand, pretending to examine it.

"Mountains ahead," I said over my shoulder. "Might hit a few air pockets, some turbulence." I brought the nose up and climbed steadily at several hundred feet per minute. One of Moran's borax mines was below us now. I could see trucks coming and going, nothing unusual. We were about ten miles west of where we'd started.

I shouted again over my shoulder: "Right on course, Moran. Why don't you take a little nap? I'll wake you when we get there."

"Funny, O'Brien. You're a regular riot, Alice."

After I got free of Moran–a plan was unfolding in my mind–I wanted to be close to the facility. I for sure didn't want to get lost out here in the middle of a billion square miles of desolate wasteland.

I glanced at Rita, who sat quietly with her back ramrod straight, her eyes opened wide. She was scared and it was going to get worse. I wanted to let her know to be ready, but

Moran's eyes stayed fix on me and he would have caught the gesture. I faced forward.

The Calico Mountains weren't that tall, just a pile of gray granite and rocky ledges a few thousand feet above the ground. But when the hot wind, racing across the desert floor, hit the mountain slopes the air above them whipped into a turbulent fury. Susie explained how turbulence was nothing to be afraid of...provided it wasn't severe. But if I flew real close to the mountaintops the little plane would be tossed about violently.

"Hang on, the wind is blowing hard. We're going to hit turbulence."

"Just get this goddamn plane to Mexico," Moran snapped.

I headed straight for the small mountain range, aiming just *below* the top of the ridge.

A few heartbeats later we were close to Calico Peak, and just as I figured, the airplane rose, lifted by the upsurge of wind flowing up the mountain's side.

At first the little plane just bounced in the air, like a boat in rough water. Then as we neared the peak, it got worse. The plane jumped and fell, whipped from side to side, dancing in a hard, violent rhythm with the wind. The left wing pointed toward the sky, then the ground. I thought it would roll. The nose lifted and we soared higher, pinning me in my seat, before dropping back in a freefall.

Moran was bellowing, but I couldn't understand his words. The Cessna shook and shuddered, ten-point-zero on the Richter Scale, but we continued to move forward, bouncing furiously; I prayed that the wings wouldn't rip off from the utter force. Then, a moment later, we shot up like an elevator and skimmed over the top of the mountain. In a matter of minutes we caught the downdraft on the mountain's backside. We sank fast. My stomach jumped into my throat. The nose dropped due to the air current, but I pushed the yoke in some more. The wind roared over the wings, sounding like a hurricane.

The plane was almost vertical, speeding to the ground. We screamed down the face of the mountain for a couple of seconds, just long enough for Moran to fall forward, losing his equilibrium.

I eased back on the controls, the throttle and yoke, and the Cessna stabilized. We were through the worst of it, flying level now, five hundred feet above the ground.

"What the hell are you doing? You got too close to that goddamn mountain!" He struggled to get back in his seat.

I leaned forward.

"What's going on? Why are you bending that way?"

I pulled the gun from my belt and put it in my lap. With my other hand, I reached down next to the seat and turned off the gas valve. Any second the engine would quit.

I held the Berretta low in my right hand, where Moran couldn't see it.

The engine coughed once and quit. The silence was eerie.

"*Goddammit*! What the fuck–"

I slipped the gun barrel in the gap between the seat backs, turned and faced Moran. Our eyes locked.

"We are experiencing a little momentary difficulty," I said.

He swung the gun away from Rita. "Get the engine started, now! *Goddammit!* I'm going to blow your brains–!"

I shot Moran in the head.

Chapter Forty-two

"Goddammit Rita! Quit kicking the seat. I gotta get the engine started."

Holding the yoke with one hand, I quickly reached down and flipped the gas valve to *open* with the other. The plane was losing precious altitude, gliding with the propeller windmilling. But almost instantly the engine caught.

The seat back jumped; Rita had kicked it. It jumped again...hard. "Hang on a minute. Let me get this thing under control." Her muffled cries competed with the howl of the engine. But right then I had other things on my mind–like how to keep us from flying into the ground.

I added backpressure to the elevator control and the little plane, with its nose high, soared into the air. It climbed smooth and serene. It was as if the Cessna sensed that Moran was dead and no longer an infection festering in its belly.

I knew I wouldn't lose any sleep over his death. The guy was evil, a greedy bastard, sacrificing others for his own gain. I did what I had to do to save Rita and myself from being killed, either during the flight or when we landed in Mexico. The only remorse I felt was that Moran wouldn't stand trial and be punished for his crimes: kidnapping, torture, and murder, just to name a few. It seemed to me that he got off easy.

The seat thumped firmly against my back. Rita's legs were like spring-loaded battering rams. I turned. She leaned forward; I hesitated, but only for a moment, then reached back and tore the tape from her mouth.

"*Ouch!* Damn, that hurt." She squirmed and turned until

her bound wrists were thrust toward me. "Here, untie me quick, Jimmy. I can't stay back here with...*him*." She nodded at Moran's corpse slumped in the seat next to her, its head lolling to the side. He had died instantly so only a small amount of blood trickled from the bullet hole that had replaced his left eye.

I trimmed the plane so that it would fly straight and level without too much effort from me. Fishing in the glove box I found the small emergency kit, matches, beef jerky, and a hunting knife. I cut the cords binding Rita's wrists.

One leg came over the seat back, exposing a lot of thigh, and then her fanny appeared. I tried not to gawk. Finally the rest of her followed. She plopped down in the passenger seat with a stern look on her face, holding her dignity intact.

"What," she said, "are you looking at? Concentrate on the flying, buster." She had a nice figure, but oh my, I'd never seen it from that angle before.

"Hey, were you scared?"

"*Scared*!" Rita exclaimed, her brown eyes flashing. "No, it's been a picnic. I love being tied up with a big gun stuck in my ribs. And it's so much fun flying around with a guy at the controls who'd ask such a stupid question."

I tried to lighten it up. "Just another day in the life of an O'Brien Law Firm associate...an associate who wants to be a partner someday, I might add."

"Don't give me that crap. I did what I had to do–"

"Just a minute. I've got to fly the plane; mountains ahead." I had to think of something to take Rita's mind off the ordeal she'd just been through or I wouldn't be able to concentrate on the task at hand. "Look in the glove box. See if there's an owner's manual in there, something that will tell me how to fly this thing."

"Oh, my God! What have I gotten myself into? I had a better chance with Moran." I glared at her and she started fumbling in the glove box. "Damn you, O'Brien."

The plane meandered. I turned the control wheel and applied a little rudder and the plane drifted back on course–the imaginary line I had drawn on the map in my mind.

"There's no manual in here–" She raised her head. "You were kidding, weren't you? You really don't need a book. Do you?"

"Don't worry, I know how to fly the thing. I was kidding. But seriously, I know you've just been through hell. We both have, but we survived."

Rita stared out at the horizon, taking a moment to compose her thoughts. "Jimmy, I was scared, really scared, and when I saw you I almost lost it. I knew you came to save me and I knew we were both going to be killed…Jimmy you were foolish to–"

"Hey, I couldn't sit there and do nothing. But anyhow, I'm proud of you, proud of your courage and the way you didn't fold up when it mattered. Are you going to be okay?"

"I'm fine now, I guess." Rita said. "But in the future can we just stick to DUI cases, maybe a little petty theft when things get dull?"

"As long as we don't do any corporate law. I've met enough big-time crooks already."

We flew at five thousand feet over the Calico range. Glancing down, I saw the complex, structures scattered like tiny toy blocks in the valley way off in the distance. I didn't mention it to Rita, but I was worried about landing the plane on that short strip. I thought about flying to Barstow or someplace where they had a longer runway, but I knew I'd get lost. For now I was doing fine, the Cessna cruising along as smooth as a

Coltrane riff.

I took a quick look at Rita. She sat quietly, alone with her thoughts, the vibration jiggling her breasts. "So, Rita, it's just you and me alone up here with a pouch full of diamonds."

"Yeah, and one dead guy in back." She turned to me. "He liked diamonds too, Jimmy."

"I thought diamonds were a *girl's* best friend."

"Right now I'd settle for a friend who knows how to land an airplane. How many lessons did that blonde give you anyway?"

"Ooh, that hurts." I frowned and thought, *Is she reading my mind?* "Hey, it's your fault we're here." I shook my head. "You and your writ. What in hell were you thinking? Just what kind of writ were you trying to serve anyway?"

"Oh, I wasn't trying to serve papers or anything. That was just an excuse. I wanted to see what was going on."

"You wanted to see what was *going on?*"

"Whoa, Jimmy, it wasn't idle curiosity. Remember I told you I got a look at Professor Carmichael's research paper?"

"Yeah, so?"

"The guy was a geologist, an expert in borax. I won't bore you with the details, but basically he couldn't figure out how the mines in the Calico area–Moran's mines–could make a profit. He knew the ore wasn't rich enough to support an operation as large as his. So he did a little investigating on his own. He came out here secretly and took a look around. And when he saw the kids working, well…"

I eased off the Cessna's throttle, which put us in a slight descent. "He figured out that with no labor costs, Moran could get rich."

"Yeah, and he planned to break the story on the college TV station. His last hurrah, before the station was sold to

Bickerton."

"So Robbie killed him before the exposé could air," I said, following Rita's thread.

"I think Moran sent Robbie to kill him." Rita nodded. "I think it was all planned. Even Robbie's religious fervor was an act. Then Moran eliminated Robbie, getting rid of that loose end and framing you at the same time."

"I'll agree that Moran killed him, or had him killed," I said. "But Robbie wasn't acting. No, he was seriously unbalanced. I met him in his cell and talked to him, for chrissakes. No one could be that good of an actor."

"If he was that good, I have a hunch he could've won an Academy Award, but he *was* acting. Think about it. The breakout, when Robbie got away, went too smoothly, had to be preplanned."

"We may never know, Rita. But, I'm just glad it's over."

"Well, it's not quite over.... You still have to land this plane."

We flew beyond the Calico Range and soared down into the valley, approaching the borax works. I made a low pass over the complex and glanced at the ground. The shootout looked to be done. The police had taken over the facility. They had the guards lined up with their hands on their heads. Numerous teens stood in small groups talking with officials, and on the road coming from Rattlesnake Lake Base I saw a line of police vehicles with flashing lights speeding toward the facility. A couple of sheriff's department prisoner transport buses led the parade, and trailing far behind was what appeared to be Hammer's car. Sol's black limo stood next to the small clapboard office.

I made a sweep over the runway, which from the plane looked about as big as a postage stamp. Rita glanced at the strip, then at me. "You can do it, right, Jimmy? I'm not worried." She tried to smile, but what appeared was more of a grimace.

"No problem," I said. "But just in case…"

"In case, what?"

"Nothing, just tighten your seatbelt."

I grabbed the radio mike. I was familiar with transceiver type radios from my days as a cop. Susie had explained the protocol of emergency aviation transmissions, the use of the 121.5 VHF frequency. I pressed the *to talk* switch. "Hey, is anybody out there? I need help!" I released the switch.

The speakers came to life. "Aircraft calling on 121.5, this is Los Angeles Center. Say your position and identification."

"I'm over the old borax works, somewhere west or maybe north…aw…south of Barstow."

"Unknown aircraft transmitting on the emergency frequency, are you a pilot?"

"No, and that's my problem," I said, turning away from Rita and speaking in a low voice. "I don't know how to land this thing, but I've got to put down on the runway at the borax works."

"Are you declaring an emergency?"

"Damn right I am."

"Roger that. Now hold tight and answer my questions. First, how many souls are on board?"

"Two right now. One just departed."

"What?"

"Two…two people on board. But I have to land this plane. It's a Cessna 172."

"Don't worry; I have a private pilot's license. I'll talk you down."

"Can you do that?"

"Yeah, piece of cake," the guy said. "Those 172s practically land themselves."

I glanced at Rita, who gave me a weak smile and tried to pretend that all was fine in her life, but the look in her eyes told me she had a few concerns. "Okay, let's go for it," I said to the controller.

"That's the spirit. Now, first we're going to dispense with the formalities. Forget about radio protocol. Just speak in a normal manner. Do you Roger that? If so, answer in the affirmative."

"Ten-four," I said.

"We don't say *ten-four*. Cops say that."

"Roger, that's affirmative."

"Look sir, just talk normally, so I can understand you," the controller said. "Now, do you see the runway?"

"Yeah, it's down there. I'm circling over it."

Rita tapped my shoulder. "Jimmy that's not the runway, it's a road—"

"Shut up, Rita—"

The loudspeaker interrupted. "Say again."

"Not you, I was talking to Rita—"

"Listen fella, just talk to me, okay?"

"Roger…I mean, sure."

I hadn't been concentrating and the plane wandered off. But the controller said he had me on radar and gave me a vector, as he called it, and soon I was circling over the facility again.

"Pay attention to what I'm going to tell you. It might get a little tricky," the controller said.

"Listen to the guy, Jimmy. We'll hit a mountain—"

"Dammit, Rita, I told you to shut up and I mean it." She hit my shoulder with her fist. I pretended it didn't hurt and pressed the mike button again. "I'm ready."

As instructed, I maneuvered the airplane until it was on the runway approach, fifteen hundred feet in the air and a couple of miles away from the end of the landing strip. I trimmed the elevator tab and the plane began a shallow decent. I settled in and flew straight, aiming right for the touch-down zone. It would've been pretty cool, sailing on a wing over the ground at ninety knots, as graceful as a gazelle and feather light...if I wasn't scared out of my wits. *Captain O'Brien at the controls, bringing her in on one engine.*

But immediately reality hit.

"Jimmy! We're gonna crash!"

"Pull up!" the controller shouted. "You're below my radar. Are you still with me?"

My heart stopped. We were too low, skimming over a building that somehow managed to move itself right to where the runway should've been. I dropped the mike, tugged back on the control and goosed the throttle. The plane jumped. We soared over the roof and continued to climb.

At three hundred feet above the ground, just when I thought I had everything under wraps, the plane veered off to the right with the wing low. *Careful*, I told myself. If I don't fix it in about five seconds, we'll hit sideways and flip.

"Hey! Why are we on our side–?" Rita covered her eyes.

I stepped on the left rudder and turned the wheel at the same time.... Oops, overdid it. I yanked the wheel back...*easy baby*. Now the plane was sinking, dropping fast and out of control again. More power! Isn't that what Susie used to say? The plane ballooned and became squishy.

Then it nosed down. I was now two hundred feet in the air and moving fast, dropping, flying crooked with that damn wing low. We flew perpendicular to the landing strip, the ground tilting every which way. *Correct it, get it straight*; okay, okay...steady. Now hold it, hang on, we're going to make it. One wheel hit the ground, banged hard–the plane bounced and was in the air again. I cut the power and we were suddenly falling. Rita remained silent, her hands planted firmly on the dashboard. She stared at the ground coming up fast.

"Come in aircraft transmitting on 121.5! Are you with me?"

"Jimmy, my God, do *something*!"

Wait! Don't cut power, *add* power! Susie's nagging voice filled my head. I jammed the throttle to the wall. It felt like the knob was going to push right through my palm and come out the other side of my hand. The engine roared.

"Answer me, Cessna!"

The strident rush of the wind, the crackling radio, the engine screaming, and Rita's fear caused my head to spin, the world a blur. *Vertigo! Snap out of it and fly the goddamn plane!*

"Aircraft on 121.5! Are you still with me?"

"Rita!" I shouted. "Reach down and find the mike, tell the guy I'm too busy to talk."

Rita grabbed the cord and with quick hand-over-hand movements she pulled the mike off the floor. "Jimmy, you'd better talk to the guy. It's probably a Federal reg, or something."

She held the mike out to me, but both of my sweaty hands were busy turning the wheel, trying to keep the plane from doing a flip. "Just tell the guy I can't talk now."

The plane responded. Finally we were stable and I heard Rita say, "Sir, the idiot...I mean the pilot at the controls is tied up for a moment. Could you call back?"

Christ, Rita made it sound like I was out going to the

potty. "Give me that damn thing," I told her. "Hey, L. A. Center, this is the *pilot* talking. Over."

"Look, guy. We're going to start over, now listen to me..." I dropped the mike and looked up. We were heading straight for the runway, zooming over the threshold.

At the last second, I let go of everything. The little plane straightened, plopped down, stayed down, and rolled effortlessly along the runway. The guy was right: these things *do* land themselves. I'll keep that in mind for the next time.... Well, I'll just keep it in mind.

When we finally stopped with a few inches of runway to spare, Rita leaned over and kissed my cheek. "Hey, Flyboy, not too bad. Sky King could've done any better." I managed not to roll my eyes.

Several patrol cars rushed up on the runway and surrounded us. I glanced out at the cops moving toward the plane and whispered to Rita that we'd talk about that partner thing later, just as soon as the cops let me leave. Sooner than twenty-five to life, I hoped.

Chapter Forty-three

On Sunday, a week or so later, Rita and I were having brunch at Rocco's, celebrating our victory over Moran and the demise of his organization. Jeanine brought my coffee and Rita's iced tea. After the waitress left, Rita sat quietly for a moment. Then she raised her glass. "You saved my life. Thank you...again."

I smiled and clicked her glass with my cup. "Here's to the future of our little firm. Oh, and that's the three hundredth time you've thanked me."

"You look a little down, Jimmy."

"Nah, I'm fine. Hey, shall we discuss that partner thing now?"

"I don't think so. Why don't we let it lie for a while?"

"Why, Rita? I though you wanted to be my partner."

"Jimmy, I need time, that's all."

"Time for what?"

"Time to think. I don't know if I'm cut out for this," she said. "You weren't exactly honest with me. Letting Mabel hide your gun, then not informing your lawyer...*me*."

"Yeah, I should've trusted you. I'm sorry; but it all worked out okay."

"Well, I may have been your lawyer but I didn't really help you. Without Moran's guards spilling their guts to the DA, and the kids talking, you'd still be a suspect."

"Rita, you did a great job. You fought the DA, came up with a plan, and if it *did* happen to go to trial I'm sure we would've won. And now you're going to represent me at the inquest."

Although there would be an official inquest into Moran's death, I was assured by the San Bernardino DA that the ruling would be self-defense.

"Jimmy, you know that's a done deal. The authorities want us out of their sight as fast as possible. The shooting will be ruled justifiable, but don't expect any accolades."

She was right. Sol and I wouldn't get medals for our involvement in the affair; medals are rarely given to those who expose corruption existing under the watchful eyes of the bureaucracy. I knew the system and I knew what to expect. When the public had learned about Moran's enterprise a firestorm had ensued, the populace demanding heads. Government agencies from the FBI on down were scrambling, running for cover, pointing this way and that, and promising intense investigations. The hoi polloi, always curious about the efficiency of their government at work, demanded to know how all of this could've been going on under the agencies' collective noses. When the smoke clears, heads will roll; at least, *one* head. As always, it'll probably be some guy way down the political food chain who'll take the fall, probably a lowly clerk in the fishing license bureau. After all, he should've known. He should've stopped Moran early on. Wasn't it common knowledge that he was using illegal bait, longjaw mudsuckers, in waters where such bait was not allowed? An early retirement for the clerk, the rabble will have their bloodlust satisfied, and that will be that.

Cathy and Tom Rogers of *The Barstow Sun* broke the story about Burt Krause, Barstow's chief of police, who had been involved with Moran. Because of their inside knowledge, Krause had been arrested and held without bail on a laundry list of charges, starting with section 187, then conspiracy and working its way down to…well, just pick a random page in the California Criminal Code and you'll find one or two of his crimes listed there.

J. Billy Bickerton was shocked. How could he have been duped by those ungodly apostates? He gave a rousing, fist-pounding sermon on his TV show damning the sin of greed. I liked the proverb he quoted: "*Greedy eaters dig their graves with their teeth*," although I wasn't sure how the quote related to Moran and his bunch. To me, it seemed a suitable proverb for a group of heavyweights meeting at their annual dieting convention.

To great fanfare, his network aired Professor Carmichael's exposé. It drew a rating of 23.6 on the Nielsen overnights, topping two highly acclaimed network shows, and because of the rating, Bickerton's Holy Spirit Network was able to raise its advertising rates by 15 percent.

The big winner—if there was a winner—had to be Sol's attorney friend, Morty Zuckerman. Sensing a buck to be made, he'd jumped in on behalf of the teens and filed a lawsuit against the Moran estate, requesting a motion for a summary judgment. Zuckerman's complaint demanded that title to all the assets held by the late Mr. Moran and/or his corporations be immediately transferred to the kids in lieu of back payment of wages.

The judgment was instantly granted. What judge in his right mind would deny *that?* Zuckerman took his customary 40 percent and with the balance helped the kids set up a sub-chapter -S corporation. An initial public stock offering is in the works. Keep an eye on the financials.

One of my concerns had been put to rest when Sol invited Rita and me to join him the following week at the grand opening of a new restaurant. He said he was part owner, and when he told me what he had done, I was flabbergasted. He'd bought the Bright Spot Café and turned it over to his partners in the venture: Maggie, the waitress who'd passed us the tip about Jane Simon…and Jane herself. I'd been worried sick that something had happened to her, but Sol was the kind of guy who took care of those who helped him. I was always proud to be his friend, but when I heard what he had done…well, let's just say I was *very* proud. I laughed when he told me that Jane had suggested they change the name of the café to *Steinbeck's*.

"So, what do think, Rita? Want to be the firm's first new partner?"

"I just don't think I'm ready–"

"Don't think you can cut it in criminal law, is that it? Want to be like Zuckerman, with his IPOs and GMOs, BSOs, and a belly that looks like it's stuffed with Spaghetti Os? Is that what you want?"

Rita shrugged. "I guess not. I staying with the firm…but, Jimmy, let's just let it go. We'll both know when the time is right."

From across the crowded room Mabel's voice rose above the clamor: "Rita, Jimmy. Look what I've got."

Mabel, wearing a faux leopard coat and carrying a huge matching handbag, waved a piece of paper above her head as she rushed to our booth.

"Hey, Mabel, what's up?" Rita slid closer to me. "Here." She patted the spot that she just left. "Sit and have brunch with us."

"Look at this," Mabel said as she slipped into the booth. "A check from Zuckerman! Sol called, told me come and pick it up. He forced Zuckerman to cut our firm in on the proceeds from the Moran lawsuit. Wow, look at the number with all those beautiful zeros!"

She passed the check around. I shook my head, said a silent prayer of thanks, and handed it back. Mabel tucked it in her purse.

Rita glanced at me and smiled. "Does this mean I can get some of my back pay?"

"Hey, we'll all get our back pay and maybe a bonus. Mabel, the brunch is on the firm, and we're going to order a gallon of the best champagne."

"I have to leave in a minute," Mabel said. "I've got a date. Gordy Payne invited me to join him for a bite. I'm meeting him here in a few. You know Gordy? "

"Sure, Mabel," I said. "He's a nice guy." I didn't mention that his wife thinks he's a nice guy, too. Rita was upset with me, and that was enough. I don't need the whole firm glaring at me all next week.

Rita shook her head. "I don't know him, Mabel," she lied. "But, have a good time."

"Thanks, Rita. Before I go…" She reached into her purse and pulled out a large manila envelope. "Here, take this, Jimmy." She slid it across the table. "It's yours. I'm tired of babysitting the damn thing."

I opened the envelope. *What the hell....* Inside was a .38 revolver. I hooked the trigger guard with my finger and pulled it out.

"*My God,* Jimmy, what are you doing? Put that thing away," Rita said.

My eyes swept the room. Nobody was looking. I started to tuck it back in the envelope, but something caught my eye.

"Mabel!" Rita said. "What's going on? Is that Jimmy's gun, the one I found behind the cabinet?"

"One and the same," Mabel said. "The killer used it to shoot Hazel Farris and planted it there, but I didn't toss it in the ocean or anything. Maybe I was dumb, but I just kept it. Now that the heat's off, no sense me lugging it around anymore. Though I did feel comfortable with it handy. A girl with *my* looks can't be too careful, ya know."

I held the gun in my hand, and even in the dim restaurant light I could see where someone had filed off the serial numbers. Suddenly, it hit me!

Rita smiled at Mabel's remark, and glanced at me. "Hey, Jimmy...Jimmy? You look like you've seen a ghost!"

It felt like I'd seen a ghost...or worse. "This is not my gun," I said.

Chapter Forty-four

I jumped up and immediately drove out to Chatsworth. When I saw that the gun had no serial numbers, I knew it wasn't mine. I mean, if someone was trying to frame me with my own gun they wouldn't file off the numbers, would they?

Being Sunday, I figured the parking lot in front of the White Front Church, Snavley's Divine Christ Ministry, would be jammed, but when I swung off Winnetka Boulevard into the lot there wasn't a car in sight.

I didn't know what to make of it. Had the church gone out of business? Had he just closed up shop? Money couldn't have been a problem. The TV show that aired on Bickerton's network, featuring *J.C. Down and Funky Dancers* or whatever they were called, must've raked in a ton. It's funny, I didn't exactly remember the group's name, but I remember vividly Snavley handing each girl a white lily. He remarked that the flower is a symbol of virgin purity.

At that moment, it came to me. I knew why the church was closed. No, it wasn't something as simple as a lack of cash that shut down the church.

I parked the Corvette close to the front, climbed out, and tried the double doors: locked. Taped on the wall was a hand-lettered notice written on binder paper: *No Services Today*.

I made my way around to the back of the white concrete structure and saw a small sedan parked next to a doorway at the end of the building. I recognized the car. It was Snavley's, the same car I'd seen when I went out to the college that night looking for Bickerton, and bumped into him instead.

The door wasn't locked, saving me from breaking in…and I would have done just that. I entered the auditorium and moved quickly but quietly to Snavley's office.

When I got to the office door, I heard Snavley's muffled voice filtering through the wall. I stopped and listened. Was someone in there with him? That could be trouble.

Leaning closer, but cautious, I held my breath and listened. No, Snavley was alone. He was mumbling some kind of prayer. Not from the Bible or a prayer book; he seemed to be making it up as he went along.

Should I knock or just barge in? I tried the doorknob: locked. I took a step back. Leading with my shoulder, I rushed the door and banged it hard. It flew open.

A disheveled wreck with a cadaverous face and lunatic eyes stared at me from across a desk. Snavley had aged a hundred years in the last couple of weeks. It looked like his brain had folded up and turned out the lights. A dirty T-shirt hung on him like an ill-fitting shroud; an odor–the smell of fear–pervaded the room. But what caught my attention was the gun–*my* gun, no doubt–on the desk, inches from his fingers.

Neither of us moved and I don't know how long we stared at each other, but an understanding like an electrical charge connected us. His hand moved and covered the gun, but he didn't pick it up.

"You know. Don't you?" he said in a lifeless tone.

"Why'd you kill her?"

"Is that important? Isn't it enough that I murdered Hazel? Do I have to explain my deed to you?"

"Confession is good for the soul–"

"Are you going to forgive me my sins? Are you a priest, Mr. O'Brien?"

"Kind of like a priest, I'm a criminal lawyer. I've heard it all, Elroy. Nothing you can say would shock me–"

"I was *fucking* her! Okay?"

Okay, I was shocked. My God, *Snavley and Hazel Farris.* The image boggled my mind. "Well, it happens, but why did you shoot her? Something to do with Moran?"

"It had nothing to do with that animal, but when I saw those kids on TV, and Robbie dead, I knew my life was over. The Lord would never forgive me..."

"Snavley, tell me, damn it. Why did you kill her?"

"You won't understand—"

"Try me."

"I went to her trailer to plead with her, to tell her we were through. I tried before but she wouldn't let me go. I saw you there and hid, waiting until you left. Then I went in. She was drunk and grew belligerent. She blamed me for what happened to Robbie, how he went crazy, all of that religious mumbo-jumbo, as she called it. My life's work was nothing but mumbo-jumbo. Then she threatened to tell the congregation that we were having an affair."

"So what? You're both adults."

"I'm married, Mr. O'Brien. How would that look? I'd be disgraced." His eyes were wide, pleading. He wanted my forgiveness, or at least my understanding.

"I see. But still—"

Snavley hung his head. "I went crazy. My whole life ruined. I had to do something. She had a gun; she'd gotten it from one of Robbie's hoodlum friends. I took it out of the drawer and shot her. Instantly I was overcome with grief, but I was scared, too. I didn't know where to turn. Then I saw your card. It said you were a lawyer. At first I wanted to ask for your help, but when I got to your office, no one was there. I went through your desk drawer looking for your address. I had to talk to someone.... Then I saw your gun...It was the same kind of gun that I held in my hand, the gun I used on Hazel."

He paused, slumped back, and whimpered. Then continued with his confession, speaking in a reverent tone, almost peaceful. "Your gun was a sign from God. *He* gave me an opportunity and I knew what I had to do. I took yours and hid the one I used to shoot Hazel behind the file cabinet..."

"But how'd you get in my office?"

"The door wasn't locked. You should lock your doors, Mr. O'Brien. You never know who might walk in."

Mabel was always on my ass about forgetting to lock the door. Maybe I should write myself a note. "Yeah, someone might walk in, like a murderer who's trying to frame me."

His hand tightened around the gun. I waited. Finally, he spoke again: "How'd you know it was me who killed her?"

"Elroy, my friend," I said. "You made too many mistakes. I guess preachers don't make good murderers. When I saw you at the college that night, you mentioned my old gray metal desk. How would you've known that unless you'd been there?

"And the white lilies. You gave them to the girls in the dance group, and you gave one to Hazel. You said they were the symbol of purity. Hazel kept hers in vase on the table next to your picture. She treasured it. She liked you, Elroy. She wouldn't have talked. You want me to go on?"

He sprang from the desk, holding the gun in his shaky hand. It was aimed somewhere in my general direction. "Shut up, just shut up…"

I approached him. He shuffled backward. "Don't come any closer…"

"Calm down, Elroy. I'm just going to use the phone."

I picked up the receiver and dialed. Snavley cowered in a corner. He slowly moved the gun to his head. "This is Jimmy O'Brien. Get a call through to Sergeant Hammer. Tell him I'm at the Divine Christ Ministry church on. Tell him I've got to the murder suspect he's looking for. The guy who killed Hazel Farris. Tell him to hurry, before he does something rash."

I hung up, walked over to Snavley and took the gun away from him. If he hadn't shot himself in the time since he'd killed Hazel, or since Robbie's death, he wasn't going to do it now.

"Make some coffee, will you, Snavley? We're going to be here a while."

I picked up the phone again and dialed. "Hey, Rita, I've got a new client for you…"

About the Author:

Jeff Sherratt was born in Los Angeles, California on September 22, 1941. When he was in grade school his father bought a cattle ranch and moved his family to Utah. But after a few years the family returned to Southern California and settled in Downey where Jeff went to high school. In his senior year he met Judy and soon after graduation they were married. They've been together for over forty years now and have three daughters, Kristin, Karen, and Holly. They also have seven grandchildren.

For most of his adult life Jeff had been in business for himself. He owned companies that made and sold food related products. But as a lark, he once became a partner in a political public relations firm. "Some of the characters in my books are based on the candidates we've handled. I guess that's why we folded the tent and sneaked away. Our guys were losers and we weren't good enough to make them look like winners," Jeff said, recalling his experience as a political spinmeister.

After selling his business, Jeff devoted his time to writing mysteries, which soon became a full time career.

Jeff Sherratt lives in Newport Beach, California with his wife, Judy. He is a member of Sisters in Crime, an organization combating discrimination against women in the mystery field, and the professional association, Mystery Writers of America. Jeff is currently working on the next book in the Jimmy O'Brien series.